POLAR VORTEX

A JAMES FLYNN NOVEL

BOOK 5

R.J. PATTERSON

J.D. KANE

PRAISE FOR R.J. PATTERSON

SIGN UP for R.J.'s newsletter to stay up to date on new releases, deals, and projects by visiting RJPbooks.com.

DEAD SHOT

"Small town life in southern Idaho might seem quaint and idyllic to some. But when local newspaper reporter Cal Murphy begins to uncover a series of strange deaths that are linked to a sticky spider web of deception, the lid on the peaceful town is blown wide open. Told with all the energy and bravado of an old pro, first-timer R.J. Patterson hits one out of the park his first time at bat with *Dead Shot*. It's that good."

-***Vincent Zandri***, *bestselling author of* THE REMAINS

"You can tell R.J. knows what it's like to live in the newspaper world, but with *Dead Shot*, he's proven that he also can write one heck of a murder mystery."

—***Josh Katzowitz***, *NFL writer for CBSSports.com & author of* Sid Gillman: Father of the Passing Game

DEAD LINE

"This book kept me on the edge of my seat the whole time. I didn't really want to put it down. R.J. Patterson has hooked me."

— **Bob Behler**, *3-time Idaho broadcaster of the year and play-by-play voice for Boise State football*

DEAD IN THE WATER

"In Dead in the Water, R.J. Patterson accurately captures the action-packed saga of a what could be a real-life college football scandal. The sordid details will leave readers flipping through the pages as fast as a hurry-up offense."

— **Mark Schlabach,** *ESPN college sports columnist and author*

ALSO BY R.J. PATTERSON

Titus Black series

Behind Enemy Lines

Game of Shadows

Rogue Commander

Line of Fire

Blowback

Honorable Lies

Power Play

State of Conspiracy

The Patriot

The President's Man

The Haitian Assassin

Codename: Killshot

Chaos Theory

House of Cards

False Flag

A Deadly Game

Brady Hawk series

First Strike

Deep Cover

Point of Impact

Full Blast

Target Zero

Fury

State of Play

Seige

Seek and Destroy

Into the Shadows

Hard Target

No Way Out

Two Minutes to Midnight

Against All Odds

Any Means Necessary

Vengeance

Code Red

A Deadly Force

Divide and Conquer

Extreme Measures

Final Strike

Cal Murphy Thriller series

Dead Shot

Dead Line

Better off Dead

Dead in the Water

Dead Man's Curve

Dead and Gone

Dead Wrong

Dead Man's Land

Dead Drop

Dead to Rights

Dead End

James Flynn Thriller series

The Warren Omissions

Imminent Threat

The Cooper Affair

Seeds of War

Polar Vortex

Polar Vortex

First edition 2024

Published in the United States of America

Green E-Books

PO Box 140654

Boise, ID 83714

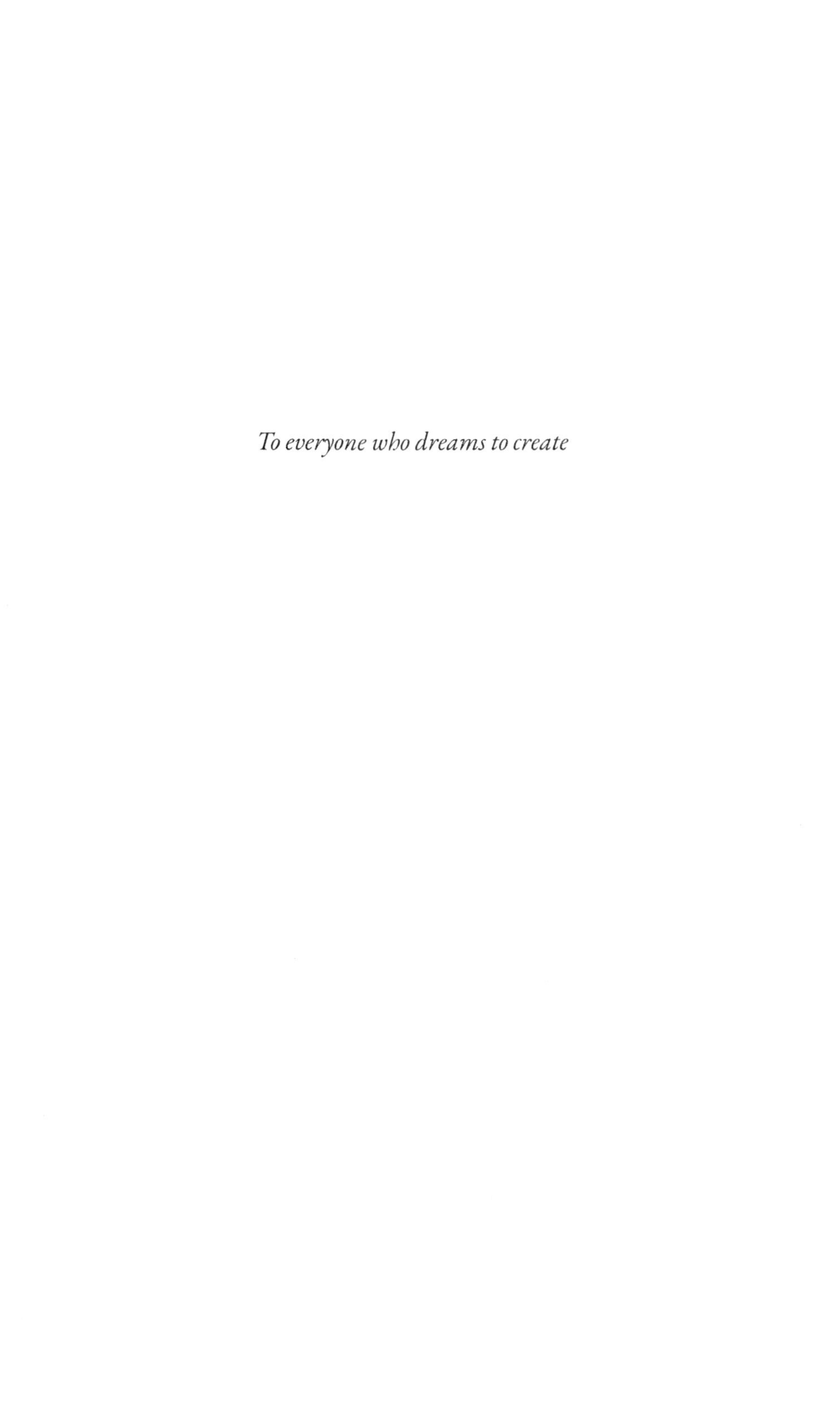

To everyone who dreams to create

POLAR VORTEX

1

COAST OF TAMPA, FLORIDA

The girl had a face and figure that Arthur Tillman imagined kings going to war over in an age long past. Many years ago, as a kid he'd tacked a poster of a bikini-clad Raquel Welch on the wall next to his bed. Every night he'd stare at the poster as he drifted off to sleep and into the fiery fantasies only a young man's brain can conjure, dreaming of gorgeous Raquel.

But this girl, dare he say it, was every bit as spectacular as Raquel Welch, circa 1970. And better yet, she wasn't just a photo on a glossy piece of paper; she was right in front of him. She was *with* him.

Debbi Dixon with her long, tan legs stretched in front of her sat on the bow of Tillman's 45-foot Formula yacht. Bob Marley wafted from a speaker, while she played a game on her phone. She more than amply filled the Carolina blue fabric of her skimpy swimsuit, and her bronze skin was a stark contrast to the pristine white of the boat's exterior.

Tillman drifted his yacht, *The Aquaholic*, in the calm waters of the Gulf of Mexico, far enough out that the Florida coast was no longer visible. A relatively new yet very competent captain, he marveled at the size of the world's majestic seas. He'd given forty-two years to the U.S. Army and had spent more time than he cared to remember in desolate places full of endless sand, dirt, rocks, or snow. When he retired from active service, he promised himself he'd spend as much time on the water as possible.

They were about thirty-five miles out; the water was smooth and the sun was bright. A light breeze wafted across the ship, carrying a sharp salty scent with a hint of Debbi's coconut tanning oil. At that moment, with Debbi at the bow, *The Aquaholic* served as Tillman's ideal picture of the good life.

He was just two months past his sixty-fourth birthday. Debbi wasn't quite yet twenty-five. No matter. There were no delusions regarding either's intentions. He was a rich man who'd cashed in big with a number of wise investments and partnerships to accompany his army pension, which wasn't anything to scoff at after ascending to the rank of general. She was an attractive young woman who knew Tillman could put her face to face with people who could fast-track her career, be it as an actress, model, TV personality, or social media influencer.

Tillman stood in the cockpit admiring the beautiful horizon as well as Debbi's striking figure in the foreground. He drained the final swallow from his tumbler and rattled the ice.

"I'm going to fix myself another," he called out to her as he held his empty glass aloft. "Can I get you something?"

She turned to face him from behind large round sunglasses and scrunched up her face in a way that somehow made her even cuter as she contemplated her options. "Mmmm, Peachy Keen?" Phrasing it more as a question than an actual request.

Six months ago, Tillman had never even heard of a Peachy Keen let alone had the slightest idea how to make one or even hazard a guess at the drink's ingredients, other than the obvious. But, keeping the company of younger women over the years had opened his eyes to many things previously unknown to him, not the least of which was the myriad of alcoholic drinks they preferred. When he first entered the dating scene after retiring from the military, a girl named Sherry (or was it Sharon? Or maybe Shelly?) took him up on a similar offer for a drink. She'd said she would like a drink that had a very suggestive name, which led to an awkward response from Tillman since he didn't immediately realize she was referring to her order.

As he stepped down toward the galley he noticed a fishing boat coming toward them. It wasn't rare to see boaters steaming by in these waters, but it was a bit late in the day for fishermen to just now be heading out. Probably just tourists on a sightseeing cruise hoping to spot some dolphins. He paid it no mind and continued inside.

Inside *The Aquaholic's* luxurious cabin, picture frames, meticulously aligned, covered nearly every bit of wall space. Inside each was a photo of Arthur Tillman smiling with some celebrity, famous athlete, or notable political figure.

There was Tillman grinning with Tom Cruise after serving as the military technical advisor on one of star's blockbusters; Tillman even landed a two-second cameo in the film where he portrayed an Army officer. His ham-fisted delivery of his single line—"You've got to be crazy!"—became a favorite quote for action movie buffs everywhere.

There was Tillman and Ronald Reagan. Tillman and Barack Obama. Tillman and Alice Cooper. Tillman and the British Royal Family. Tillman and Derek Jeter. And so many more. For a career military man, he'd become quite the celebrity himself.

Since retirement, he'd also become well-traveled through the talk show circuit, often appearing as an expert whenever a military conflict sprang up across the world. He'd even been urged on more than one occasion to get into politics. Many believed he had the charisma, demeanor, and stone-chiseled good looks to one day possibly become president.

Tillman turned down all invitations into the political arena. Too many skeletons in his many closets. And he wasn't about to give up the Debbi Dixons of the world simply to be a bureaucrat in Washington. No. He had life just the way he wanted.

He mixed Debbi's drink, consulting a handy book that was filled with all manner of standard and exotic cocktail recipes. He then tipped a generous pour of Jim Beam over ice for himself and eyed his cellphone that he'd left on the countertop. He took a sip, placed his tumbler on the counter, and reached for the phone.

He had already read the text message. More than once. But its contents weighed on him, and he was compelled to take another look.

Tillman, known for his connections and influence, was facing a dilemma unlike any other in his life. His discovery of sensitive information had put him in an awkward position. He had considered going public with the intel, a thought that had not gone unnoticed.

The text message on his phone carried a tone of familiarity and threat.

> Art, I know what you're planning to do with the information you've stumbled upon. I urge you to reconsider. While I understand your moral stance, you must think about the bigger picture. Everything will be handled with utmost discretion; you have my word. But be warned, refusing my offer and going ahead with your plans could have dire consequences. It's not a path you want to tread. Let's not escalate this.

This message was different from the usual requests Tillman received from his political and celebrity acquaintances. It was not just a plea for information but a veiled threat, an indication that his actions could trigger a chain of events beyond his control. This was no idle threat; the sender had the means to carry out the most menacing of deeds. He knew he was in a precarious situation, where every move he made had to be calculated with the utmost care.

Tillman involuntarily balled a fist. The text had come just after he and Debbi set out for the afternoon. He'd offered no reply. Texting was fine for quick communication, but this type of conversation needed to occur in person. He wasn't about to be intimidated. He hadn't gotten to where he was by being a push-over. The plan was to spend the night on the water, but when they got back to shore, he was going to get the answers he wanted. About that he had no doubt.

"Arthur," Debbi yelled from above.

He put down the cellphone and scrambled to the deck.

The fishing boat he'd seen in the distance had picked up speed and roared along the port side of *The Aquaholic's* hull, causing it to rock from its wake. Tillman couldn't get a look at the driver, only seeing that the man was dressed in a black t-shirt, dark glasses, and a black baseball cap pulled low across his brow. Tillman grabbed onto the railing of the stairs that led up to the bridge to steady himself as his yacht rolled to the right and then back to the left. Debbi tumbled a bit on the deck but managed to stabilize herself.

"What the hell?" she shouted.

"Just some idiot tourist," he said. "It's okay. Here's your drink. There's nothing to worry about."

He lied.

2

TAMPA, FLORIDA

James Flynn smoothed the whiskers of his fake mustache and adjusted his costume glasses one last time before he approached the building. It had been some time since he'd gone undercover to the degree that required an actual disguise, but doing so felt like putting on an old comfortable suit.

He was told not to be dropped off nor park near the site of the meeting, so he had the cab drop him a few blocks away and approached the building on foot.

Even in the dark Flynn could tell the place was rundown, almost certainly abandoned. There were no lights outside, and the windows offered no sign of activity inside. For a moment he wondered if he'd transposed the numbers of the address and had accidentally gone to the wrong location. Maybe he'd been sent on a wild goose chase. It wouldn't be the first time.

I'm here. Might as well play it out.

Flynn followed a narrow alley around the back—getting a whiff of rotting food and garbage. He took long, slow, deliberate strides, moving as stealthily as possible. Midway through the alley he stopped.

What am I doing? Old habits die hard.

He was no longer a government agent. He was a legit and respected journalist on a bona fide assignment. He had been invited to this meeting and had nothing to fear. There was no need for the cloak-and-dagger approach.

The group was called Ultra, an underground society of conspiracy theorists who met regularly to discuss and argue the existence of any number of nefarious plots aimed at undermining one's individual freedoms and their right to know the "truth."

Flynn, an investigator of conspiracy theories by trade, had spent the past several years exploring a number of popular would-be conspiracies—the D.B. Cooper case, Area 51, and of course the JFK assassination, among them.

Prior to his career as an investigative journalist, Flynn had served as an officer for the CIA, working undercover in some of the world's most dangerous places and getting a firsthand look at what happens behind the curtain. "You never want to see how the sausage is made," his father warned him when Flynn told him about his desire to work for the agency. But that didn't deter Flynn. And during his career, he'd been part of plenty of clandestine operations, most of them never to be known by the American people. In each case there was a clear objective, and secrecy was vital to keep American intelligence and military personnel safe from organizations and governments that would otherwise do them harm. The overarching purpose of these missions was to protect American lives. The covert approach allowed the men and women of the CIA to do their jobs and make the world a better place.

Tonight's meeting wasn't a covert affair. It was simply another interview. And he'd been invited.

Although he'd never worked with Ultra before, Flynn was keenly aware of the organization's existence as well as its reputation for being a collection of eccentrics and wacko extremists.

Theresa Halston, Flynn's boss and the editor of *The National* magazine, had been contacted by someone claiming that the U.S.

government was experimenting with mind control as part of a secret military operation. A breakthrough had occurred that actually allowed scientists to read the minds of some of their test subjects, or so the rumors suggested. Theresa wanted Flynn to investigate these rumors on behalf of *The National*.

Flynn figured the people at Ultra would be plugged into all the pertinent details related to the experiments, real and imagined. His own reputation as one who exposed various conspiracy theories earned him the opportunity to attend their latest meeting which, as it happened, was being held in the Tampa Bay area not far from Flynn's home.

On Ultra's website, the flat-Earthers and moon-landing deniers ran wild with speculation regarding the alleged mind-control experiments, embellishing what they'd heard from their own "sources," creating quite a panic that ran crazier than their usual state of paranoia.

To Flynn, it was nothing more than fodder for online discussion forums. Similar stories managed to live lengthy existences among conspiracy theorists, the far-fetched tales' hearts kept beating via a consistent flow of new developments and alternate theories via the internet.

"We don't swim in those waters," Flynn had argued to Theresa.

"Typically, no. But this time we do," she said.

"What makes this any different?"

"Blaine Jacobs," she said.

"*The* Blaine Jacobs?"

Theresa nodded. "The one and only. He wants something huge. Apparently he's big into conspiracy theories, especially ones that involve the government acting shady."

As with nearly every print publication, times were tough and money was tight at *The National*, so when one of the magazine's top investors, a social media billionaire like Jacobs, urged the magazine's publisher to explore a topic, that topic was going to be explored.

Flynn urged Theresa to put someone else on it.

"This is a nothing story built by a bunch of crazies who are looking for something to hold their interest while they're not out chasing flying saucers and spotting Elvis at Denny's," he said. "What about that new girl? Leslie Vander-something. Send her instead."

"Leslie Vander*waal*," Theresa said. "And, no. She's on something else right now. And besides, Jacobs asked for you specifically. Said he wants, and I quote, 'the big guns.'" She chuckled as she said it.

Flynn told her it was a waste of time. She agreed that it probably was before delivering the final word on the matter: "But you're going to look into it nonetheless."

Yeah, I'll look into it alright. As Flynn strode toward the meeting, he regretted not standing up to Theresa more vigorously. Did he really want to embrace the rules of this so-called secret society?

Ultra had accepted Flynn's request to attend their meeting but asked for him to show up in disguise and answer to the name John Smith. His contact inside the group was concerned that if Flynn, who was gathering some notoriety for his many investigative pieces, was recognized, it might spook some of the group's members, a particularly private and jumpy bunch.

Flynn had agreed. But now, standing in front of the building engulfed by the darkness and the smell of rotting garbage, he changed his mind. They wanted to talk to him; he wasn't trying to join the club. He wasn't looking to impress anyone. And he sure as hell wasn't going in disguise.

He pulled the fake mustache away from his upper lip, grimacing as the glue fought to adhere to his skin. He removed the non-prescription eyeglasses and slipped them into his jacket pocket along with the fake facial hair.

At the end of the alley, Flynn approached the base of a set of stairs that led up to a solid industrial door that featured no name or address just as the instructions from his contact had outlined. There was, however, an intercom wired next to the door that looked like it had been installed recently and looked very out of place compared to the dark and abandoned surroundings.

A cool light-blue ring illuminated the talk button. Flynn pushed it and spoke the password that he had been given.

A few seconds later, a hum and a hardy *click* signaled that the door was unlocked.

"Ahh, Mr. Smith." A tall man with a wide smile that stretched across his narrow rectangular face greeted Flynn as he pushed open the door. He reached out and shook Flynn's hand with the enthusiasm of a zealot meeting the Almighty.

"Pleased to meet you in person at last. I'm Oswald. We spoke on the phone."

"Thanks for the invitation."

Oswald. Flynn knew the members of Ultra used aliases but didn't expect such an obvious reference to the most infamous name from history's most-debated conspiracy plot.

Oswald's jubilant expression melted into one of concern bordering on despair.

He bent at the waist to lean close to Flynn, his voice dropping to a whisper. He pointed to himself and drew an imaginary circle around his own head with his bony index finger.

"Mr. Smith, your face. It looks very familiar, I'm afraid."

Flynn extended his palm toward Oswald's chest and nudged him back to a suitable distance.

"Yeah," Flynn said. "I decided to come as myself. Imagine that."

Oswald craned his neck to look back over his shoulder. He and Flynn were the only ones in the room.

"Yes, but Mr. Smith ... Mr. Flynn. This is *not* what we discussed. This is ... your attendance ... is going to be ... disruptive. These are very private individuals. A celebrity journalist here could unnerve them."

Flynn smiled. "I don't know if I'd consider myself a 'celebrity.'" He'd written a couple of books and regular features for *The National*, but he was never entirely comfortable with his growing notoriety. "It's not going to hurt if a few of your members recognize me. If they know my work, they know I protect my sources. I'm not going to spill club secrets to *The New York Times* or anything."

A gust of frustration exhaled from Oswald's nose. He no longer appeared to be excited about Flynn's presence and seemed more annoyed by an unwanted guest.

"You are known to this group and you will be recognized," Oswald said. "It's unexpected."

"I can leave," Flynn said, turning back toward the door. He was completely willing to walk out on Oswald and go back to tell Theresa the story was a no-go.

Oswald grabbed Flynn by the elbow. "Please, Mr. Flynn," Oswald said, his voice calm. "I apologize for my reaction. Please join us for the evening. Talk to the members. They'll be excited to speak with someone with your reputation and credibility."

Oswald released his grip, and Flynn smoothed the sleeve of his jacket.

"Lead the way," he said before following Oswald down a flight of stairs.

The first thing Flynn thought as he entered the large room was that he had stepped into a comic book convention. Ultra's members were an eclectic bunch, some dressed in suits and ties, while others wore outlandish outfits and even outright costumes. One unbelievably tall man was dressed as Bigfoot and held a sign that read, "Has anyone seen me?" Another man had a full-size rubber "Gray" alien draped on his back piggyback-style. A young woman wore a particularly tight t-shirt with "1984" emblazoned on the front and "I survived Big Brother" printed on the back. Some people wore ornate and creatively designed tinfoil hats, and Flynn wondered if they were trying to be ironic or had merely discovered a fashionable way to support their paranoia.

Tables lined the perimeter of the room where some Ultra members tried to sell books, be they pulp-style science fiction tales, memoirs of alien and/or government abductions, or nonfiction investigations exposing all manner of hidden truths. Others sold trinkets or distributed pamphlets. Flynn noted one that outlined practical steps to check any room for unwanted listening devices. Another explained how to build an underground shelter to survive the impending end times.

Oswald led Flynn through the crowd, and more than one Ultra member turned to eye the famed journalist, whispering to each other and pointing at him. Their attempts to be inconspicuous were about as successful as a pre-teen girl trying to remain calm in the presence of their pop star du jour. Flynn was, to put it mildly, the focal point of the event. Some reached out and shook his hand, welcoming him. Everyone smiled. His presence did not seem to unnerve anyone, as Oswald had feared.

Flynn followed Oswald through the large conference room to what appeared to be a coat-check area. An Ultra member stood behind a banquet table with a set of steel lockers and a coat rack behind him. He straightened his posture as they approached.

Oswald placed his arm around Flynn and introduced him to the man behind the counter. "This is Victor Nellis, Mr. Flynn," he said. "Nellis handles the security during our meetings."

"Security?" asked Flynn. "Worried about a heated conversation about the Loch Ness monster getting out of hand?"

Nellis narrowed his gaze on Flynn.

"Ultra members are extremely well-behaved, and respect for others' opinions is a hallmark of our organization. No, Mr. Flynn, our security measures are to ensure that our guests—outsiders—don't get out of hand."

Flynn eyed Oswald and then turned back to Nellis. The mood had shifted. Minutes ago Flynn had felt like an honored guest. Now he felt as though he was something just short of an enemy. The smiles that had greeted him just minutes ago were replaced by a stern face and piercing eyes.

"Outsiders," Flynn said. "Like me? Let me remind you that you cleared me to be here."

"Of course, Mr. Flynn," Oswald said, his voice sounding like it was mustering up all the good cheer possible. "You're our guest. Nellis is just being cautious. I'm sure you can understand."

Flynn smiled and nodded.

"Your cellphone," Nellis said as he produced a small plastic basket on the counter in front of Flynn. "It will be safe in one of the lockers here. It will be returned to you when you are ready to depart."

"That's not going to work for me," Flynn said. "I use my phone to record my interviews to make sure I quote my sources accurately. It protects them and it protects me."

Nellis waited a moment before saying, "Ultra does not allow audio, video or photographic documentation of its meetings. I must insist."

Flynn felt his body tense up and wondered if Nellis noticed. He stared at the guard for a long moment, the man holding his ground, not flinching, not smiling, not turning away. Flynn recognized the look. Nellis, he surmised, had some legit security training and likely a military background. He stood tall with one hand clasped over the other, belt-high in front of his body like a nightclub bouncer.

They were at an impasse. It wouldn't be worth it to escalate the situation.

Flynn pulled his cellphone from his pocket and dropped it into the plastic basket.

The two men continued to lock eyes for an uncomfortable interval, causing Oswald to break in.

"Let me introduce you to some of our members, Mr. Flynn," Oswald said.

Flynn kept his eyes on Nellis for another beat before turning to acknowledge Oswald again.

"Let's do that," Flynn said.

Nellis slid the basket into a locker and handed Flynn a claim check with the locker's number printed on it.

Oswald grasped Flynn's arm once again and directed him back toward the throng of Ultra members who had broken into pairs or small groups engaged in a dozen separate conversations. He led him to a table where two men had been watching Flynn from a distance. Oswald extended an arm toward one of the members, a gray-bearded man in his late sixties. He wore a dark suit and maroon tie and appeared to be much more mentally stable than anyone else in the room.

"Mr. Flynn, this is Brice Holland, one of Ultra's most senior members," Oswald said. He then motioned to the other man, younger than Holland, but also dressed in a suit and tie. "And this is David Bailey. They've requested an opportunity to speak with you."

Flynn took a seat across from the two men, and Oswald excused himself and stepped away.

"I'm a big fan, Mr. Flynn," Holland said. "I've read your books. I truly admire your work."

Flynn still wasn't used to the compliments he often received from strangers. He certainly enjoyed the praise, but was never quite sure how to respond.

"Thank you," he said.

Holland rambled on, raving about how Flynn handled different conspiracy plots, reporting actual facts uncovered by solid research and firsthand interviews with people directly involved. He also said he admired Flynn for how he conducted himself on national TV when a CNN host grilled him about his research.

"That little bastard was smug, but you stood your ground and put him in his place," Holland said.

To Flynn's memory, the interview in question was nowhere nearly as contentious as Holland made it sound. He didn't recall the interviewer being "little" or "smug," and he definitely didn't remember putting anyone in their place. He had learned over the years that his fans were often quite defensive. It was understandable; they held unpopular opinions and were consistently labeled as weirdos or worse. They viewed him as a champion of sorts and celebrated him for finding answers that were often difficult to uncover.

Flynn smiled. "I appreciate the support, but I doubt you went through the trouble of inviting me to your secret meeting to talk about my fifteen minutes of fame on CNN," he said.

"Oh, you're right about that," Holland said. He cleared his throat and began to speak, but his words were clipped as Bailey interjected.

"Gakona, Alaska," Bailey blurted.

Bailey's eyes widened. He had been champing at the bit to get to the matter at hand. But, as quickly as the words came out, his enthusiasm melted, the heat coming by way of a stern glance from Holland.

"I know about the not-so-secret research facility there," Flynn said. "It's called HAARP for High-frequency Active Auroral Research Program. I know that they study the Earth's ionosphere and the effects of heating the air to facilitate communication with submarines as well as locating various minerals in the ground. At one point, the Russians believed the U.S. military was creating a new type of secret weapon there. I've also heard the rumors about alleged experiments on human behavior, specifically mind control. That's been all over the internet for years. The theories about questionable research projects have more or less been debunked."

"Which is it, Mr. Flynn?" Holland said.

"What do you mean?" Flynn said.

"More? Or less? Are you saying with complete certainty that the reports about the HAARP facility are false?"

"I can't say that definitively. But I'm pretty plugged into the military community. I have high-ranking sources in every branch. It's unlikely that I wouldn't have gotten a whiff from someone if things were sketchy."

Holland eyed him carefully. "How keen is your sense of smell tonight?"

Flynn leaned forward, his eyebrows raised in curiosity. "What are you trying to say?"

"You called us to see what we knew. Here's what we know," Holland said before nodding to Bailey. "Show him."

Bailey reached into his jacket pocket and took out a black and white photograph. He laid it on the table in front of Flynn.

Flynn's eyes flickered with uncertainty.

"That's Dr. Nestor Keller," Holland said. "He's the lead researcher at HAARP. Has a reputation for being a genius. That's the man you want to talk to."

Flynn, sensing something was up, said, "What's the catch?"

Holland and Bailey exchanged glances.

"We have reason to believe he's missing," Holland said.

"Missing?"

"Vanished," said Bailey. "According to a source who contacted us last week, no one at HAARP has seen Dr. Keller in some time."

"The source goes by TruthSeeker47," said Bailey. "We have every reason to believe this person is either inside the Gakona facility or has a direct connection to the research being conducted."

"What makes you believe this TruthSeeker47 is reliable?" Flynn said.

"That's why we were so willing to invite you to our conference," Holland said. "We would love for someone of your skill to investigate what's going on up there. It's really quite serendipitous that you reached out to us at the same time as this TruthSeeker person."

Bailey chuckled. "Mr. Nellis is suspicious of the timing," he said. "Said it was 'too convenient.'"

"Yeah, I don't think Nellis cares much for me," Flynn said.

"He doesn't like many people," Bailey said. "Don't take it personally. It's his job to not trust outsiders."

Flynn exhaled. "I can look into this, make a few calls, see what I can uncover, but I have to tell you this TruthSeeker47 angle feels flimsy. If I had a nickel for every anonymous source that popped up on the internet—"

"We believe the source is credible," Holland said.

Bailey handed Flynn a slip of paper.

"Login information for our private messaging app," he said. "We've created an account for you so you can check it out for yourself."

Flynn tucked the paper into his inside jacket pocket and promised the two men he'd investigate their lead. As he stood to leave he was nearly knocked off balance by a small, round man who stumbled directly into him. The man appeared to have had too much to drink. He wore a beanie made of aluminum foil, and his face was red and dappled with sweat.

"Take this," the man said to Flynn. He thrust a handful of foil into Flynn's palm. "Find the son of Zeus. Find the truth."

The man wobbled off leaving Flynn holding the makeshift aluminum hat. Flynn looked at a bewildered Holland and Bailey, and shook his head.

I gotta get out of here.

3

ST. PETERSBURG BEACH, FLORIDA

Flynn grimaced hearing Theresa laugh.

"Literal tinfoil hats," he repeated as he opened the door to the beachside motel that he called home. "I just walked in the door, putting you on speaker."

He laid his cellphone on the desk next to his laptop and switched the computer on. The light from the screen spilled into the room enough to allow him to navigate to the refrigerator and grab a bottle of water. The room was an efficiency apartment that had been used by the motel's owner back when the place was built in the late 1950s. Now it was labeled as a "suite" and rented by the week. Flynn used some money he'd earned on his latest book to rent the place for the past three months. His future there was indeterminate, but he loved living close enough to the water to hear the waves hit the beach while he lay in bed at night.

"Sounds like you made some new friends," Theresa said, still chuckling.

"Yeah, well, there's not much to this that I didn't already know," he said. "As far as the alleged missing Dr. Keller, I told them I'd make a few calls, turn over a couple of rocks, and see what I could find out. It won't likely amount to much. He probably just moved on to another facility. Or maybe he retired."

"Well, it better amount to something. Jacobs is expecting a story. And a good one too."

"I don't think you're hearing me," Flynn said. "The story about the HAARP facility at Gakona isn't a new development; it's old news. It isn't even secret anymore. They even give tours of the place to the general public. We're not talking Area 51 here. These Ultra weirdos are clinging to conspiracy theories that have been debunked for years. I don't know who this guy is, this TruthSeeker47, but he's having some fun at Ultra's expense, and it seems they're taking Blaine Jacobs along for the ride."

"I'm sure you'll find something to write about once you actually see the place," Theresa said.

"When I *what*? You're crazy if you think I'm going to Alaska."

"I already booked you a flight to Anchorage. You leave out of Tampa International at four-thirty on Monday. Take a coat. I hear it's cold. Good luck, Flynn."

She hung up. Flynn closed his eyes, drew in a deep breath and let it out slowly; it was a technique he often used to soothe his rage. It never really worked. He banged his fist on the desk. The last thing he wanted to do was freeze his ass off on some half-baked wild goose chase in the Arctic.

He logged into the secure Ultra website using the credentials from Bailey and Holland. A private message was waiting for him:

TruthSeeker47: PROJECT TITAN

Flynn responded to the message:

J_Flynn: What is Project Titan?

He waited a moment and took a bottle of water from the refrigerator. He twisted the cap off and took a long pull.

. . .

TruthSeeker47: ASK TILLMAN.

J_Flynn: Who is Tillman?

TruthSeeker47: YOU SHOULD KNOW.

J_Flynn: I was told to contact you for information. I'm not here to play games or solve your riddles. If you want to know the truth, you need to help me out. Give me something I can use.

TruthSeeker47: TILLMAN. PROJECT TITAN.

[TruthSeeker47 has logged off.]

FLYNN CURSED OUT LOUD. These people were boarding the crazy train and taking him along for the ride. Project Titan. Son of Zeus. Tinfoil hats. Mysterious online informants. Secret research facility in Alaska of all places. This was shaping up to be the weirdest assignment of his career, and he'd dealt with some real zingers in the past.

He googled "Tillman Project Titan," which didn't return anything of value. The top hits for "Tillman" were articles about former NFL star-turned-Army Ranger Pat Tillman, who was killed in combat in Afghanistan back in 2004. Most of the other search results linked to profiles of various high school, college and professional athletes, as well as a local plumbing business owned by someone named Bill Tillman.

Flynn scrolled to the second page and stopped.

Arthur Tillman. Of course.

4

GULF OF MEXICO

Debbi had once told Tillman she'd always dreamed of spending the night on a boat.

"Not like a cruise ship," she'd said. "Everyone had done that and it was so cliché. Or a dinky fishing boat—*ewww!* But a nice boat. Like a really nice boat."

Tillman was wide awake in bed, staring at the ceiling with Debi curled up next to him, running her fingers along a scar on his chest.

"Is this a nice boat?" Arthur asked.

Tillman's music played low on the stereo. She blurted out the names of the songs she recognized but didn't know many of the titles or the artists. The playlist wouldn't have been her first choice, but she'd grown to appreciate music from the late 60s and 70s, just as she'd learned to appreciate Tillman, even if he, too, had not been her first choice.

She climbed on top of him, pressed her forehead against his and whispered. "This is a *really* nice boat, Arthur."

She pushed both palms against his chest and sat up straight, staring into his eyes. It was late, but the moon and stars provided just enough light. She closed her eyes and swayed a bit to the groove pulsing from the speakers and gentle waves lifting and releasing the boat.

"Who is this one?" she said.

Tillman didn't answer right away. He seemed to be almost in a trance. Debbi smiled.

"The Moody Blues," he said after a moment.

"Nights in White Satin?"

"That's the one, baby."

The music played on, and the boat rocked in the water.

* * *

DEBBI SAT STRAIGHT UP in bed. They had struck something. The *thump* and sudden jolt startled her from a deep sleep. *The Aquaholic* rolled to one side and then the other, again thumping against something solid on its port side.

Tillman popped up. It took him just a couple of seconds to clear the drowsiness from his brain.

We didn't hit anything—something hit us.

She watched as he stood and pulled on a pair of shorts, steadying himself against the rocking motion.

"What happened?" she said.

"It's nothing. Go back to sleep."

He reached into a drawer and pulled out a large handgun. He held the weapon and grimaced. He looked right at her and shook his head.

"Arthur! What's going on?"

"Don't worry."

He glanced at the revolver and paused for a second. He looked at her again before he left the cabin and closed the door behind him, leaving her alone in the darkness.

5

ST. PETERSBURG, FLORIDA

Flynn took a shower before bed, already dreading the 10-hour flight to Alaska.

He imagined the ridiculously cold weather he was about to endure, and the hot water that pelted him in the shower felt wonderful in contrast. Theresa wasn't going to let this go, so he was going to have to find an angle, *something* to write about. The steam from the shower relaxed Flynn, and he began to recount the events of the evening with a new sense of clarity.

As much as he didn't want to go to Alaska, and as crazy he thought the Ultra folks were, something felt off to him. Something about that security guy, Nellis. Was it the way he'd looked at him? Flynn was certainly no stranger to people staring at him hard, trying to intimidate him. No, it wasn't that.

His mind changed gears back to his conversation with TruthSeeker47.

He'd heard of Arthur Tillman and was surprised he didn't recall the former general as soon as that online nut job mentioned his name.

Although their paths never crossed, Flynn knew that Tillman

was a fringe player in American intelligence operations. Tillman had an ego and was fond of speaking his mind—and doing so loudly—to people who weren't used to having the truth pushed so brutally in their faces. Flynn had heard that Tillman was a shoo-in for a position with The Company, but the old man opted to retire and spend more time in the public eye.

Kinda like me.

Nothing that he found online linked Tillman to a Project Titan, but it was common knowledge that Tillman was close to a lot of secret military research initiatives. Flynn would need to make some calls.

Loud banging jolted his concentration. He poked his head out of the shower, straining to hear. The banging repeated. Someone was knocking at his door, and they didn't sound patient.

Flynn shut off the water, eased out of the shower, quickly dried himself, and stepped into a pair of gray sweatpants with "U.S. Air Force" printed down one leg in dark blue letters.

The frantic pounding at his door continued.

"Hold on," Flynn shouted. "I'm coming."

He peered through the peephole, but could only see the extreme closeup of the head and shoulder of a man who was apparently leaning against the door.

Flynn yanked the door open, and the man fell forward into his room. He collapsed onto the floor, and Flynn jumped backward to avoid being toppled.

The visitor was dressed in a light gray suit, and Flynn recognized him as the short, pudgy man who had given him the tinfoil beanie at the Ultra meeting after he'd talked to Holland and Bailey. He seemed to be unconscious. Flynn bent to inspect the man for injuries but found none.

The man uttered a sound that was equal parts giggle and groan.

"Ooof, I'm sorry," he said as he attempted to gather himself and stand.

Flynn jolted back to avoid the overpowering aroma of cigarettes and bourbon on the guy's breath. The guy smelled like he'd gone ten rounds with Jim Beam and was behind on the judge's scorecards. Grabbing the man's elbow, Flynn yanked him to his feet.

"Liam Baxter," the man said, extending a sweaty palm. "But my friends call me Bax. If I had friends, that is."

At this, Baxter laughed until his round face bloomed red.

Flynn accepted the handshake with his right hand and steadied the man's upper arm with his left, partly to help Baxter not fall over and partly to prevent him from getting too close. Flynn was always wary of people invading his personal space. His most fervent fanbase tended to lean toward the type with unstable personalities, and he was always alert when someone approached him. Baxter seemed harmless enough, but Flynn didn't take risks with anyone.

Baxter's boisterous laugh was abruptly murdered by a series of rattling coughs, and the man bent forward at the waist holding a palm toward Flynn as he tried to catch his breath.

"One. Second. Please," he said, the words laboring to come out in three separate gasps.

Flynn backed up a step.

Baxter got his breathing under control, smoothed a few thin wisps of hair across the top of his otherwise bald scalp, and tugged the wrinkles out of his suit in an attempt to compose himself. He asked Flynn for a glass of water, which Flynn filled from the tap and placed on the counter near Baxter's reach.

Baxter drained the glass in one long gulp and wiped his mouth with the back of his chubby hand.

"Much better. Mind if I sit?"

Flynn said nothing.

Baxter stumbled toward the small couch against the wall and plopped onto the worn cushions. He exhaled and took in the room like a new student on the first day of school. He certainly looked to be drunk for sure, but there was more to it than that.

His eyes bounced around, looking at everything, except directly at Flynn. His attention finally rested on the digital clock that was nearby. A few minutes past one A.M.

"Apologies for the hour," he said.

Flynn realized his front door was still wide-open. He leaned to look outside. Nothing appeared to be out of the ordinary.

He turned back toward Baxter.

"Did you drive here? Where's your car? No way you walked all the way from downtown Tampa."

He shut the door and locked the deadbolt.

Baxter flinched at the lock's resounding clunk.

"It's a hot one out there tonight," Baxter said. "Every time I come to Florida I forget how suffocating the humidity can get."

Baxter stood to refill his glass at the sink. He did so without much struggle, Flynn observed. The man seemed less inebriated, and his limbs had magically regained their coordination. Baxter's eye met Flynn's with a tiny flash of recognition that he'd been caught. He dropped his gaze and once again feigned an inability to control his motor skills while he staggered back to his spot on the couch. It was quite the dramatic display.

Baxter gestured toward the sliding glass door that led from the back of the apartment to the shore of the Gulf of Mexico just a few yards beyond.

"I bet you see a lot of bikinis out there," he said, his words slurred together more so than previous, really playing it up.

The guy wasn't drunk, or not nearly as drunk as he wanted Flynn to believe he was. But why the act?

Why come all the way across the bridge from Tampa and stumble into my house at one in the morning pretending to be three sheets to the wind?

"Just get to it," said Flynn.

Baxter's face flashed more sense of clarity than the man intended but then sagged again to bluff inebriated disorientation. Even if he knew his ruse was exposed, he was intent on playing out the string.

Before Baxter could respond, Flynn asked, "Was it Ultra? Did they send you here?"

Baxter shook his head, his expression uneasy. "No, it's... it's not them. It's him. He... he knows."

Flynn leaned forward, his curiosity piqued. "Who? Who knows things?"

"Not *him*. It's..." Baxter hesitated, struggling to find the right words, his eyes darting around as if seeking an invisible prompt. "I can't remember. Son of Zeus. I can't..." He trailed off, clearly frustrated by his inability to articulate.

Flynn, sensing Baxter's distress, changed tack. "What is it? Talk to me, Bax."

Baxter smiled and then his eyes flickered with a mix of fear and urgency. "I was part of something... a messenger. They said it would help, but it didn't. It changed things in here." He tapped his temple with a finger, his hand trembling.

Flynn sat back, processing this.

Baxter went on, really straining to concentrate and get the words out. "Conversation. But not words. It's hard to explain. They don't talk. Son of Zeus."

"What do they talk about?" Flynn pressed, intrigued despite his skepticism. "What is the Son of Zeus?"

"Warnings, ideas, fragments. Something important, but I can't piece it together. It's like a puzzle—" Baxter was exasperated.

"Why come to me?"

Baxter leaned in closer, his voice dropping to a whisper. "Find the pieces."

"I don't understand."

Baxter shook his head and began to sob. "I can't... I don't have the words. It's like they're on the tip of my tongue, but I can't." He stared straight into Flynn's eyes. "Help me."

They sat in silence for nearly half a minute. Flynn sensed something was about to go awry. It was nearly imperceptible, but his training had taught him to spot even the slightest change in a person's demeanor. He would later describe the tiny transformation in Baxter's disposition only as an involuntary tic, but even that didn't quite tell the whole story. Baxter himself was almost certainly totally unaware that he'd given himself away.

In a flash, Baxter launched himself from the couch straight toward Flynn. Gone was the visage of a drunken buffoon or a distraught victim, replaced by that of an enraged maniac.

Flynn was ready for the attack but totally underestimated the squatty man's quickness. He tried to sidestep the lunge, but Baxter, shockingly, was too agile and slammed into Flynn, tipping him and his chair straight back to the floor.

Flynn's neck whiplashed from the impact and he struck his head on the floor. For a split second everything flashed bright white and Baxter was on top of him compressing two sweaty hands around his neck.

The ambush worked, but Flynn expected Baxter to lack any real fighting skills, relying only on brute force and adrenaline to gain the upper hand.

Flynn was wrong.

Baxter barred his left forearm across Flynn's throat, choking off his air. On the brink of blacking out, Flynn grasped Baxter's right arm, outstretched for balance and the source of his unyielding pressure on Flynn's neck. Flynn drilled his thumb into a pressure point in Baxter's wrist with a sharp squeeze. Baxter winced. It was the opening Flynn needed.

He surged upwards to roll the rotund man toward his right side. Baxter still held his left arm against Flynn's neck, but his right arm was useless and he had no leverage to stop the sudden forceful rotation toward the floor. Flynn regained the upper hand.

Or so he thought.

With a last-ditch attempt, Baxter flailed a heavy fist and struck a massive blow against Flynn's temple.

Everything went black.

6

WASHINGTON, D.C.

To call Quinton Danbury an honest man would be a relative statement. He was as honest as anyone in Washington, which is to say he was as honest as he needed to be, given each particular situation. The longtime senator from Virginia did, however, have the reputation as a straight shooter, at least when compared to his peers on Capitol Hill. Not necessarily above making an empty promise or embellishing his own accolades in the pursuit of votes, Danbury did have a particularly admirable public stance on one topic: He was staunchly opposed to receiving financial backing from special interest groups and large corporations that might otherwise steer his decision-making. He was, and always had been, all about Virginia.

Not that there weren't clever—and not so subtle—ways around his number one rule.

Campaign contributions came from all directions, and tracking down and vetting each source seemed unrealistic and unnecessary in Danbury's mind. For example, he wouldn't accept donations from organizations that expected favors, but money from the individuals within that organization was welcome with open arms and an open deposit slip. If the CEO of a well-known Virginia-based bank or aeronautics company wanted to contribute personal funds to his re-election war chest, who was Danbury to complain? It may have been a small distinction but it was one that played well to the TV cameras and his constituents, who viewed Danbury as a Maverick who followed his own conscience and wasn't in the pocket of some corporate fat cat.

Danbury took the money with a wink and a nod. He knew the contributor often wanted to steer the senator toward legislation that would be favorable to their desired outcome, but Danbury made no promises. He knew that whoever believed he could be expected to vote one way or the other on a particular issue would be better served with him in office than one of his opponents on the other side of the aisle. Chances were good that he would naturally take action that would favor groups and industries that supported him. It was worth their while to keep him in office regardless whether they were actually pulling his strings or not.

That way of doing business had served him well. Danbury had cemented himself as a fixture on The Hill and a major player in the U.S. political landscape. His face was well-known, and his smooth Virginia drawl made one feel comfortable, like they were talking to a favorite uncle. He was generally liked, and even earned the respect of his political foes for being a man who could compromise for the general good of the majority.

But, politics are politics, and there was always someone looking to take his seat at the table. In the case of this upcoming election, that someone was a young up-and-comer from Roanoke. Thirty years younger than Danbury and handsome in a way that Danbury never was, Blake Calloway possessed every bit of the older man's southern charm along with fresh ideas and a lot more money to throw around on the campaign trail. The young challenger was gaining serious momentum, and recent polls even showed him having the edge over Danbury. What would have been unthinkable even just a few months ago was becoming a dreadful reality for the incumbent senator.

It was Calloway's sudden surge in popularity that led Danbury to attend the evening's event: a fund-raising dinner on a massive yacht in Chesapeake Bay. He hated things like this but had come to the realization years ago that such events were necessary to maintain a successful political career. Like all business operations, his campaign needed money to be successful, and parties like this one were often the best way to generate some serious revenue.

Danbury, seeking a brief break from glad-handing, stood on the deck near the yacht's bow, leaning against the railing and admiring the glittering Virginia Beach skyline. Politics aside, he truly loved his home state and believed he was doing all he could for the benefit of Virginians as well as all Americans. He'd taken a few questionable actions during his political career, but every decision he made was made with good intentions. In every case, Danbury believed the ends justified the means.

The fundraiser was, for lack of a better word, a bomb. Far fewer people attended than expected, and the checks in the white envelopes, although very much appreciated, were considerably smaller than he'd hoped for. Even at $2,500 a plate, the total take was looking to be a drop in the bucket.

Danbury nursed the last few sips of his drink. It felt like it was all about to be over soon.

"Senator Danbury?"

The man's voice startled him, and he quickly spun around to face a slender man dressed in a dark blue suit. The man was built with straight lines and crisp angles, like he was constructed from diagrams pulled from a geometry textbook. His suit was immaculately cut, and the man's complete appearance was impossibly clean, almost unnaturally so. Something about the thin man unnerved Danbury right away.

He immediately shook off the uneasy feeling. It was time to go to work.

"I have to admit you caught me off guard there, friend," Danbury said with a wide smile. "I was lost in my thoughts on this beautiful night and didn't know anyone else was out here. I'm Quinton Danbury. What can I do for you, Mister...?"

Danbury extended his arm to shake the man's hand, but the slender man seemed to not notice.

"You can call me Mr. White. I represent an organization that can get your campaign back on track," the man said. "We are willing to provide a sizable contribution."

Danbury said nothing, but gave a look that encouraged the man's sales pitch.

"A new federal research project is going to come before your committee soon, seeking a great deal of funding," the man said. "The people I work for would like to see that funding denied. We know you carry a great deal of influence on the committee that oversees these research projects, and we'd be grateful if you could close the door, so to speak. It's crucial that this project ceases."

Danbury knew there was a slate of projects that were competing for limited available funds. Ones deemed unnecessary would be scheduled to have their funding cut or eliminated entirely to move money into other areas that were considered a higher priority. Budgets were tight, and Danbury was known to be a conservative spender of taxpayer money. He quickly ran through the list of funded research projects in his head. He wasn't an expert in their details but knew enough to be surprised that any of them would have such passionate opposition with, apparently, deep pockets.

"You can rest assured that I'll do my best to make sure that all programs that are in the nation's best interest and strengthen the general well-being of the majority of Americans will maintain all the support and funding they need to continue," Danbury said.

Mr. White's expression was vacant within the outline of his triangular face.

"No," he said.

"No?" Danbury said. "No, what?"

"This is not a press conference, and your canned response is unacceptable. If my organization is going to contribute to your re-election, we will need nothing short of a promise that money for this research program will be cut off as soon as possible."

"Well, I hate to tell you, but that's not how it works," Danbury said. "I don't play ball like that. People who want to donate to my campaign do so because they have faith in my integrity. My track record speaks for itself. I don't make promises that aren't in my constituents' best interest. I can tell you that I'll look into your pet project, and if it makes sense to do so, I'll do my best to curtail its existence."

The man turned to walk away but stopped briefly.

"I wonder," he said. "How will your integrity serve this nation after you lose the election?"

Danbury clenched his jaw as the man left. The senator stood so fixated on his departing visitor's stinging retort that he didn't even notice his campaign manager, Barry Meadows, seemingly appear from nowhere.

"Who was that?" Meadows said.

Danbury snapped out of his brief trance. "Dammit, Barry, Where were you? Why are you never within earshot when I actually need you? Isn't your job to help me? It'd be nice to, I don't know, actually get some help once in a while."

Meadows' face drooped like a puppy that had been called out for peeing on Danbury's favorite rug. "I was below deck with your guests, Quinton," he said. "Singing your praises. Drumming up votes for you. Shaking the proverbial money tree—for you. Why are you up here instead of down there working the room?"

Danbury sighed and shook his head. He gave Meadows' shoulder a firm squeeze. "I know," he said. "I'm sorry. It's just that ... I can see the end of the road. I'm gonna lose this thing. You know that as well as I do. And men like that, they just piss me off."

Meadows looked toward the door where Mr. White had left. "Who was that guy?"

"Him?" Danbury said. "He could be everything we need."

7

TAMPA, FLORIDA

Arthur Tillman's boat had been towed in and moored to the pier. Yellow tape stretched from one piling to another, preventing pedestrians from getting close. A uniformed Hillsborough County Sheriff's deputy stood on the outside of the tape, and a few onlookers craned their necks to see what the fuss was about.

FBI Special Agent Wayne Minter flashed his badge to the deputy and ducked under the tape and strode up the gangway onto *The Aquaholic*. He took a deep breath and inhaled the salt water air before he looked skyward and eyed a pelican swooping low across the pier. Down the beach, he spotted sun worshipers lugging chairs and coolers across the sand in search of the perfect spot to relax.

Wonder what that would be like? he mused to himself. Shortages at his field office had him working all the time. He couldn't remember the last time he'd had two consecutive days off. Then for a moment, he wondered what he was doing there.

Tampa Police determined the murder had occurred in waters that fell within the county jurisdiction and were more than happy to turn the case over to the Hillsborough Sheriff's Office. Realizing who the victim was, the county made a call to the local FBI field office for assistance. Minter was stationed at the FBI's Tampa office and had been directed to take the lead on the investigation.

Once onboard, Minter walked through a mixed team of FBI and local law enforcement already on scene. A pair of uniformed officers stood, each with a cup of coffee, talking about yesterday's Gator game, which Minter knew had been a 35-21 win over LSU.

Minter, a shade under five-foot-nine with a wide body and short, yet powerful-looking arms, approached the men with a wide smile across his face.

"How ya doin'?" he asked with an exaggerated southern accent.

The two deputies smiled back. "Doing just fine, thanks for asking," said one.

Minter was jovial, as if speaking to one of his old Army buddies. "You two doing any actual police work this morning or are you just playing grab-ass at my crime scene?"

The uniforms, caught off guard by the question, looked at Minter and then toward each other and then back at Minter. After a moment, one of the deputies spoke. "You FBI?"

Minter held the deputy with a stare that answered his question. "Special Agent Minter."

The other deputy began to ask to see Minter's credentials but his partner hushed him and led him off the boat back to the pier.

Minter surveyed the scene and the gaggle of bodies crammed into the tight space. He cleared his throat.

Everyone went silent and looked up immediately as if they'd been hauled into the principal's office. No one moved.

Minter waved a hand toward one of the FBI forensics guys.

The man nodded and said, "Alright, people, let's give Special Agent Minter some room."

Slowly, each of the law enforcement officers filed past Minter and off the yacht. All but one.

"Sorry, Wayne. It just sort of got out of hand," said Minter's partner, Special Agent Samantha Blackwood. "First it was just the CSI guys. Next thing I know I'm up to my armpits with these County rubes trampling everything. Word around the office travels fast. As soon as we heard it was Arthur Tillman, even some of our own people started slinking around, trying to get a peek."

Minter grunted something that made Blackwood believe he accepted her apology. She stepped back to give him room to approach the scene.

Arthur Tillman's body was crumpled against the door frame heading down into the yacht's cabin. A thin rod of stainless steel protruded from the center of his bare chest, and blood ran from the wound down his torso and pooled on the white fiberglass deck.

"County marine unit spotted the boat around six a.m.," Blackwood said. "Found a young woman on board. Scared out of her mind. They said she was huddled back in the bedroom tucked into a cabinet."

"Who is she?"

"Not his daughter, we know that," Blackwood said. "Escort maybe? Girlfriend? We don't know. She's at the hospital. Poor thing was really shaken up. She didn't want to go home, and I knew you'd want to talk to her, so we've got her under protection."

Minter slipped on a pair of rubber gloves and crouched down next to the body. He gestured toward the shaft sticking out of Tillman's chest.

"Crossbow?"

"Speargun," Blackwood said.

"Well, that's a new one. Prints?"

"Clean. Found a cellphone in the kitchen. No prints on it, either."

Minter looked up at Blackwood and shielded his eyes from the sun. "What'd the girl see?" he asked.

"Not much. Report from the deputy on the scene says a boat came alongside late last night. General Tillman and the girl were down below, sleeping. Tillman, Colt .45 revolver in hand, went out to investigate. The girl hid until the marine unit arrived early this morning."

"Where's the gun?"

Blackwood motioned down the steps toward the galley. "On the floor. No prints."

"Sounds like a theme."

Minter descended and crouched near the .45 revolver. "Nickel-plated. Pearl grip," he said. "It's certainly on brand for the General. Tillman was never shy about making a grand appearance. Gun like that definitely makes a statement."

Blackwood leaned in from above. "It's not loaded," she said. "What was Tillman planning to do, throw it at the guy?"

"Maybe he wasn't expecting to have to use it," Minter said as his partner came down the steps into the cabin. "Probably grabbed it just for show, expecting whoever it was to run off. You see a guy like Tillman waving this hand cannon in your face, what are you gonna do?"

"Shoot him in the chest with a speargun."

Minter smirked. "Don't get cute. Ninety-nine out of a hundred guys see this gun, they're gonna run."

"Maybe." Blackwood sounded less than convinced.

Minter peeled off the latex gloves. "What I'm wondering: Why'd the killer let the girl live?"

Blackwood shrugged. "She didn't see anything. Maybe the shooter didn't even know there was anyone else on board."

The yacht's interior was pristine. A couple of glasses were on the counter—both empty.

Minter scanned the galley and stopped when he got to the cellphone on the counter. "Tillman's?"

Blackwood nodded and handed Minter a red folder. PROJECT HERMES - EYES ONLY was typed across the front.

"What's this?" Minter asked.

"It's empty" Blackwood said. "It was under the cellphone."

"What is Hermes?"

* * *

Debbi Dixon recalled the events of the previous day. It was the same story she told the Hillsborough County deputy who found her huddled inside the boat.

"Did you hear anything after General Tillman left the cabin?" Minter asked.

"I heard him yelling," Debbi said.

"General Tillman? What was he yelling."

Debbi shrugged. "I couldn't tell. He was really pissed though."

"Did it sound like he knew the guy? Were they talking back and forth?"

The girl was quiet for a second before responding. "I couldn't tell. I heard Arthur yell and then nothing. When he didn't come back in after a few minutes, I freaked. I was certain they were going to kill me. I covered my eyes. I didn't want to see it. I didn't want to see Arthur. I didn't want to see what they did—"

Debbi leaned forward and cupped her face with her hands and began to sob. Minter looked at Blackwood and then nodded toward Debbi.

Blackwood put her hand on the girl's back.

"We know this is tough," she said with a soft, soothing tone. "We want to find whoever did this, and anything you can tell us is helpful."

She handed Debbi a tissue.

The young woman wiped her eyes and sat up. She craned her neck to get a look toward the hallway where a police officer stood guard. "Are there TV reporters out there?"

The FBI agents looked at one another and then back to Debbi. "No," Minter said. "We've managed to keep this quiet so far, but the media will be all over it by lunch time."

Debbi laid back and rested her head against the pillow.

"We can keep you in protective custody for a while if you're looking to avoid the media," Blackwood said. "We'd prefer you don't say anything publicly right now; it could hamper our investigation. Eventually we could help you craft a statement."

"Miss Dixon, did you ever go outside to check on General Tillman?" Minter said.

"Check on him? He was dead."

"But you didn't know that. He could have just been injured. He could have fallen overboard."

"I knew he was dead," Debbi said. "I knew it. I laid there with my eyes shut tight, praying they wouldn't kill me, too. I heard the other boat rev up and speed away. I didn't look up for at least a minute or two. I couldn't look at him. I couldn't go out there."

Blackwood spoke up. "What else?"

Debbi sat silent and motionless as if she were reenacting the events in her mind. After a moment she said: "I finally opened my eyes and sat up. I was so scared. I expected them to come back. I don't know why. I just did. So, I crawled inside a cupboard next to the bed and hid inside. I didn't know what to do. So, I hid."

"You didn't call for help?" Minter said. "You had your cellphone on the boat."

"I had it but I forgot it on the counter, and once I was inside, I wasn't going back out there. No way."

"You stayed in that cabinet for ten hours?"

"Is that how long it was?" Debbi asked.

"Give or take."

Blackwood spoke up again: "Can you think of anyone who would want to kill General Tillman?"

Debbi bit the inside of her lip as she thought about it. "I mean, Arthur had plenty of people who'd like to see him knocked down a peg or two," she said. "You ever meet him? He's so charming — *was* charming, I mean. He was in his sixties but in better shape than some guys I know who aren't even thirty yet. And he knew it. He could rub people the wrong way with his attitude. People thought he was arrogant. But I can't think of anyone who'd want him dead."

"What about jealous boyfriends?" Minter asked.

"Me?" Debbi asked. "None crazy enough to kill a man."

"Are you sure?" Minter asked, pushing her. "You never know how a guy might react, he sees his pretty young girlfriend on the arm of a man old enough to be her grandfather, sticking it in his face."

"I never did anything like that."

Blackwood broke in. "I never met General Tillman, but I've seen him on TV. Handsome, those eyes."

Debbi brightened up. "I know, right? I mean, I know he has a reputation. Lots of younger women, likes to run with celebs and get on TV, but we had a connection. It was real. Not saying we were going to last forever, but I ... I loved him."

Minter stifled a groan as Blackwood shot him a look. She knew him too well. She was good with people in a way that he could never be.

"No, I understand," Blackwood said. "Age. It's just a number, right?"

"Exactly," Debbi said. "Thank you. Finally, someone gets it."

"He ever talk about money?" Minter jerking the conversation back on track. "I mean, clearly the guy had done well for himself, but a boat like that has a hefty price tag, even for a decorated ex-general with a lot of celebrity connections."

Debbi dabbed her eyes with a tissue. "He never talked about where he got it, but money was never an issue. There was always enough. I know he talked about his investments a lot. He would sometimes say, 'Once this product hits the market, we'll be dancing.' I never really knew what product he was talking about. I didn't ask, and he didn't say."

"Dancing?" Minter asked.

"Yeah. That was Arthur's word for it. You know, like we'd be living it up after a big payday — he always said we'd go dancing."

The girl began to cry again.

Minter was feeling an end to the usefulness of the interview. "I think we're good here," he said.

Blackwood reached out and touched Debbi's shoulder and

handed her a card. "Thank you," she said. "If you can think of anything else, please give us a call."

The FBI agents turned to leave the room, when Debbi Dixon said: "They always get my name wrong."

Minter pivoted and said, "Who?"

"The media. It's Debbi, with an 'i.'"

8

ST. PETERSBURG, FLORIDA

Flynn sat across the table from Leslie Vanderwaal. He was halfway through a western omelet, while she sipped her second cup of coffee. In the short time he'd known her, Flynn had never seen the woman eat a single thing. She seemed to be fueled entirely by a steady stream of caffeine.

Vanderwaal had been with *The National* for just over six months. She was young and wore serious dark-framed glasses and her hair pulled back tightly into a perfect and completely no-nonsense bun. She dressed exclusively in black pants suits with dark-colored blouses that ranged from Navy blue to deep maroon to somber gray. Her makeup was minimal, and her speech was crisp with enunciation so precise that it would make a vocal coach swoon. Everything about Leslie Vanderwaal's appearance screamed "serious journalist," and although Flynn knew she was indeed a talented writer and tenacious reporter, he also could see that her entire image was little more than a costume.

The diner was a quick walk from Flynn's motel and had become his favorite hangout. They had the best grouper sandwich in the Bay Area—cheap prices, and a perfect spot for people-watching, something Flynn enjoyed.

Breakfast that morning was Vanderwaal's idea. She'd been trying to pick Flynn's brain for weeks and finally decided to set up a meeting on his turf. So eager she was to meet with him that she flew from New York to Florida just for the day. He knew that level of enthusiasm likely had no end, so he figured the path of least resistance was to sit and talk with the woman to get it over with.

"A government mind-reading lab in Alaska," Vanderwaal said. "You always get the best gigs."

Flynn looked up with a mouthful of omelet and an expression that was caught somewhere between confusion and irritation.

"No?" Vanderwaal asked, taking another sip of caffeine.

Flynn spoke with his mouth full. "Hardly."

"But secret government projects—"

"There's nothing secret about what's going on there. I told Theresa as much."

"Then why are you going?"

"Who says I am?"

"You're not?"

"Not today."

"Gonna talk to the police first?"

How did she know?

"I'm a nosey reporter, Flynn," she said, sensing his surprise. "I know things. You reported an intruder at your cozy little beach-front motel. I assume he's the one who gave you that nice bruise."

Flynn lightly touched the side of his head. It was embarrassing enough to have been caught off guard by a lucky haymaker from Baxter, but to have Leslie Vanderwaal make a point to acknowledge the injury made it all the worse. Flynn knew that even just a few years ago, a guy like Baxter could have never gotten the jump on him like he did last night. He'd been out of the field for a while now, and he could feel his self-defense skills slipping just a bit. He made a mental note to get his ass back in the gym ASAP.

Every day was a new adjustment to his moderate level of fame.

He'd spent his previous career in the shadows as an unknown operative, so it was still an uneasy feeling to be recognized by strangers. Once he realized that some of those strangers would boldly intrude into his daily life, it made him uncomfortable. He wrote extensive magazine features and full-length books to inform his readers; that's what he gave to them.

But they wanted more. His fans wanted to be close to him, to really know him. Sometimes it creeped him out. People wanted to learn his secrets. People like Leslie Vanderwaal. How she had a source inside the St. Pete PD was vexing.

"Doesn't sound like you," she said. "Calling the cops."

"What does that mean?"

She shrugged. "You did the right thing."

She was right; he didn't typically get the local police involved in his affairs. He'd spent years working alone and solving his own problems. Why did this one feel different?

"We should work on something together," Vanderwaal said, pulling the topic back toward herself.

I'd rather stab out my own eyes.

"Like what?" he asked.

Leslie put a finger to her lips and thought for a moment. "I don't know. Something juicy. Like that piece you did on the JFK assassination. But something more 'now,' more 21st Century."

"I don't really do team projects," he said. "I'm more of a one-man operation."

"I saw you on TV talking about UFOs in New Mexico," she said. "That interview made me want to do this for a living, you know? I was working cops and courts at a newspaper in Fort Wayne. I saw you on CNN and knew right away I wanted to do something better, something bigger."

"Well, here you are," he said. "Living the dream."

"You're making fun of me."

Flynn smiled and went back to his omelet. "Not really."

"You are," she said. "But that's okay. I'm just a girl from the sticks, and you're a big deal, getting your books on bestseller lists and your face on TV. I'll get there, too, you know. I have time. What are you, like sixty?"

Flynn put down his fork. "Forty-one," he blurted. "You think that's what this is about—being a celebrity?"

She raised her eyebrows and made an expression that illustrated that she was ready for some sage advice from a veteran in her field.

"It's not," was all he said.

She slumped back against the booth and watched him for a moment as the waitress fluttered by to warm up their coffee.

"This Alaska thing sounds sexy," she said with renewed spirit. "A secret organization meeting at undisclosed locations, a clandestine government research facility in the arctic. Mind-reading conspiracies."

Flynn shoveled an extra large bite of eggs into his mouth. *How did she know all of this?*

"Why can't I get assignments like that?"

"They're not assignments," he said. "I dig this stuff up. There's a lot of work that goes on behind the scenes. Any half-decent journalist at a podunk daily can whip up a piece handed to them from an editor. If you want to make waves, you have to be ready to go where most reporters don't want to go."

"Where's that?"

"Anywhere it takes you. And you can't take shortcuts either, not to mention you can't burn people. Half this job is creating solid relationships, often with people you can't stand to be around."

"But Theresa gave you this story. You didn't dig this up."

"And you see what I'm dealing with," he said. "It's a waste of time. My reputation got this thrown in my lap. People are dying for a juicy story. They believe I can deliver one. They forget. I don't write novels. I report on facts, and sometimes the facts just aren't that exciting."

"Maybe I could go," she said.

"Alaska? Be my guest. I actually suggested it."

Her eyes went wide. "You did?"

"Theresa shot it down. Said you had another assignment."

Vanderwaal huffed. "Some assignment. Profile piece on Quinton Danbury. The guy is a total snooze-fest. He's going to lose—big. Not sure why we're even going through the trouble."

Politics bored Flynn, and politicians annoyed him. He signaled the waitress that he was ready for the check.

"Everybody has to start somewhere," Flynn said. "No one just hits the ground running with their first assignment."

The waitress glided by and dropped the bill on the table.

"You did," Vanderwaal said, reminding him of his first big story in *The National* that earned him instant worldwide acclaim.

"You're not me," he said.

"Obviously," she said. "*I'm* still excited about uncovering the truth."

Flynn chuckled. "Is that what you want to do? I thought you wanted to be a star."

"Those things aren't mutually exclusive, Flynn. Besides, don't tell me you don't like the notoriety. I've seen you talk to major TV news hosts, having the time of your life being a big shot. It's not something to be ashamed of, you know."

"It's an unavoidable product of the job," he said. "I could take it or leave it."

She smiled and nodded with a heavy dose of sarcasm.

"Newbies always think about the praise and accolades that follow a big story. You never think about all the hard work that goes on beforehand."

"Tell me more, Grandpa," she said with a grin.

"You'll see someday."

"Will I?"

"The good ones do. I guess the jury is still out on you, though."

"Seems to me the good ones could balance the fame and still maintain their enthusiasm to track down a juicy lead. But I suppose no one stays on top forever. There's always a time when new blood needs to inject life into the job."

Flynn felt his irritation rising and he stood to leave. "You ever hear the saying, 'To be the man, you've got to beat the man'?"

Vanderwaal smiled again. "It definitely sounds like something a man would say. An insecure man. Lucky for me, I'm not a man."

Flynn dropped a twenty on the table.

"It was nice talking to you, Leslie. Coffee's on me. No charge for the life lessons," he said.

Leslie Vanderwaal looked up at him. She slid the twenty-dollar bill back toward him. "Thanks anyway, Flynn," she said. "But I can afford my own coffee. And, don't forget to check in with the boss before you leave town."

* * *

THE DETECTIVE WAS a shade under six-feet tall and tipped the scale well north of three-hundred pounds, with hulking hands and fat, stubby fingers. Flynn pictured him trying to dial a phone and wondered how he was able to press just a single digit. He imagined the detective probably opted for a stylus of some sort because those sausage fingers would be no good for precision work.

His name was Block.

Flynn had talked to him the previous night when the detective arrived on the scene outside Flynn's apartment. He'd given the St. Pete Police an abbreviated account of what had happened, being careful to not disclose details about the Ultra meeting, leaving out the name of the organization, its members, and the location of its gathering.

The detective had left his card with Flynn and urged him to call, "in case anything else comes to mind during the night."

The vagueness of Flynn's report and his apparent lack of cooperation had clearly agitated Block, who greeted Flynn this morning with an aggressive handshake and a salesman's phony smile.

Flynn assumed the invitation was just an excuse for Block to get him away from the comfort of his motel room and tighten the screws on him. But his training had made him an expert in resisting interrogation, and he wasn't about to divulge any details that would compromise his source.

Detective Block lumbered into the interview room, one of his pudgy hands clutching a small Styrofoam cup. He asked Flynn if he wanted some coffee or perhaps a bottle of water. Flynn declined, and Block shut the door behind him.

Flynn sat at the table that divided the room, which was typically used to interrogate suspects. The room's intended purpose didn't go unnoticed and neither did the observation that Block chose to stand. He was edging for any psychological advantage he could muster. Flynn appreciated the effort.

"Let's go over last night again, if you don't mind, Mr. Flynn."

"I'll tell you what I can," Flynn said.

"Let's start with where you were and who you were talking to." Block getting right to it.

"As I explained last night: I'm an investigative journalist. I was on assignment. My sources count on me to protect the confidentiality of our conversations."

Block spread his arms wide, exposing dark, wet stains under the armpits of his white button-down shirt. "I'm not asking for details about your conversation. A man breaks into your motel room and knocks you silly, I think you'd be anxious to supply as much info as you can to make sure we get him off the streets."

How about I knock you silly?

"He's not coming back," Flynn said.

"How can you be so sure?"

"He got lucky and he knows it. Caught me off-guard. It won't happen again."

"Pretty cocky for a guy who got knocked out in his own house. Maybe you made sure it won't happen again."

Flynn went silent for a moment and then understood. “Baxter’s dead, isn’t he?”

“Are you asking me?”

“Well, is he?”

“You tell me, Mr. Flynn.”

“Look, the guy came to my room, attacked me, knocked me unconscious. When I got up, he was gone. I called you. That’s all I know.”

“You seemed pretty confident that you weren’t going to have to worry about dealing with Baxter ever again.”

“I don’t think he was there to hurt me, not seriously, anyway,” Flynn said. “I think he was there to ask for help.”

“What kind of help?” Block was growing more and more irritated by the second.

“Beats me.”

“You wanna know what I think?”

“I know what you think,” Flynn said. “You think I went out last night and settled a score with the unfortunate Liam Baxter? I was the last one to see that man alive. That makes me a suspect. No explanation of the night’s events is going to change that. But we both know I didn’t kill anyone, and these questions are just wasting time that could be spent finding the real killer.”

Block smiled. “Well, I gotta say, you don’t disappoint, Mr. Flynn,” he said. “You’re exactly the man she said you were.”

Flynn began to ask who *she* was, but answered his own question. “Theresa,” he said.

“I got off the phone with Ms. Halston about thirty minutes before you came in. Nice lady,” Block said. He pulled a file folder from a small cabinet behind him and took a seat across the table from Flynn. “Let’s see: A group of weirdos call themselves Ultra and meet up for some kind of clandestine conspiracy theory comic-con. You talk to a couple of them—Misters Holland and Bailey—about government mind control experiments in Alaska, and some pathetic nerdy bastard follows you home, knocks you upside the head and dies of a stab wound not four blocks from your motel room. That sound about right to you?"

Flynn said nothing.

Block leaned toward him and pointed a kielbasa of a finger in his face.

"Look, Flynn. I don't give a rat's backside about your magazine, Ultra, secret government facilities at the North Pole or stories about little green men from outer space. What I do care about are dead bodies in my town, so you better smarten up and play ball with me while you still have a chance to stay on my good side."

"This is your good side?"

That earned a little chuckle from the fat man. "Hard to believe isn't it?"

"If you had all that info, why ask me questions you knew I wasn't going to answer?" Flynn said.

"I wanted to see what kind of man I was dealing with. Now I know."

Flynn wasn't sure what to make of that, but there was no time to worry about Detective Block's opinion of his character.

"The killer was either very good or very lucky."

"How's that?" Flynn said

"The blade pierced the aorta. It was a fatal strike, even if it was going to take a few minutes."

"What else can you tell me? Who is this guy Baxter?"

Block tightened up. "It's an active murder investigation. There are details I can't share with the public."

This guy. Flynn inhaled deeply, held it for a second and released a slow exhale. "I'm not the public," he said. "The man died after leaving my motel room. He assaulted *me*. I'm in this."

"I agree," Block said. "That's why I was hoping you'd come talk to us. You were the last to see Baxter alive, and anything you tell us could be beneficial in helping us find his killer."

Help them? The thought stabbed at his brain.

"I can help you by being part of the investigation," he said.

Block laughed, causing the hair on Flynn's neck to stand up. "You're not a detective, Flynn. You're not any kind of law enforcement. Hell, you're not even a private investigator. Do me a favor: write your stories and leave the police work to the professionals."

* * *

NELLIS SAT in his car across the street from the St. Petersburg Police Department. He'd been following James Flynn all morning, and waited for him to exit the building. Nellis wondered what Flynn told the police. How much did they know? What exactly did Flynn know?

9

ANNAPOLIS, MARYLAND

Wayne Minter's flight from Tampa had been uneventful, pleasant even. To his surprise, his experience at the rental car counter at the Baltimore airport had been equally agreeable, and his drive to Annapolis proved to be as smooth as he could've hoped for given the Beltway's rage-inducing traffic. But, nevertheless, Minter's stomach was tied in a knot with aggravation.

The Tillman murder case was driving him crazy. The General was a brash man; no doubt he had some opponents and rivals, enemies even. Minter could see Tillman catching a random left hook to the jaw from some angry adversary tired of the old man's blustering. He could even imagine a jealous boyfriend or husband in a white-hot rage going after the General. Situations like that could get out of hand and people sometimes ended up dead.

But for someone to take a boat and track Tillman thirty-plus miles into the Gulf of Mexico and shoot him point-blank in the chest with a by-God speargun? That was a different thing altogether. It was intentional.

It felt professional.

Minter wanted more information on Tillman and knew one man who could likely shed some light on the general's private affairs.

By the tone of his voice, Vice Admiral Paul Barrow sounded happy to hear Minter on the other end of the line.

"Wayne," he said, "how have you been?"

Minter and Barrow had gone to the Naval Academy together before Minter realized a career in the military was not going to be to his liking. Barrow stayed in, played football for the Midshipmen, and climbed the ladder to earn distinction among his peers.

Despite their branched career paths, the two men stayed close and still managed to talk regularly, even though it became harder to do so as the years went by.

"I'm fine," Minter said. "How's Kathy?"

"What can I say? I'm a lucky man."

Minter didn't want to jump right into the Tillman case so he voluntarily suffered through small talk about the unseasonably warm weather, the general state of college football, and tales of Barrow's two grown children, who were living their dreams as hotshot lawyers.

Minter was never adept at hiding his disdain for banter, and Barrow obviously noticed his friend's lack of reciprocation in the conversation. Minter never felt the need to share details of his personal life—a trait, which not so ironically, led to the two divorces—and wished others would do the same. There hadn't been any kids in either marriage and he doubted anyone sincerely wanted to hear about his retriever, Grit.

Barrow chuckled. "I get it. Enough chit-chat. I'm sure you didn't call to hear me complain about the Redskins changing their name, so speak up, Wayne. What's on your mind?"

Minter couldn't help but smile. He knew he was a tough nut to crack and he truly appreciated Barrow accepting his personality quirks and remaining a loyal friend.

"Arthur Tillman," he said.

"Ol' Art. What'd he do? Get a college cheerleader pregnant?" Barrow laughed at his own joke.

"He's dead."

The phone went silent for a few seconds before Barrow finally spoke.

"Aww, hell," Barrow finally said. "Well don't I just feel like a horse's ass? I'm real sad to hear that. What happened?"

"He was murdered on his boat in the Gulf."

"Who would want to kill Art Tillman?" Barrow said. "And I ask that somewhat rhetorically, because I know plenty of people who flat-out didn't like the SOB. But murder?"

"That's why I'm calling, Paul. I'm in town and I'd like to get together and pick your brain a little. I mean you knew Tillman, right?"

Barrow paused before letting out his words very slowly. "Yeeeaaaahhh, I knew him. I mean we weren't drinking buddies or anything, but—you say you're in town? You mean Baltimore? Washington?"

"Your town. Annapolis," Minter said, sensing a bit of fresh tension in his friend's voice. "Flew into Baltimore and drove straight here. I came straight from the crime scene this morning. I'm a little tired and a lot hungry. Was hoping you could point me toward some crab cakes and cold beer, and we could talk about this case. Quite frankly, I'm stumped."

"What made you come to me?"

"I need to talk to someone who knew Tillman, someone who worked with him. Someone I can trust."

Barrow paused for a moment. "Sure, I understand that. Makes sense. I'm just not sure I can really help you. Like I said, I knew who he was, but that's about it."

"I'm grasping at straws here," Minter said. "You never know what could be helpful. You have a few minutes for an old friend?"

"Sure, Wayne," Barrow said. "How about we meet at the Boatyard Bar & Grill off Fourth at seven o'clock. I'll see what I can do to help. But I can't make any promises."

"Thanks. I'll be grateful for anything. One thing I wanted to run by you real quick if I could though, because I want to get back to my partner if there's something to it: You ever hear of something called Project Hermes?"

Minter thought the call was dropped. "Paul?" he said.

Barrow didn't reply for another five seconds.

"Yeah?" he finally said. "I mean, no. Project what? Hermes? No. I don't know what that is. Where'd you hear that?"

"There was an empty folder at the crime scene, labeled *Project Hermes*," Minter said. "I know you used to serve on committees that dealt with military research, as did Tillman. Just taking a shot in the dark that maybe you knew what this was."

"Sorry, no. I have been a part of a lot of discussions about funding for hundreds of projects. It's possible this Hermes was one of them, but I don't recall the name. Look, Wayne, I have a few things to finish up here. I'll see you at seven."

Before Minter could say good-bye, his phone went silent.

10

ST. PETERSBURG BEACH, FLORIDA

Afternoon sunshine invaded the otherwise dark confines of Flynn's motel apartment. On the laptop screen in front of him, Blaine Jacobs was in the midst of an intense weight-training workout, sweat beaded on his forehead. Occasionally a droplet splashed onto the camera lens, creating momentary distortions in Flynn's view.

"Flynn," Jacobs said, his tone brisk, "I keep hearing about these mind control experiments in Alaska. The public's alarmed. If there's truth to it, it's big. I need you on it. Theresa says you're pushing back a little. Can't have that on this one."

Flynn felt his jaw tighten. This guy was not his boss and he didn't appreciate the tone.

"I decide which stories to pursue," he said. "And from what I've gathered, this Alaska rumor is just conspiracy talk. *The National* won't be swayed by mere public alarm, especially when the panic is unfounded. I've vetted these rumors. Most stem from conspiracy groups and don't hold water. We'd be chasing ghosts."

Jacobs set down his weights and stared straight into the camera.

"Sometimes those ghosts lead to substantial revelations. *The National* has a history of breaking big stories. It'd be a shame to see it falter on account of ... hesitations."

Flynn's voice sharpened, "Mr. Jacobs, I've been in this game for years. The research facility in Gakona's been picked apart, time and again. It's been debunked. Going after it would just fuel misinformation. It would make me and my publication look just as unhinged as fringe organizations like Ultra."

Jacobs took a slow sip from his water bottle. "It's not just about Gakona. It's about the bigger picture, the trajectory of *The National*. I've supported its mission, believing it wouldn't shy away from such challenges."

Flynn felt a flash of anger. He understood the implication—the jobs of his colleagues hung in the balance.

"Listen. I get it," Flynn said. "But trust my years of expertise to know when a story is worth the chase, and when it's not. I worry about *The National* too. About good people, like Theresa, who'd bear the long-term repercussions of whimsical decisions."

Jacobs' smile was thin, almost predatory. "Then we're on the same page about understanding stakes. All I'm suggesting is that you consider the broader implications. For everyone."

Flynn didn't attempt to hide his irritation. "I'll re-evaluate the leads. But understand this: my integrity isn't up for negotiation and it won't be held hostage. Not now, not ever."

Jacobs ran a hand through his sweaty hair, pausing to collect his thoughts. He spoke softly as he continued.

"I do understand what you're saying and I respect your professionalism. It's why I asked for you specifically. You're the best. Just know that more than profits, more than influence, I value the truth. The unequivocal, unvarnished truth. If there's nothing sinister happening up there, fantastic. That's great. But if there is something, it could be a monumental revelation. Either way, we'd have clarity."

Flynn crossed his arms, clearly unmoved. "As far as every credible source is concerned, the truth *is* definitive. HAARP's history has been scrutinized. The wild tales? They've been debunked."

"You're a journalist, James. Curiosity is in your blood. Don't you want to know for yourself? Don't you want that irrefutable evidence?"

Flynn didn't mention to Jacobs that Dr. Keller, HAARP's lead scientist, was missing. That part of the mystery did ignite his curiosity.

"I'll even offer you my private jet," Jacobs said. "My pilot will fly you to Alaska today. Take a look and come back with your findings."

Flynn could read between the lines. It wasn't only the missing scientist who intrigued him now but the man in front of him. Why was Jacobs so insistent? What was the billionaire truly after?

"Fine, I'll check it out," he said after a long pause. "Not because I believe in the rumors, but because I care about the people I work with. And as for your jet? Thanks, but no thanks. I'll fly commercial."

"Suit yourself," Jacobs said. "I knew your innate curiosity would win out. Safe travels, James."

As the call ended, Flynn stared at the blank screen, a storm of thoughts swirling. This wasn't just about Gakona anymore. It was about unraveling the enigma that was Blaine Jacobs.

* * *

A TEXT MESSAGE from a hidden number appeared on his phone. The caller identified itself as TS47.

There's more going on than you realize.

Help me out. You seem to have the answers.

I don't have the answers but I can help you ask the right questions.

I'm listening.

Are you, James?

I'm starting to think you're just a flake out here trying to waste my time.

Arthur Tillman is dead. But you know that already.

I don't even know Tillman. Who killed him?

Project Titan

What is Titan?

You'll have to go there to find the answer.

Go where?

You know where.

I'm not investigating Tillman's murder. I'm not a cop.

Step back. See the bigger picture. You don't have a lot of time. General Tillman's murder is the beginning. It's the key.

11

ANNAPOLIS, MARYLAND

Minter arrived at the restaurant fifteen minutes early and asked for a table near the corner. The place was crowded, but he dropped Admiral Barrow's name and was seated almost immediately. Like every restaurant in the entire Chesapeake Bay area, this one boasted the best crab cakes in the world and displayed the press clippings from *The Baltimore Sun* and other regional publications to prove it.

It had been a long day, and Minter ordered a beer, which the waitress brought promptly. While he waited for Barrow, Minter decided to check in with Blackwood, who'd spent the day going through Arthur Tillman's top-floor condo in Tampa.

"Nothing," she said when Minter asked what she found. "The place was immaculate, like no one even lived there."

Minter grumbled.

"Yeah," agreed Blackwood. "The cellphone we found on the boat? Its data was wiped clean, but we're having the guys check the number to see if it had any incoming or outgoing calls prior to the murder. Should have an answer by morning. How'd it go with Barrow?"

"Strange," Minter said. "He started off cracking a joke about Tillman like he was an old college buddy, but as soon as I told him the General had been murdered, he acted like they were barely acquainted. He wouldn't say anything over the phone. I'm meeting him here in a few minutes in person."

"Let me know what you find out. I'm probably not going to get much sleep tonight, so call me, even if it's late."

It always felt weird when she said things like that. Samantha Blackwood was one hell of an investigator and the best partner Minter had ever worked with. But she was also an attractive woman, and no matter how hard he tried to treat her just like any other special agent, he couldn't look past that fact. He enjoyed working with her. He respected the way her mind worked, the way she could see things he might otherwise miss. His weaknesses were her strengths; they made an effective team.

But he also just loved talking to her. The invitation to call her later was nothing more than business. Blackwood was serious about her job and tenacious when it came to solving mysteries. She simply wanted to be kept in the loop with any new developments regardless of how small. Minter knew that, but he couldn't help but wonder what could've been had they not both been bureau employees.

Her voice snapped him out of his daydream. "Wayne? Are you still there? I think you lost reception for a second."

"No. I'm here," he said, grateful that she couldn't see him blush. "That sounds great, Sam. I'll let you know how it goes here. Talk to you then."

"Awesome," she said. "Good luck with Barrow. I'll be waiting for your call."

He sipped his beer and ordered the world's best crab cakes. If nothing else, he was going to get a free meal out of Barrow.

Minter promptly polished off two crab cakes and was happy that they lived up to the hype. Except for maybe New Orleans, he believed the coast of Maryland offered the best seafood in the country. Not that he was any kind of expert. He was typically dazzled by a simple platter full of fried fish, shrimp, oysters, and clams, and his favorite meal was often his most recent meal.

He drained the second of his two beers and glanced at his cell phone. It was after eight o'clock, and he'd not heard from Paul Barrow. He'd never known his friend to be even a few minutes late to anything, let alone tardy for over an hour without so much as a text message to explain the situation.

Paul had been weird on the phone, and his absence was odd if not downright concerning. Minter's eyes swept the dining room and shifted toward the entrance for about the hundredth time, anticipating the arrival of Admiral Barrow. The weight of his investigation into Tillman's murder weighed heavily on his mind.

The waitress, who had taken Minter's order earlier, approached his table, holding a large envelope.

She leaned in close and spoke into his ear. "Are you Mr. Minter?" Her voice was soft and a bit shaky.

He nodded, "Special Agent Minter, yes."

She slid the envelope across the table to him and snapped her hand back to her side as if it were hot. "Admiral Barrow sends his regrets. He won't be able to meet you tonight," she said.

Minter placed his palm on the envelope and stared at it.

She turned to leave, but he grabbed her arm.

"Did you talk to the admiral?" he said, gently turning her back toward him.

She shook her head. "Someone just dropped this off. Said to deliver it to the man sitting at Admiral Barrow's table and said to tell him—I mean, you—that the Admiral would not be coming."

"Did you see who delivered the envelope?"

She hesitated, making it clear that she had.

"It's okay," he said. "You can tell me. I'm a close friend of the admiral's."

"He was kinda creepy," she said after a few seconds, again leaning close to him to make sure no one nearby would hear her.

"Creepy, how?"

"He was like, weird-looking. Super skinny. And he didn't

smile. I mean his face didn't really move at all. It was just creepy, like I said."

"What did he say? How did he sound?"

"I told you," she said, sounding anxious. "He said to give you this and tell you Admiral Barrow isn't coming."

"That's all?" he asked.

"Yeah," she said, irritation rising in her tone. "Look, I need to get back to work. I have other tables. They don't allow me to stand around and chat."

Minter realized he'd been holding the girl's arm the whole time. He looked at his hand and released his grip, and she drifted away to wait on other customers. He started to thank her, but she was gone.

Minter looked back at the envelope with dreadful anticipation.

The large envelope was sealed and he slid the dull edge of a butter knife under the flap to open it up. He looked up and scanned the restaurant to see if anyone was watching him. The diners were all in their own separate worlds, enjoying their meals and polite conversations without giving him the slightest bit of attention. He reached his thumb and forefinger into the envelope and removed a small stack of photographs.

Throughout his career, Minter had witnessed crime scenes that would churn most stomachs. Yet, the images he now held were so harrowing that he swiftly tucked them back into the envelope. Casting a wary eye across the room once more, he realized this venue was ill-suited for such grim contents. The last thing he needed was a horrified patron getting a peek and throwing up the evening's special.

Minter, still gripping the envelope, broke for the men's room with a brisk pace. To even the most observant onlooker, he'd appear to be nothing more than a man who'd had his fill of beer and crab meat and needed to excuse himself with moderate haste.

He took a seat in one of the stalls and latched the door. The accommodations weren't ideal, but at least he'd be able to look over the packet of information in private.

The photos were labeled as "Project Hermes." They displayed a collection of violent scenes that involved U.S. military personnel. All four branches of service were represented, and each image was more horrible than the last.

A note was attached that read: "Walk away from this. Don't make the same mistake Tillman made."

Minter was afraid for Paul. Did his friend send these images to him? The mere mention of Project Hermes had spooked him earlier. How was Barrow wrapped up in whatever this was? How did it all connect to Arthur Tillman's murder? And, who was the thin man who'd delivered the package to the waitress?

The pieces of the puzzle were beginning to reveal themselves, but how they all fit together remained a mystery.

Minter knew he was on the right track.

* * *

WAYNE MINTER LEFT THE BOATYARD, his mind fighting to sort through the myriad of implications the photographs had unearthed. The crisp Annapolis air greeted him, and he appreciated the upcoming twenty-minute walk back to his hotel. It would give him time to piece together various theories on how this all connected to not only Arthur Tillman's murder but Paul Barrow as well.

He pulled his coat tighter against the chill and tried to decipher the dilemma that was Project Hermes. Was he witness to an experiment gone wrong? Or was Hermes an investigation into brutal attacks against U.S. servicemen and women? If it were the former, what could possibly be the goal, and if the latter, who was responsible for such brutal bloodshed?

As Minter contemplated the potential origin of the violence in the photos, streetlights cast pools of golden light on the cobblestone pathway, and the distant murmur of the Chesapeake Bay provided a calm ambience for his walk.

He thought about Barrow.

What have you done, Paul? What do you know?

Once he checked in with Blackwood, Minter would call Barrow, if for no other reason than to be sure he was safe. If a well-known figure such as Tillman could be a victim, whoever was responsible for his death wouldn't hesitate to take out a garden variety Naval officer, no matter how high his rank.

As if on cue, his phone vibrated in his pocket. A text from Blackwood: "Any updates?"

He quickened his pace. He'd decided to wait and call her after reaching his room. The information that had fallen into his lap was too sensitive and too complicated to discuss over text. Besides, he wanted to hear her voice. In the security of his room, he'd brief her. They'd piece this puzzle together as they had with so many cases before.

Minter finally reached his hotel and pushed through the front doors, giving a quick nod to the young man at the front desk as he made a beeline for the elevators where he pushed the button for the third floor. Once he reached his room, he slipped the keycard into the lock. The door clicked open and he hurried inside. He tossed the envelope with the photographs onto the desk and pulled out his phone. He scrolled through his contacts to Blackwood's name and pressed the call button.

Just as the first ring echoed in his ear, the room went dark, the only faint light slipping through a seam between the drapes that covered the window. Minter reached inside his jacket for his Glock 19 nine millimeter, but not even his highly-tuned instincts allowed him to react fast enough.

A strong grip seized his right wrist and another hand reached to take away his weapon.

A man's voice broke the silence. "I wouldn't."

Minter froze. The lights came on, and two men bracketed

him; one to his right held his gun in one hand and pointed another at his chest, while the second man, seemingly unarmed, stood directly in front of him. He snatched Minter's cellphone and ended the call before Blackwood picked up.

The man in front was clearly in charge. Despite possessing an almost impossibly slight build, he exhibited an air of authority. This thin man, who was obviously the one who'd given the folder to the waitress, felt ominous to Minter. He sized up Minter with a look of bemused indifference on his gaunt face.

"I understand you're quite the detective, Special Agent Minter. But this time you're playing checkers while we're playing chess," he said. "You simply fell into some information by happenstance. Far from exemplary police work, I'm afraid."

Minter eyed the man. "Chess, eh? Then who's the grandmaster? Barrow? Tillman?"

The thin man laughed, a hearty sound not quite matching his wispy physique. "Barrow and Tillman are merely pawns, much like you. But as you know, pawns can be promoted if they manage to hang around long enough and reach the other end of the board. Or they can be sacrificed."

Minter's thoughts raced. "Project Hermes, the photographs—what's the endgame?"

Mr. White examined himself in the mirror that hung on the nearby wall. He flicked at a few stray hairs, settling them back into place, and turned back to Minter.

"You haven't a clue," White said. "Hermes is no longer in the game. There's a bigger gambit afoot. But don't worry. You're still an important player in the strategy, even if you're oblivious to your role."

"What about Barrow? Is he another pawn?"

"Admiral Barrow has acted as instructed. He's fine. You should be more concerned about your own next move."

Mr. White's words hung in the air, a chilling prelude to an unfinished chapter. Minter tried to back away but the room seemed to close in on him. For the first time, he fully grasped the danger that he had stumbled into. These men, who'd allowed him into their world, were not mere messengers.

As they lingered in the room, their unspoken threat loomed larger than any words, leaving Minter with the grim realization that his next moves could very well be his last.

White nodded to his partner, a silent command to move. Minter felt the hard muzzle of the other man's gun press against the small of his back, nudging him toward the door. They led him past the elevator to the stairs at the end of the hallway. White twisted the handle to open the door while his partner muscled Minter toward the staircase.

They took the stairs two levels up and stepped off onto the windswept roof.

The gunman grabbed Minter's arms and twisted them behind his back. Mr. White then typed a message on Minter's phone. The gunman, who used his hulking strength to hold Minter, led him to the edge of the building.

"Special Agent Samantha Blackwood will miss you," White said. He sounded sincere, almost apologetic.

Minter's heart pounded. He felt a wave of cold terror crash over his body. This was it. He was running out of chances.

"Blackwood will come looking for me," he said. "She'll bring the full force of the FBI on top of you. You can't win."

Mr. White eased comfortably back into his sadistic persona.

"I'm counting on Ms. Blackwood," he said. "She also has a part to play, a more important one than your own, to be honest. It's a shame you won't be here to see it. I'm really quite excited to see how she does—better than you, I hope."

Mr. White cast a final, penetrating glance at Minter. Then a near-imperceptible nod.

With a forceful shove from the gunman, Minter went airborne. It was over in seconds as the sidewalk five stories below rushed up to meet him. In that fleeting moment, his final thought was of Samantha.

His body struck the pavement with a gruesome thud.

Mr. White looked down from the rooftop, his eyes devoid of emotion. He pressed "send" on Minter's phone, delivering the faux suicide note to Samantha Blackwood.

12

TAMPA, FLORIDA

Admiral Barrow's voice was friendly, almost cheerful, thought Blackwood. She'd called the man's personal number that she lifted from Minter's files and expected Barrow to be annoyed or at least wary of someone contacting him on his private line.

Instead, the admiral was accommodating and seemingly not the least bit surprised to hear from her this morning.

"First, let me express my sadness over Wayne's death. He was a good friend," Barrow said after Blackwood introduced herself and explained why she was calling. "Yes, I met with him yesterday, here in my office. He was hoping I might have some insight into who would want to kill Arthur Tillman."

"And..." said Blackwood.

"Did you ever meet General Tillman, Ms. Blackwood?"

"*Special Agent* Blackwood," she corrected. "No, sir. I did not."

"Tillman was a polarizing figure. Some people were mesmerized by his charisma, and they absolutely loved him. Others were turned off by his brash behavior and oversized ego. It's not hard to imagine that he might have an enemy or two."

"There's a lot of ground between being annoyed with a guy who craves attention and wanting to shoot him in the chest with a speargun. Wouldn't you agree?"

"It's not my forte to analyze the reasons why men choose to do one thing over another. To get to the heart of your question about my conversation with Agent Minter: No, I have no idea why Tillman was murdered, but I can see how he might be a target more so than someone else who exhibited a less explosive personality."

Blackwood noted Barrow's use of "Agent Minter." He was distancing himself from his relationship with the man whom he initially referred to as "Wayne."

"Project Hermes," Blackwood said, just letting it hang there.

Barrow said nothing at first, and the silence carried for more than a few seconds. After a moment, he said, "I can't speak to that."

"Did Wayne ask you about it?"

He hesitated.

"I don't recall," his voice clipped.

"After he left your office, Special Agent Minter checked in with me," she said. "He told me about your conversation. He said he asked you about Project Hermes and that you planned to meet with him last night."

"We had planned to have dinner together. Agent Minter and I were once old friends, but we haven't spoken much in the past few years. He wanted to catch up." Barrow paused. "It was—awkward, I guess would be the word—for me. I had barely spoken to the man in over a decade, and then he shows up out of nowhere seeking some sort of reunion. I didn't want to disappoint him, but I wasn't nearly as enthusiastic as he was over an evening of small talk."

Blackwood knew that an evening of small talk was the last thing Minter wanted as well. Any friend of his would certainly know he was not exactly the type to chit-chat about the good old days over dinner.

"How was your dinner with Wayne?" she asked.

"I'm afraid I didn't go. I remembered I had an important meeting in the morning that I needed to prep for. I called Agent Minter and apologized, but told him to enjoy dinner on my tab."

"How did it go?"

A pause. "How did *what* go?"

"Your meeting," she said. "This morning. I hope I'm not keeping you from something important."

"No," he said. "I mean, actually, *yes*. I'm afraid I don't have much more time for you Ms. Blackwood."

Special Agent.

"I just have one more question, Admiral Barrow, and then I'll let you get to your ... meeting. Did Agent Minter—your friend, Wayne—strike you as the type who would jump off a five-story building?"

Barrow said nothing.

She continued: "Did he seem particularly upset or agitated when you met with him? Is it possible he was so distraught by your failure to meet him for crab cakes that he went back to his hotel and threw himself off the roof?"

The image of Wayne falling to his death pierced her imagination and she squeezed her eyes tight. For the first time she was happy this interview was happening over the phone.

Barrow still said nothing.

"Admiral Barrow?"

She waited another few seconds.

His voice barely rose above a whisper. "I don't know. I'm not aware of Agent Minter's emotional state or the quality of his mental health. I am sorry for his death, but I'm afraid I can't give you any answers. I apologize, but I must be going now. Please don't hesitate to let me know if I can be of any more assistance."

The line went silent.

Blackwood slid her cellphone into the front pocket of her slacks.

Minter's death was not a suicide. No way.

The text she'd received last night had to be faked. It certainly wasn't written by Wayne. The man hated text messaging. The only texts she'd ever received from him were brief, often one-word snippets—"Lunch?"

The floral prose in the "suicide text" was definitely not written by him. Barrow would know better. If he was trying to cover up Minter's death, he'd have done a better job. Blackwood didn't make Barrow for the murder, but he definitely knew more than he let on. He was stonewalling her, pretending to not know anything at all.

She'd spoken to investigators who were at the scene. They said Minter's gun and cell phone were missing, but his wallet, credit cards and $120 in cash were still on his body when they found him. A passerby could've taken his gun and phone, but why leave the cash?

She'd called Minter's phone immediately after receiving the bogus text, but it just rang and went to voicemail.

Blackwood's phone vibrated in her pocket. She reached for it. The incoming call was labeled as UNKNOWN. She answered. It was Barrow.

"I know who killed Tillman," he whispered.

"I'm listening," she said.

Blackwood waited.

"The killer's name is James Flynn," he said.

13

RICHMOND, VIRGINIA

Danbury's campaign manager handed him a towel as he stepped off the stage following a rousing speech in front of an enthusiastic crowd of faithful followers who'd packed a high school auditorium to show support for the man they believed had their best interests at heart.

When he was at his best, Danbury could mesmerize an audience with the charisma of an evangelical minister preaching at a tent revival. Today was one of those days.

"It was classic Danbury," pundits said after the event, praising the veteran politician's charisma and skill to rally his base.

He took the towel from Meadows and used both hands to wipe the sweat from his face. He felt energized and exhausted at the same time.

The senator and his small entourage exited the building to a parking lot of cheering constituents who hadn't been lucky enough to get inside to see the sold-out event in person. On their way to their black SUV, Meadows escorted Danbury through the crowd, many of whom held signs that declared, "DANBURY

FOR VIRGINIA! DANBURY FOR AMERICA!" and other messages of support.

Like most campaigning politicians, Danbury was behind schedule, but Meadows didn't rush him; he didn't dare. If there was one city that Danbury could still count on to make him feel like a winner, it was Richmond. Lynchburg and the small towns between here and there could wait a few extra minutes. The supporters had come out in droves, and Meadows knew the senator needed this.

Danbury waved. He smiled. He shook hands and took selfies with adoring fans. It felt like a true victory.

As they approached the SUV, a familiar face in the crowd caught Danbury's attention. It was the mysterious Mr. White from the other night, leaning in ever so slightly to make eye contact with the senator.

"Senator Danbury." The man's voice was crystal clear despite the raucous cheers and perpetual applause from the crowd. He didn't seem to be yelling or straining to amplify his voice, but Danbury heard him all the same. "Might I have a word?"

Danbury's gut told him to ignore the man, but something compelled him to motion the thin man toward him. He was in his element among his most fervent supporters and wanted this angular stick-drawing of a man to acknowledge his political muscle. Danbury signaled to security to allow the man through.

"Thank you," White said as he stepped forward. He craned his neck to take in the scene. "Quite a turnout."

Danbury, full of fiery confidence, smiled in affirmation. "I'm in a bit of a hurry."

"I was hoping I could get a few minutes of your time." He motioned toward the throng of supporters. "This must have you feeling pretty good."

Danbury continued to smile and wave.

Mr. White continued. "But, I wonder if you saw the latest poll numbers released this afternoon. No one expected you to struggle in Richmond. But, Virginia is a big state, and you're lagging behind in most of it."

Danbury stopped waving, but his handsome smile did not fade. One of his men held open the back door of the SUV, and Danbury took a seat.

"I really have to go," he said. "Call my office. They can get you on my schedule early next week."

The door was shut, and the SUV pulled away.

Mr. White stood there with his arms clasped in front of him. After just a few yards, the SUV stopped abruptly. The rear tinted window slid open and Senator Danbury looked back at him. The man stood there with a smug expression, a smirk that screamed "you know you need me."

As much as he hated to admit it, Danbury did need him.

The SUV door opened. Mr. White walked at a deliberate pace toward the vehicle and got in.

14

ST. PETERSBURG BEACH, FLORIDA

Flynn's thoughts swirled in his head like the ferocious twisters that he'd endured as a boy growing up in Oklahoma. He shuffled the past day's events through his mind and prowled back and forth over the length of his hotel room, his bare feet carving a very noticeable groove in the already well-worn teal-green carpet.

The conversations with Blaine Jacobs and the mysterious TruthSeeker47 created more questions than answers. Online search results revealed what TS47 had told Flynn hours earlier: Arthur Tillman had been killed.

He pulled up an article from *The New York Times* that had just a couple of paragraphs about the murder with a few sketchy details followed by a lengthy profile on Tillman's life. The portrait *The Times* painted was of a larger-than-life character who was equal parts All-American war hero, movie star, and serial philanderer. The man had been popular with heavy hitters in business, entertainment, and politics, but had also racked up an impressive roster of detractors along the way.

The article detailed how after retirement, Tillman profited

significantly from numerous investments amid whispers that he leveraged his military connections to facilitate lucrative deals for private firms seeking government contracts. Speculation ran rampant that Tillman either received kickbacks or cashed in on investments he made in these companies and projects based on privileged information. However, these claims remained unproven, while always managing to keep Tillman's military background and celebrity status at the forefront of the rumors.

Cable news networks were already deep into speculation about what had happened to Tillman. Theories that listed potential suspects included jealous husbands and boyfriends of Tillman's many female companions, business rivals, fanatic admirers, Russian mobsters, and just about anything in between. A retired FBI agent tapped to provide his expert analysis said unequivocally that Tillman's murder was a professional hit.

Flynn wasn't completely sold. The whole thing was too ... what was the word? *Theatrical*, Flynn thought. The media leaked that Tillman had been shot in the chest with a crossbow, which was bizarre enough. But just minutes later, news anchors reported that the murder weapon was potentially a speargun. In Flynn's experience, it just didn't feel like the work of a professional hitman, who typically would go for a well-planned and less-colorful manner of execution. It felt more like an argument that had just simply gotten out of control.

TruthSeeker47 had initially said, "Ask Tillman." That clearly wasn't an option now, but even after the general had been killed, the enigmatic source doubled down on urging Flynn to follow the lead. How was Tillman connected to the rumors surrounding HAARP. And what is Project Titan?

To compound his frustration, the incident with the now-deceased Liam Baxter made Flynn leery of Ultra and the group's motives. It wouldn't make sense for them to ask him to investigate a story and then send someone to his home to violently attack him. Had Baxter acted alone or was someone else pulling his strings?

And then there was Blaine Jacobs. Why was he pushing so hard to have Flynn investigate the HAARP facility in Alaska? Was it a genuine concern for the public good, or did Jacobs have hidden motives, perhaps financial or political gains to be made from the information he might uncover? He couldn't shake the feeling that there was more to Jacobs' interest than met the eye. The more he thought about it, the more he realized that Jacobs, with his extensive resources and deep connections, could easily have chosen any number of investigators for this task. Yet, he had chosen Flynn, a former CIA operative turned investigative journalist. Why him?

Flynn considered where to start. It was clear that breaking through the veil of secrecy surrounding "Titan" and HAARP would require an ally with resources and insights that went beyond his own.

Michael Harrison answered on the first ring.

"Flynn," Harrison said, his voice full of energy.

Harrison was a veteran reporter at *The Washington Post*, who had a reputation for tracking down information in the nation's capital that either slipped through the cracks or had been swept under the rug. Flynn knew of no better source for Washington, D.C. dirt.

Flynn brought Harrison up to speed.

"Titan doesn't ring a bell for me, buddy," Harrison said. "I mean Tillman has, or had, I should say, his fingers in a lot of pies. If we're talking about a codename for some secret project, anything is possible. Those names aren't released to the public. Do you have any more context?"

Flynn didn't want to expose his interaction with Ultra or Liam Baxter. Harrison was a friend but he was still a journalist who would jump at the chance to dig his claws into a juicy story. Flynn owed it to Ultra to protect the confidential nature of their relationship.

"I've got a source who told me to 'Find the son of Zeus'," he said.

Harrison stayed silent for a few seconds before responding. "Hmmmmmm," he said. "This may sound crazy, and I'm almost certain it's not what you're looking for, but when someone says 'Titan' and 'son of Zeus' to me, the first thing I think of is the old Titan rockets."

"Like from the sixties?"

"Nineteen fifty-nine, to be precise, but yeah."

"How does this connect to a research facility in Alaska?" Flynn asked.

"I'm not saying it does," Harrison said. "You're throwing some words at me, and I'm just telling you what pops into my mind."

"What's the son of Zeus thing?"

"Are you serious, Flynn? Didn't you pay attention to Greek mythology in school? I thought you were supposed to be smart. Didn't you used to be in the Central *Intelligence* Agency? Must have been a bad year for recruiting." Harrison chuckled.

"Yes, very clever," Flynn said. "Are you gonna enlighten me or not?"

"I'll do my best. Titans *are* the sons of Zeus. You know, Apollo, Hercules, Ares? Those guys. All sons of Zeus. Each of them a titan."

"Then I wonder how this connects to Tillman?" Flynn asked.

"Atlas."

"Another son of Zeus."

"Right. And coincidentally, the name of a family of rockets and ICBMs used by our government for decades. They don't still use the Atlas for missiles anymore, but NASA's Atlas V is still very much in service for manned and unmanned space missions."

"Rockets," Flynn said. It wasn't what he was expecting to hear, but at least it was a thread to pull. "Did Tillman have any connection to outer space exploration?"

"Not that I'm aware of," Harrison said. "But I'm no expert on the general. I'm playing catch-up on this story like everyone else. I can do some digging, but you have to promise to share anything you learn with me. We can both help each other out on this one, Flynn."

Flynn agreed to exchange information on the Tillman case, thanked Harrison for his time and hung up. He checked the time and realized he was in very real danger of missing his flight to Anchorage.

If this "son of Zeus" thing really did involve rockets, Flynn knew the woman to ask.

15

NEW YORK CITY

Theresa Halston sat across from Christopher Mays in his office, the dark glossy surface of his desk reflecting the light from the large circular lamp that hung down from the vaulted ceiling.

Mays, *The National's* publisher, had a reputation for being as ruthless in business as he was enigmatic in his personal interactions. Theresa had worked for him for the past five years after *The National* was sold to a private equity group who installed Mays as publisher.

As far as bosses went, Mays was slightly better than most. He stayed out of Theresa's way most of the time and let her run the magazine as she saw fit. Mays didn't come from a publishing background, which made his role an odd choice, but it also kept him out of her hair. The story was that he knew someone who was related to someone who owed someone a favor, and that's all it took for him to get the big chair in the corner office.

Mays was, as far as Theresa could tell, an astute and competent businessman. He didn't worry about the deadlines, headlines, cutlines, or bylines, but focused his attention solely on the bottom line.

If the money rolled in, and the profit margin was acceptable to the board of directors, Theresa never heard so much as a peep from the publisher. But when sales were down and revenue was short, Mays got involved. And it was never pleasant.

So, when she got the call to come to his office, she knew there was a financial crisis at their doorstep.

"It's bad," he said. And said nothing more.

Theresa wasn't sure if she was supposed to speak up or if her boss was trying to make a point with some sort of dramatic pause.

Christopher Mays was in his late thirties, at least fifteen years younger than Theresa. He was overweight and soft, a feature that his expensive tailored suits couldn't hide. Mays' hands were small and smooth, and had likely never beheld a callous.

"Your man Flynn is doing good work for us," he said. "Blaine Jacobs is pumping a lot of cash into *The National* while Flynn tracks down this whatever it is mind-reading pet project of his. It will get us through the year, but forecasts for Q1 are not favorable."

Theresa, like most journalists, hated to hear about the business side of her chosen career. Budget talks far too often resulted in fiscal cuts, which meant staff reductions and fewer people to produce quality work that people were willing to pay for, which led to less revenue, perpetuating a negative cycle.

"We have good pieces in the works," she said. "We're starting a multi-part series on—"

"What about that new girl?" Mays interrupted. "You have her on the Danbury profile, right?"

Theresa was surprised that Mays knew what Leslie Vanderwaal was working on, or that she even existed. Mays rarely talked about the words and photos that were in the pages of their magazine or the people who put them there. Apparently, he'd been paying more attention to things than she realized.

"She's set to fly down to Virginia tomorrow," she said. "She's going to meet him at his farm. We're sending a photographer with her to get some rustic pictures of the senator, some real Norman Rockwell stuff. It should really hit a home run with his base."

The National was well-read by people who considered themselves patriots and looked back at past decades as being the sweet spot of the American experience. Mays was never shy about pandering to their emotional nostalgia. Theresa knew this and wanted to make sure that the publisher knew her people were ready to serve up some American apple pie to hopefully connect with an audience who still wanted to buy magazines off the rack —and the advertisers who coveted that demographic.

Mays steepled his hands. He nodded slowly, almost as if in a trance. Theresa was unsure if he'd even heard what she'd said, but clearly something was going on in that brain of his. He sat silent for an awkward moment, and Theresa glanced at her phone to check the time. She had things to do, and watching her boss stare aimlessly into the void wasn't at the top of her list.

"I don't think," he said. "That Norman Rockwell is what we need."

Theresa waited for Mays to clarify.

He continued, "Let's change gears. What we need is something that will generate conversation, maybe even some controversy. Danbury has a clean image, right? 'Mr. I Don't Take Special Interest Money'? Well, I don't buy it. Let's take a deeper look into who Quinton Danbury really is. Do you think your girl is up for that?"

Theresa knew that Leslie would jump at the chance to sink her claws into a "real story." She was young and eager to make a name for herself. If ambition was the key, she'd be the perfect woman for the job. But Theresa wasn't buying into this plan.

It wasn't the kind of thing *The National* did. The magazine never shied away from hard-hitting topics, but neither had they ever set out to do a hit piece on anyone, let alone a U.S. Senator.

And Theresa didn't think the young reporter was ready for that type of assignment. She was planning to ease her in and let her get her feet wet first with some easy ones before throwing her in the deep end.

"I don't know, Chris," she said. "She's brand new. I'm trying to toss her an underhand softball, and you're talking about putting her in the box against a big league fastball."

It was clear Mays didn't get the reference. The man had probably never attended a single baseball game in his life.

"Besides," she said, "I've already prepped her for the profile interview. She leaves first thing in the morning. There's no way we can get her ready for a full-on investigative piece in one day."

"Have faith, Theresa. A great deal can be accomplished in a short time when one puts her mind to it."

"She's just not ready. And I think the type of piece you're talking about can damage the magazine's reputation. This isn't what people come to us for."

"Haven't you noticed? They don't come to us for anything anymore. Not like they used to. And every issue sees fewer and fewer readers, save for when Flynn drops a JFK bombshell or finds alien artifacts in New Mexico."

Mays took a file from a drawer and placed it on his desk. "I'd like to talk with Miss Vanderwaal," he said. "And I've already invited her to join us."

Theresa stiffened. "Don't do this, Chris. Not while I'm in charge. You pay me to run the magazine. You have trusted my leadership and judgment for the past five years. I'm asking you to keep trusting me."

Mays tugged at his bottom lip for a moment as if he were actually considering her plea.

"Please," she said.

A beep from the intercom on Mays' desk interrupted them. He pushed the button. "Yes?"

"Miss Vanderwaal is here for you," Mays' receptionist said.

He never stopped staring at Theresa. Finally he smiled.

"Send her in," he said. And then to Theresa: "You're right. I do trust you."

Theresa exhaled a breath she hadn't realized she'd been holding.

"I trust you to do your job and follow directions," he said, his tone sharpened.

Leslie Vanderwaal entered the room.

"Ah, Leslie," he said. "Welcome. We were just discussing you and your impressive skills. We have a slight change in your Danbury assignment. Unfortunately, Ms. Halston has a pressing engagement and cannot stick around with us. Please, have a seat."

Mays held a hand toward an empty chair in front of his desk, still looking squarely at Theresa, his face telling her it was time to go.

As Vanderwaal approached the desk, Theresa stood to leave.

"Can we catch up later?" Vanderwaal asked Theresa. "I have some more questions for you before I leave tomorrow."

Theresa didn't answer. She simply looked back at Christopher Mays and marched out of the room.

16

CAPE CANAVERAL, FLORIDA

Flynn drove the two hours from St. Pete to Kennedy Space Center, killing any chance he'd have at boarding his scheduled flight, which was set to leave that afternoon back in Tampa. Theresa would be irked, but he had to get someone to shed some light on this Tillman situation before he made the trip to Alaska. And that someone was Dr. Sierra Keegan.

Flynn had called ahead and his visitor's pass was waiting for him. He navigated a maze of corridors before he found himself standing before a door marked "Dr. Sierra Keegan, Aerospace Engineering."

He paused for a moment, collecting his thoughts. Flynn recalled with clarity his previous encounter with Dr. Keegan; an article he wrote had quoted her on the speculative existence of alien spacecraft technology at NASA. Keegan believed they were speaking candidly, but Flynn never explicitly told her that her comments were off the record and used every word she said about the very real possibility of the existence of alien tech. The article stirred up quite a controversy, putting her in an uncomfortable spotlight. Now, he was back to seek her help, hoping she wouldn't hold the backlash of their first meeting against him.

Framed patents and awards adorned the walls of Dr. Keegan's office, showcasing her many achievements. Models of rockets and spacecraft occupied the shelves, a testament to her contributions to space exploration. It was the office of someone who lived at the frontier of human knowledge, pushing the boundaries of what was possible.

Keegan, thirty-eight years old, was one of NASA's leading aerospace engineers and astrophysicists. After earning her Ph.D. in Aerospace Engineering from MIT, Keegan wrote a groundbreaking thesis on new rocket fuel formulations that garnered significant attention from the aerospace community.

Since then she'd dedicated the majority of her career to advancing space exploration technologies, particularly focusing on propulsion systems and the feasibility of manned missions to Mars.

Dr. Keegan, tall, slim, and athletic, stood by a large window, overlooking Kennedy Space Center. She turned as Flynn entered, her expression guarded and serious.

"James Flynn," she said. "I must admit, I didn't expect to ever see you again, especially not face-to-face in my office."

Flynn stepped forward, feeling more awkward than he'd expected. He looked at her dark brown eyes that locked onto him with unwavering focus.

"I'm just as surprised as you are, Dr. Keegan, believe me," Flynn said. "I know after our first meeting—I know it put you in a tough spot."

"Tough spot? That's putting it mildly."

"I didn't handle it the best I could have."

"Is that some half-assed apology? I had my reputation ripped at and attacked from all corners of the aerospace world, and all you can say is 'I didn't do my best'? Well if that is your idea of an apology, you're still not giving me the courtesy of your best effort."

"I am sorry," he said. "But you knew who I was and why I was there. I had no obligation to go off the record with you. I'm sorry that your colleagues reacted poorly to your words, but they *were* your words, Dr. Keegan. I didn't make anything up. I quoted you fairly."

The thinnest of smiles creased her face and she shook her head slowly.

"Before we spoke the first time, I did my homework on you," she said. "I had an acquaintance at Langley who told me to watch my step around you. 'Flynn always needs to be the smartest man in the room,' he'd said. He'd told me you would do anything to make sure you come out on top. I thought I'd listened to him. I was wary of you, as I am of all of you journalist types who would sell your own mother for a scoop. But apparently I didn't really listen, because I let you in and I trusted you. And I got burned in the process."

"I'm not sure what to say."

"You know exactly what to say, but your ego won't allow you to say it. So just get on with it. What brings you here?"

"Arthur Tillman," he said.

"Tragic," Keegan said with a tone that expressed not even the slightest bit of sympathy for General Tillman's fate. "Are you working homicide these days instead of writing your little articles about aliens?"

He ignored the dig. "Not a fan of the late general, Dr. Keegan?"

"I'm not a fan of you, Mr. Flynn. Please get to the point so you can be on your way. And before we start, this entire conversation is *off* the record."

"Noted. I'm not looking for quotes. I just need some information. Your name will not be used in anything I write. You have my word."

Keegan huffed a cynical laugh.

Flynn explained to her all of the pertinent details he'd learned from Harrison and asked if she knew of any connection between

General Tillman and rockets, more specifically any space projects named after Greek mythology.

"Are you kidding? The entire space program was built off of mythological names: Mercury, Gemini, Apollo. We took about a forty-five-year break from that nomenclature, but we're back with the Artemis program aimed at getting humans back to the moon. And that doesn't even get into the ICBMs like Atlas, Jupiter, Thor, Titan, Minotaur, and others. They're not all Greek. Some are Roman, but it's all basically the same idea."

"Titan rockets?"

"Sure," she said. "But those are old news. The first Titans were introduced in the 50s. Variations of that platform were used as intercontinental ballistic missiles for the US military for decades, but they've all been decommissioned at this point. And there certainly isn't anything secretive about them."

"What about Tillman? Was he ever involved with the space program or missile projects?"

"Tillman was involved with anything he could get his hands on that could make him happy or rich, but I can't think of anything that he got into that had a name from Greek mythology. Unless you count a 23-year-old research assistant named Cassandra. The esteemed general definitely had his hands all over her."

"That's it?"

"That's it," she said. "Now please leave."

17

ST. PETERSBURG, FLORIDA

SWAT was already on the scene when Samantha Blackwood pulled into the parking lot of the beachside motel James Flynn called home. Dressed in black, encased in body armor, and carrying automatic weapons, the federal SWAT operatives had the building surrounded and were stacked at the door of Flynn's apartment ready to bust in with a blaze of glory.

"Hold on there, cowboy." shouted Blackwood. "We're not dealing with Osama Bin Laden here. Did anyone try—I don't know—knocking on the door?"

The lead field officer, Carlson, approached Blackwood holding an MP5 submachine gun.

"Affirmative," he said. The man was all business. "There was no answer from inside the structure. We were about to breach the entryway and infiltrate the interior."

"I bet you were," Blackwood said. "Let's hold off on the breaching and infiltrating for just a minute. There's no reason to blow the door off this motel unless we have to. Just give me a minute."

Disheartened, Carlson told his team to stand down. Blackwood could almost hear their collective groan of disappointment.

Carlson watched Blackwood walk to the motel office where the frightened manager stared out the window with both palms flat against the glass. Blackwood spoke to the man for a moment or two before coming back outside. She held up a finger with a ring and a single key dangling from it.

"Let's try it this way," she said.

She went to the door and placed the key in the lock and turned the handle. The SWAT guys to either side of the door flexed.

Blackwood couldn't help but shake her head. "Y'all are just a buncha Rambos, aren't you?"

She held her Glock 9mm in her right hand and pushed open the door with her left.

"FBI," she called out. "Is anyone here? Mr. Flynn?"

As soon as she entered the room, the SWAT team filed in and searched the apartment.

"It's clear," Carlson said.

Blackwood snapped off a dramatic salute. "Good job, soldier. Now please remove your team from my crime scene."

Her curt reaction made her think of Wayne and his rough demeanor when too many people contaminated his investigation.

The SWAT team trudged out of the apartment, leaving her alone.

She'd done some quick homework on Flynn after Barrow dropped his name. He was an investigative journalist, and apparently a good one. He'd written a few books and seemed to enjoy the spotlight on cable news shows and was a popular featured speaker at a number of journalism seminars and workshops throughout the country. He published articles primarily in *The National*, but had freelanced for some other big-name publications as well.

Prior to his journalism career, Flynn was a CIA field officer, although the majority of that information was classified. He came up through the Air Force, but his dates of service were unavailable in the searches Blackwood conducted.

There was absolutely no criminal record—not even a speeding ticket for Flynn. On paper, this guy was a real-life Captain America. Blackwood couldn't find any connection between Flynn and Tillman, but Flynn's background as a spy and Tillman's in-depth knowledge of secret military programs opened plenty of possibilities.

Flynn's apartment was likewise immaculate. No clothes on the floor. No leftover pizza boxes or fast food burger wrappers. No dirty dishes in the sink.

She opened his dresser drawers and rifled through his clothes, mostly t-shirts and military style cargo pants. Nothing fancy. No printed logos or graphics. Everything folded neatly. In one drawer she found a blue plastic case that held a SIG Sauer 9mm semiautomatic pistol and two full magazines.

She thumbed through a stack of files, hoping to find something about Project Hermes or some other link to Arthur Tillman. Most of what she found were articles on various conspiracy theories: aliens, assassinations, cover-ups, and ... secret government research projects.

One folder was left out on the desk. It was labeled "HAARP." It was apparently Flynn's latest assignment dealing with rumors of military mind-control experiments being conducted in a secret facility. Blackwood snapped photos of each page.

On her way out, she gave the apartment a final once-over, looking for anything that seemed out of place. That's when she spotted the mismatched section of paneling in the wall.

One of the wide vertical boards had been cut, removed, and placed back into the wall upside down, its grain not lining up at all. Blackwood cursed herself for not seeing it earlier—the damn thing stood out like a pair of sneakers at a ballet recital. She always carried a small pocket knife and used it to pop the odd piece of panel from the wall.

"Well, hello," she said, peering inside.

Tucked into the wall was a JBL Elite model speargun.

* * *

FLYNN GLANCED AT HIS PHONE. His flight to Anchorage would be taking off right about now. He had an interview scheduled with the head of HAARP tomorrow, and there was no way he would be able to book another flight and make it on time. The trip to visit Keegan was going to wind up wasting half of his day and put him far behind schedule to get in and out of Alaska and put this entire dreadful assignment behind him.

The last thing Flynn wanted to do was take Jacobs up on his offer to use his private jet, but he believed answers were waiting in Alaska, and Jacobs provided his only option to stay on schedule.

He dialed the direct line Jacobs provided and spoke to the man, who did nothing to try and hide his smug satisfaction that Flynn was reaching out to him for assistance.

"I've had my people on stand-by," he said. "They'll be ready for you as soon as you arrive."

It was an easy drive to Orlando and the small airstrip where Jacobs' sleek Cessna Citation Latitude waited for him. An attractive, young woman stood at the bottom of the steps that led to the interior of the handsome jet.

"Hello, Mr. Flynn," she said, flashing him a well-rehearsed smile. "We've been waiting for you. We'll be in the air shortly. Please make yourself comfortable."

The woman followed Flynn onboard and pressed a button inside the cabin that raised the steps and closed the door. Flynn, the lone passenger on the aircraft, took his place in one of the plush leather seats, and the plane began to move almost immediately.

Once in the air, the attendant arrived to place a package on the table in front of Flynn.

"Courtesy of Mr. Jacobs," she said.

He opened the package to reveal a heavy parka, gloves, and a thick knit beanie. Jacobs was being very accommodating, and Flynn was happy to have him on his side, even if he didn't completely trust his motivations.

The hum of the engines created a soothing backdrop to the pulse of his anticipation. He was en route to Gakona, Alaska, a place as enigmatic as the crazy rumors that swirled around it.

Flynn pulled his MacBook Pro from his bag and flipped it open. An email from Jacobs contained an attachment labeled "HAARP_Official.pdf."

The document was an official release that outlined The High-Frequency Active Auroral Research Program (HAARP) being conducted in Gakona by the University of Alaska Fairbanks. It explained in detail HAARP's benign scientific endeavors, its focus on studying the ionosphere, and how its array of 180 antennas were probing the atmospheric layers to understand their effects on communication systems. The official line was clear: HAARP was about protection and enhancement of critical technological infrastructures.

Flynn's gaze lingered on the words. For years he'd honed his instincts to read between the lines and find truth in what was left unsaid. This document was too clean, even for a sanitized piece of PR written by the government. Something was missing. He closed the laptop with a snap, his mind already sifting through the possibilities, the hidden threads that lay beneath the sterile words of the official statement.

Flynn rubbed his eyes. He was worn down. They were starting to get him to buy into all of this mind-control nonsense. He needed a solid night of sleep. He was willing to settle for a quick drink. He called over to the flight attendant who brought him a whisky with ice.

The jet banked gently, Alaska drawing nearer with every passing minute. Flynn downed his drink in one hard swallow, leaned back, and closed his eyes. He wasn't sure what he was going to find when he got there, but whatever HAARP truly was, the key to unlocking its secrets lay in Gakona. And he was determined to find some answers.

18

WESLEY CHAPEL, FLORIDA

Samantha Blackwood transformed her dining room table into a workspace cluttered with files, photographs, and a myriad of notes related to Arthur Tillman's murder case. Living alone, she had the luxury of spreading her work out, turning her condo into a makeshift command center.

She focused on identifying a potential motive that would cause James Flynn to murder Arthur Tillman. She tried to construct a theory that would place Flynn at the scene, miles off the coast of Florida with a speargun, but nothing made sense with the bits and pieces of information she'd been able to collect on the two men.

Why would Flynn target Tillman? She had someone at the Bureau put together a list of articles Flynn had written as well as the titles and subjects of his three books. Examining Flynn's work, Blackwood saw virtually no common ground between Tillman's interests and the controversies Flynn covered.

Without a clear motive, the suspicion cast upon Flynn seemed increasingly questionable. Blackwood's instincts as an investigator told her that motives were rarely hidden so deep without reason.

If Flynn had no clear reason to kill Tillman, then perhaps the narrative being constructed around him was flawed.

"Time to look at this from a new perspective," she said aloud to herself in her empty living room.

Instead of seeking ways to fit Flynn into the role of the murderer, she began to consider the possibility that he was being positioned as a scapegoat, a convenient target to distract from the real perpetrator. But why?

The next logical step was to retrace Flynn's steps, to uncover the latest story he was chasing and how it might intersect with Tillman's life and death.

She ran an internet search for HAARP and was overwhelmed by the sheer volume of conspiracy theories surrounding the research facility. From machines that controlled the weather to experiments that centered on mind manipulation, the allegations were as creative as they were implausible.

She knew that understanding Flynn's interest in HAARP was paramount to unraveling his involvement in Arthur Tillman's killing. If Flynn was onto something big, something that might expose dangerous truths, could Tillman's death have been a message to stop digging? Or was Flynn being framed, his investigation into HAARP a convenient way to divert attention?

As Blackwood continued to search the web for details about the goings on at HAARP, one storyline kept coming to the forefront: the disappearance of their lead researcher, Dr. Ethan Keller, who apparently just vanished off the face of the planet.

According to one article, the Alaska State Troopers say the investigation is on-going but they have no solid leads as to why Keller went missing or any information regarding his current whereabouts.

She dug into Keller's background and discovered that after he'd graduated from the California Institute of Technology, Keller quickly established himself as a big deal in the field of communication systems. A few years after college, Keller accepted a position at a prestigious research lab in Silicon Valley, where he led a team dedicated to pushing the boundaries of communication technology.

In the years that followed, Keller's work led to breakthroughs in quantum encryption and the development of new protocols for secure data transmission. His reputation as a visionary in the field grew, as did the list of publications and patents bearing his name. However, Keller became increasingly concerned with the ethical implications of his work. He saw the potential for misuse of technology in surveillance and control and began advocating for transparency and ethical standards in tech development.

Blackwood skimmed the rest of Dr. Keller's bio, which was basically just a list of accomplishments, each one more impressive and prestigious than the last. She was about to move on to something else when something caught her attention.

Five years ago, Keller was hired by another tech giant to spearhead an ambitious program that aimed to develop interfaces that could directly link human brains with digital networks and promised to usher in an era of "next-level human communication and understanding."

The program was called "Hermes."

The man who'd hired Keller was Blaine Jacobs.

19

GAKONA, ALASKA

The plane touched down at a small public airstrip nestled atop a flat ridge just above the Copper River. Jacobs had a car waiting for Flynn. It was late, and after a short drive from the airstrip, Flynn checked into the Explorer's Inn, an oversized, two-story log cabin that appeared to have been plopped down in the middle of the Alaskan wilderness. Despite snoozing on the plane, Flynn collapsed on the bed just seconds after stepping into his room and slept until morning.

He ate breakfast in the small restaurant attached to the inn and noticed a woman watching him from across the room while he shoveled in large mouthfuls of scrambled eggs doused in hot sauce. The woman tried to play it cool, first peeking at him over the top of her menu and then glancing at him sideways before quickly turning away. But he had caught her looking.

Flynn ascertained she was a fan, probably saw him on TV or possibly even bought one of his books. She was quite attractive, and Flynn considered the idea that maybe being recognized in public wasn't always such a bad thing, although he'd never admit it to anyone else.

He was aware of what his growing notoriety was doing to his ego. It was one thing to get recognized at a Barnes and Noble in New York City just a few days after a new release and obligatory book signing. But catching the eye of a woman at an end-of-the-Earth hotel restaurant in Alaska really raised the awareness that he was becoming known on a global level.

He poked at his eggs with his fork and smiled. She shifted her weight from one foot to the other, her breath hitching as if she wanted to say something but didn't. Once he was finished with his breakfast, he planned to walk over and introduce himself and offer to sign her book, or a napkin if she didn't have a copy with her. She'd no doubt want to snap a selfie.

Why not? Anything for a fan.

He stabbed the last bit of egg and popped it into his mouth and approached his female admirer.

But, she was gone.

He had to laugh at himself.

So much for being an international celebrity. Get over yourself, Flynn.

Outside it was twenty-five degrees Fahrenheit, which was apparently warmer than average for the time of year. The morning air stung his face as he slogged his way through the snow to his car, his nose growing numb.

"Mr. Flynn?" a woman called out from behind him.

It was the woman from the restaurant, waving a mittened hand toward him. Flynn stopped, and the woman bounded over to him, smiling.

"I thought it was you!" she said. "I just knew you'd end up here one day." She dropped her voice to a whisper. "Y'know, the whole mind-control thing?"

Flynn said nothing.

She continued, pausing barely long enough to take a breath and continuing at a rapid clip.

"I saw you sitting in there and I just didn't want to interrupt your breakfast. I'm not a rude person. I had to run out to my car and grab my book. I mean your book. I mean my book that you wrote—the book that I bought that you wrote."

She let out an exasperated breath and then offered the book, a hardcover edition no less, to Flynn.

"Can you sign this for me? Make it out to Natalie. That's me, Natalie Mercer."

Flynn took the book.

"I don't have a pen," he said.

Natalie frowned as if she hadn't considered this potential setback.

"I'm sure they have one inside," Flynn said. "Let's go back in and I'll sign it for you."

Back inside the Explorer's Inn restaurant, they took a table by the wall, and the waitress brought a pen, which Flynn used to autograph Natalie's book. He handed the book back to her and stood to go, but Natalie grabbed his hand.

"It's not every day that a famous writer visits us here in Gakona," she said. "Don't go just yet. Please stay for just a moment."

Flynn looked around. Many of the inn's patrons were looking toward them. He sat down and pulled his hand back.

"I really have a busy day today," he said. "I'm hoping to get what I need and get back home as soon as possible."

Natalie leaned in and lowered her voice. "What do you need?"

"I'm looking into some background info on a story I'm working on," he said. "I'm in a bit of a hurry and hope to be out of here later on today."

"HAARP, right?"

"I really can't say."

"What else could it be?" Natalie paused. "All the weird stuff that goes on out there, I'd love to read an article from someone who's willing to print the truth. I'm excited to see you here. I know you could uncover the truth that most of us up here already know."

"What truth is that?"

She smiled. "A-ha! I knew that's why you were here."

"I never said that," he said with a grin. "I could be up here looking into the feeding habits of brown bears."

"Ahhh, brown bears. Very interesting. Very mysterious."

"They are the most secretive of the bears."

"Is that so?"

"Not many people know that."

"I can hardly wait for the article."

"Could be my best one yet. But let's just pretend for a moment that I wasn't here for brown bears. Let's say I'm writing a story about, I don't know, rumors of mind-control experiments from a secret government research facility."

"Sounds crazy, but okay," she said, playing along, smiling.

"Crazy, right? But what were you saying about weird stuff going on around here? Just in case the brown bear thing falls through, I'd like to have a backup plan since I came all this way."

"Just in case?"

"Just in case I decide to look into that sort of thing."

Natalie reached back and clutched Flynn's hand again, this time with both of hers. She held him with a firm grip and stared into his eyes.

"If you're going to do this, there are some things you need to know," she said, "starting with you need to be very careful."

Flynn had to cut his conversation short with Natalie Mercer to make it on time for his scheduled appointment with Dr. Simon Grant, who was in charge of the research at HAARP.

Natalie said she was a guide who led adventurous tourists through the Copper River and the surrounding region on various types of hunting, fishing, hiking and camping excursions. She claimed to have seen some "crazy stuff that I can't begin to explain" and offered to fill Flynn in on more details later that afternoon.

He was starting to believe that HAARP was more than it

claimed to be, but he wasn't willing to jump to the conclusion that mind-control experiments were its deep secret. Natalie seemed sincere about whatever it was that she saw, and Flynn was curious to hear more about it.

20

GAKONA, ALASKA

Dr. Grant greeted Flynn with a warm, yet measured smile, engaging in a minute of small talk before the senior researcher offered to show Flynn what HAARP did. They started their tour outside, among the towering antennas.

Dr. Grant swept his hand outward with a proud flourish toward the impressive expanse of antennas.

"These are the stars of our ionospheric research," he said. "We have one-hundred and eighty antennas spanning thirty-three acres that send high-frequency radio waves into the ionosphere, allowing us to study its properties."

Flynn aimed to jot down notes, but as he walked beneath the massive array of antennas, its sheer size and complexity momentarily stunned him. The operation was far more extensive than he'd anticipated, leaving him temporarily awestruck.

Grant smiled and allowed Flynn to absorb the scene.

"Amazing," Flynn said after a moment. "What practical applications do these studies have?"

"Primarily, it's about understanding the ionosphere's impact on satellite and radio communication. But it's also useful for navigation systems, such as GPS."

They continued on in silence. Flynn felt the vast network of antennas gave off a very strong science fiction vibe. He could see how someone's imagination might run wild after visiting the facility. Such wild imaginations could easily turn reality into fantasy.

Grant led Flynn beyond the antennas to a large building and inside to a control room. Employees bustled across the room where dozens of screens displayed real-time data and graphics. Two armed guards wearing laminated security badges stood stone-faced near both exits.

"Here's where we control the transmissions," Grant said. "We can manipulate the ionosphere to analyze its behavior. This includes creating artificial auroras, which are harmless but spectacular to witness."

Flynn observed the technicians at work, their focus unwavering.

He asked, "Have there been any unexpected results from these experiments?"

"The world of science is full of surprises, but rest assured, all our findings are within safe and expected parameters."

As they walked through a corridor lined with offices and labs, Flynn noticed one door labeled "Restricted Access."

"What's behind there?"

Dr. Grant's demeanor shifted from tour guide to security guard. "That room's just for storing sensitive gear," he explained. "I'm sure you're referring to the 'Restricted' sign? It's mainly for our own team. We've got a lot of new faces around here—short-term employees and students. Not everyone's up to speed on handling our more delicate, high-tech equipment. So, that sign's there to prevent anyone unfamiliar with the protocols from just walking in."

They continued, with Dr. Grant showing Flynn more of the facility—a room where they simulated various atmospheric conditions, and another where data from global ionospheric studies was analyzed.

Throughout the tour, Flynn was prepared for evasion or half-truths, yet Dr. Grant had seemingly been open and helpful. Contrary to Flynn's expectations of someone hiding secret experiments or hidden agendas, his interactions with Grant revealed nothing but Grant's genuine commitment to the facility's stated research objectives.

Dr. Grant shared information freely, contributing to the conversation without any obvious attempt to steer Flynn's questions. It didn't feel at all like a cover-up, making him reconsider his initial suspicions.

But, TS47's words hung ever-present in his mind. If his source was reliable, there were answers to be found here regarding Tillman's murder.

Might as well get to it.

"What can you tell me about the allegations that HAARP's conducting experiments involving mind control?" Flynn asked, the question's sole intent meant to see how the doctor would respond.

Grant chuckled and clapped his hands together.

"I wondered how long it would take you to get to that one, Mr. Flynn. I assumed from the beginning that's why you came to see me. Your reputation—as an examiner, shall we say, of all manner of conspiracy theories—has preceded you. I was beginning to worry that you wouldn't ask. It would have been so disappointing."

Flynn waited for an answer.

"Not a week goes by that we don't address these rumors," Grant said. "Even though we've opened our doors and have been transparent in our research efforts, these wild accusations still manage to hound us regularly. We are doing serious research here, and continually needing to respond to such queries gets in the way of the true scientific efforts we conduct daily. That's why I was so willing to talk to you today. I hope that you can write your article and put this entire matter to rest."

"So that's a 'no,' then?" Flynn needling the man just a bit.

"We conduct scientific experiments on the planet's ionosphere. All of the work that we do here is documented and available via the Freedom of Information Act. You can request the paperwork and see for yourself."

Flynn smiled. "My apologies, Doctor. I guess my sources are wrong on this one. It happens. You should see some of the whackos I deal with."

"I can only imagine. Since we've opened this facility to public tours, I've been asked about so many bizarre things. We could probably trade hilarious anecdotes."

The laughing waned, and then Flynn jabbed the needle deep: "What can you tell me about Project Titan?"

The tone turned grave as Grant stuttered for a moment as he started to respond. The flustered response was barely noticeable, but Flynn caught it. A tiny flinch, a sudden shock in the doctor's eyes. And then it was gone. Grant's quick recovery told Flynn that the man was used to concealing sensitive information even when he wasn't expecting it.

"That's not one of my projects," Grant said.

"So someone else is in charge of it? Dr. Keller, perhaps?"

"It's not a study that I'm aware of is what I meant. It may well exist, but it's not something that is being conducted here at HAARP."

"I can quote you on that?"

Dr. Grant stared at Flynn as though he couldn't decide whether to answer the question or punch Flynn in the face.

Flynn continued before Grant could answer. "What can you tell me about Dr. Keller's disappearance?"

"Nothing that I haven't already told the police," Grant said. "Is this an interview or an interrogation? Am I mistaken or are you law enforcement? May I see your badge, officer?"

Flynn eyed Grant silently.

"I don't owe you an answer, Mr. Flynn, but I will give you one all the same, simply as a professional courtesy," Grant said. "Dr. Keller has been gone for three months. I don't know where he is or what happened to him. We worked together for two years here at HAARP. I respected the man as a scientist, but we were colleagues, co-workers. We weren't best friends. His disappearance was unexpected and unprofessional if you want my opinion, but we have kept our research running smoothly despite the change in leadership."

"Thank you for your candor, Dr. Grant. I'm sorry if my questions sound a bit aggressive. I am not law enforcement, as you know, and you are not obligated to respond to me. But, I am interested in Dr. Keller's whereabouts because I believe his disappearance is integral to the article I'm writing. If there's anything you could tell me that could potentially shine light on what may have happened to him, I'd be very grateful."

"I don't know where Dr. Keller is," Grant said.

"And you've not spoken to him since he went missing?"

"I have not."

And, there it was. Grant's eyes flickered for a split second, darting to one side before refocusing on Flynn.

The doctor was lying.

Almost as if on cue, one of the technicians slid between the men and addressed Grant face to face.

"Doctor," the man said, "the results you asked about are in. I knew you wanted to be alerted as quickly as possible."

Grant nodded. The technician left, and Grant apologized to Flynn that he needed to step away for a moment.

Flynn watched as Dr. Grant followed the technician to the other side of the room. They were out of earshot, but Grant's face tightened into an expression of irritation. He snatched a printout from the technician's trembling hands, only to thrust it back with such force that the technician staggered backwards. The paper crumpled against the technician's chest, a symbol of Grant's disdain. With a fearful glance, the technician clutched the mangled document and scurried away, his steps quickening as he disappeared down the corridor, eager to escape Grant's wrathful presence.

Grant took a deep breath and returned to Flynn.

"I'm afraid I have to cut our tour short," he said. "A situation has come up that I need to attend to immediately."

Of course you do.

"Please see yourself out," Grant said, gesturing toward the lobby doors that led outside. He forced a smile. "Thank you for your visit and don't hesitate to contact me again if you have any further questions about our research. Have a safe flight back home to Florida."

After Dr. Grant excused himself, Flynn's mind wrestled with the problematic pieces of his visit. Grant clearly was not telling the truth about Dr. Keller, and the "Restricted Access" sign nagged at him, an itch he couldn't ignore. He waited in the lobby, feigning a preoccupation with his phone as if he were checking the weather forecast or the latest headlines, until he sensed the opportunity—a shift change, perhaps, or a momentary lapse in the staff's awareness.

He removed his beanie and tucked it into his coat pocket. With no one watching, he edged his way back from where they had just come. He retraced his steps back to the main transmission room where he was stopped by one of the armed guards.

"I believe I dropped my hat while Dr. Grant gave me the tour," said Flynn, tapping the top of his head. "I don't think I want to go wandering outside without it. I'm pretty sure I remember where I left it."

The guard waved him through without a word, seemingly annoyed that he had to move at all.

Flynn made his way to the secured door. Grant had dismissed it as simply a storage room, which made Flynn want to get inside even more. All of the technicians were busy staring into their computer monitors, no doubt fearful that Grant could bust in at any moment. The look on that one technician's face told Flynn all he needed to know about what kind of operation Grant ran.

No one even noticed Flynn as he placed his hand on the door handle. He held his breath, fully expecting an alarm to go off, or at the very least for the door to be locked. But as he rotated the handle clockwise, it moved, and with a click, the door opened.

Flynn slipped into the room and eased the door shut behind him, careful to not make any unnecessary noise. The room was full of cardboard boxes. Flynn flipped open a few of the flaps to find computers and other lab equipment. It was just as Dr. Grant had said. Merely a storage room.

He examined the room further, his attention drawn to a sturdy metal cabinet in the corner. It was locked, but that was a minor obstacle for someone with Flynn's skill set.

Using a paperclip he snagged from a nearby stack of papers, Flynn jimmied the lock open. The door creaked as the drawer slid open, revealing rows of neatly arranged files and binders. He rifled through them, looking for anything that hinted at the mind-control research he suspected was being conducted here.

Instead, Flynn found a stack of folders labeled "Emory Research: Dr. Janel Hart." Curious, he opened one and quickly skimmed through its contents. The papers detailed extensive studies on the effects of nutrition on the immune systems of lab rats. It was comprehensive and scholarly, but completely innocuous for his purposes. There was nothing about mind control or secret missile bases or any other clandestine government projects—just straightforward scientific research.

Flynn felt a twinge of disappointment. This was a dead end, far from the explosive discovery he had hoped for. He carefully replaced the files, ensuring everything was as he had found it. This part of the facility held no dark secrets, just the earnest work of scientists studying rodent health.

As he left the storage room, Flynn's earlier suspicions began to wane, replaced by a dawning realization that perhaps the Gakona facility was indeed just the straightforward scientific research center Dr. Grant had always insisted it was. But he knew Grant had more information about Dr. Keller's disappearance than he let on. That was enough to keep Flynn's curiosity piqued.

He left the room and followed the hallway back toward the lobby, holding up his hat and smiling to the guard as he walked by.

Standing at the front door with his arms folded across his chest was Dr. Grant. A satisfied grin stretched across his face.

"Did you get lost, Mr. Flynn? I apologize if my directions were not adequate to help you find the exit."

"Your instructions were fine, Dr. Grant." Flynn said. "I saw exactly what you wanted me to see."

21

UNKNOWN LOCATION

A small, weak fluorescent tube flickered, fighting to cut into the darkness. Dr. Nestor Keller stabbed the numbers on his cellphone with a sense of urgency. The room was cluttered with scientific equipment and monitors, which hummed quietly in the background. He paced back and forth.

Next to him, on a bed, lay a patient—awake but quiet, the restraints holding his arms and legs strapped firmly in place. He wouldn't be a problem.

"Who is asking questions," Keller spoke into the phone, his voice tight. "A journalist? Why is he here?"

The man on the other end of the call explained that Flynn's visit was expected, and that he'd be taken care of in due time. Keller drummed his fingers on the counter as he listened.

"Alright. Just handle it," Keller said. "I don't want any complications. No more interruptions."

The man on the phone reassured Dr. Keller that everything would be fine and then ended the call. Keller cursed at his phone and dropped it into the pocket of his white lab coat.

Turning back to his work, Keller approached the bed where

the soldier lay. The young man took shallow breaths, his face gray and gaunt. The soldier was thin, and his hands were bruised and beaten as if he'd been punching solid rock for days. Wires and tubes connected him to nearby monitors, which displayed his vital signs.

"This will help," Keller said softly, almost reassuringly, as he prepared a syringe filled with a clear liquid.

The soldier's eyes went wide, revealing a mix of hope and fear, before closing slowly. Keller injected the serum into the soldier's arm, his hand steady despite the tension from the phone call and the unsettling visit to his facility from James Flynn.

For the moment, the injection produced positive results. The soldier's breathing returned to a normal cadence, and his other vitals began to improve almost instantly. Keller checked the monitors; it was working.

His optimism was short-lived. Keller felt his heart sink as the monitors erupted like a shrieking ensemble of warning beeps and buzzes. The soldier's body convulsed, his heart rate spiked. Keller rushed to administer aid.

It was too late.

The soldier's body finally lay completely still, the monitors emitting a continuous, haunting tone. Cardiac arrest.

Keller froze, staring at the lifeless body. With a heavy sigh he disposed of the empty syringe in a nearby receptacle. He had failed, but at least the young man was at peace.

There were more left to save.

22

VIRGINIA BEACH, VIRGINIA

Quinton Danbury, seated in the back of his luxury SUV, felt the exhilaration of victory along with an uneasy conscience. His campaign had just hit a jackpot as a surge of donations began to spill in. His campaign team called it a testament to his growing influence and the confidence voters had in his ability to represent them. He smiled at the thought, his mind imagining his eventual moment of triumph.

Among the list of donations, a striking pattern emerged. Contributions were flowing in from areas where Danbury had previously struggled to gain a foothold. Notably, there were multiple donations from Chesapeake, a region where Blake Calloway had held a firm grip. These donations were not just token amounts; they were significant, suggesting a shift in the public's allegiance. Each donation from Chesapeake was like a small victory, chipping away at Calloway's stronghold.

Another surprising development was the influx of funds from Norfolk. Historically lukewarm to Danbury's influence, this area was now a source of robust support. Among the contributions was a notable sum from a group of small business owners, a collective that had been openly critical of Danbury in the past. This change of heart was not only a boost in resources but also a symbolic win, hinting at a broader shift in public opinion within the region.

"True Virginians know what's best," he said out loud as he looked over the report listing his windfall of financial support. The donations weren't just numbers; they were affirmations, people believing in his vision, his leadership. But that glow was dimmed by the looming shadow of Mr. White, a reminder that success often came with strings attached. And Danbury didn't like to be made to dance.

Mr. White, the ominous figure who had entered the Senator's life just days earlier, had shown up again earlier in the day, unannounced as always and seemingly out of nowhere. His words were still ringing in Danbury's ears.

"I hope you're happy with the results," he'd said. There was a promise in his tone, a hint of more to come, but also a chilling threat. "But if you screw us over—"

Mr. White let his words hang.

Danbury shook his head, trying to dispel the menacing tone. He still had no idea who "us" referred to. He'd agreed to vote to kill funding to a Project Titan, a secret military experiment that had somehow gone awry. He didn't recall the project and didn't have any details as of yet, but he'd get them ASAP. What was one less military initiative in the overall scheme of things? This one favor was going to keep him on Capitol Hill, where Danbury knew he could do some real good for a lot of people.

He turned to Barry Meadows, his campaign manager, who was eyeing him with curiosity. "Just a pesky donor," Danbury had lied. He couldn't afford to let Meadows know the depth of the waters into which he was wading.

The SUV rolled on, the city lights blurring past. Danbury's thoughts were interrupted as he discovered a report, mysteriously placed in the seat next to him.

He frowned, "Who put this here?"

No one knew.

Curiosity piqued, Danbury opened the folder. The first glimpse of its contents sent a jolt through him. Meadows leaned in from the front seat, trying to catch a peek, but Danbury flattened the report against his chest, keeping it out of plain view.

"Classified," he said. "Sorry, Barry. You know the rules."

Meadows shrugged. He was used to being out of the loop. He turned back to face the road in front of them.

Danbury looked again. His heart pounded.

What have I gotten myself into?

Needing to escape the confines of the SUV, Danbury asked the driver to stop. He stepped out into the cool night air. He walked a few steps in front of the vehicle clutching the classified report in his hand. His mind was racing.

Opening the report again, he stared at the images. Murdered bodies, their stories untold, but their ends violent. The photos were labeled "Project Titan." Danbury felt a wave of nausea. There was a typed note paper-clipped to one of the pages with a simple four-word message:

"Do the right thing."

In that moment, under the Virginia night sky, Quinton Danbury stood at a crossroads. He'd made a decision that would likely lead to his re-election, but he wondered who else was going to benefit and who might suffer. One thing seemed clear: If this Project Titan led to the loss of innocent lives, he'd have no problem cutting its funding.

23

GAKONA, ALASKA

Natalie Mercer sat at the same table against the wall where Flynn had spotted her earlier that morning. It was late afternoon, and the dinner crowd was filing in, their chatter creating a lively backdrop as he approached her. He reached the table and noticed a discernible shift in her demeanor—a mix of anticipation tinged with caution. An unconvincing smile greeted him as he sat down.

"You're back," she said.

"Surprised?" Flynn said.

"*Relieved* may be a better word for it."

"Was there any doubt?"

"There's always doubt when that place is concerned," she said. "You went inside?"

Flynn nodded. "I did. Dr. Grant seemed a bit defensive. But honestly, I didn't see anything that seemed all that out of the ordinary. I got the feeling he wasn't telling me everything about Dr. Keller's disappearance, but that doesn't mean he's experimenting with mind control. There are a dozen reasons why Keller may have run off, and none of them have to involve anything nefarious. And it's not uncommon for someone to lie to protect a colleague."

Natalie glanced around the dining room, which was nearly full now. She lowered her voice. "There's more to that facility than what you saw."

Flynn raised an eyebrow and leaned in toward her. "How do you know?"

She hesitated. "I can't really talk about it here."

He leaned back in his chair and stared at her through squinted eyes.

"What?" she asked.

"Enough with ambiguous insinuations," he said. "I need to know what you know. I can't take this any further without more information. If you have something to say, say it. If not, I'm going home."

Flynn's threat was a weak con. He couldn't leave until he had more info on this secret Project Titan, whatever the hell it was, and how it connected to Arthur Tillman's murder. He needed answers. He hoped Natalie would fall for his ruse and open up.

She bit her lip, hesitating to respond.

"Can we go somewhere else? Somewhere private?"

"I've got a room upstairs, unless you're worried that someone has it bugged." He smiled.

Some of the tension in her face melted away, and she almost laughed.

"No," she said. "That will work just fine."

Flynn led Natalie up the stairs to his small room. He stood in the corner and she took a seat on the bed.

"Let's just say what they're doing goes beyond standard research," she said. "It involves the mind. It's just not atmospheric studies or whatever they claim."

Flynn turned serious. "What proof do you have?"

"It's complicated," Natalie sighed.

He reached for the door and twisted the knob.

"I think we're done here," he said. "I have a flight to catch back to St. Pete. I told you I don't have time for games."

"No, wait," she said.

Flynn took his hand off the door.

After several moments of tense silence, Natalie finally broke down. Her voice wavered between fear and resolve as she revealed her secret.

"Sergeant Richard Mahler, my boyfriend, is an Army Ranger," she said. "He was called to Gakona two years ago for a special assignment. It was supposed to be just six months. I wanted to see Alaska, so I tagged along with him, figured it'd be a nice vacation, a unique experience, and a chance to get to know each other better. We'd talked about getting married. This felt like a good test."

Her eyes drifted just a bit, and Flynn figured she was reliving those initial days of adventure and uncertainty as she began her story.

"It was exciting at first, the idea of being in this wild, remote place together. I was outside studying the area, the wildlife, the weather, the people. But then things . . . changed."

She went silent and clasped her hands together, fingers interlocked.

"Changed how?" Flynn said, urging her on.

"Richard started acting differently," she said. "He was always so strong, so confident before. But in Gakona, he became distant, secretive. He'd leave at odd hours, come back looking exhausted and ... troubled."

Flynn was well aware how military assignments could change a person, especially in remote places like Alaska where it was easy to feel isolated and secluded.

Natalie said, "He wouldn't talk about his work, said it was classified. But I could tell something was weighing on him, something more than just the usual stresses of his job." She took a deep breath to steady herself. "Shortly before he disappeared I found him in our kitchen scribbling on a notepad. Page after page he kept writing this one word: Hermes. I think it's connected to the HAARP facility, to whatever they're doing there."

Flynn felt a spike of adrenaline surge through his body and he sat up straight. "Hermes?"

"It DOES mean something to you," she said. "I knew it would. It's why I approached you. When I saw you, I knew it was a sign. You're here to find Richard and find out what's going on in there."

Flynn said, "Find him?"

"I haven't seen him for three months," she said. Tears welled in her eyes. "I called his family; they haven't heard from him. I called the Army; they said his current duty is classified. I even reached out to Dr. Keller. He told me Richard had been dismissed from the program, but he wouldn't say anything else."

Flynn nodded. He realized that Natalie wasn't just a fan or an informant; she was a woman driven by love and fear, desperate to uncover the truth. He wasn't sure how Hermes fit in with Tillman's murder and the conspiracy looming over HAARP, but he'd brushed up enough on Greek mythology in the past few days to know that Hermes was a titan, a bona fide son of Zeus. And that meant he was getting closer to unraveling this mystery.

24

The door clicked shut as Natalie Mercer left Flynn's hotel room. Flynn stood by the window, marveling at the pure darkness of the night dotted with the bright white lights from more stars than he'd ever seen in one sky. He looked down toward the parking lot in front of the inn and watched Natalie get into her car and drive away.

Flynn tapped a message on his phone to TS47:

Hermes?

The messenger of the gods. He was cunning and mischievous.

How does he connect with Tillman and HAARP?

Tillman freed Hermes.

From who?

Your friend who is not your friend. Your enemy is not your enemy.

No more games!

You're right. There's no time to waste. Find Keller. Do what Tillman could not.

What couldn't Tillman do? Dammit! Give me a straight answer!

Flynn stared at his phone for a full minute, but it was clear that TruthSeeker47 had said all they were going to say.

Flynn churned this latest cryptic message through his mind, trying to decipher yet another riddle. He concluded that he needed a drink, as the words and their mysterious meaning muddled his brain like a muddy stream through which he attempted to wade.

He ambled downstairs to the lounge and took a stool at the end of the bar.

At the other end was a group of men looking his way. They were having a good time laughing with one another, and Flynn soon realized he was the object of their good humor. Content to let it go, he looked straight ahead and drank his beer. No reason to get worked up over some drunk Alaskans who likely considered him to be a conspiracy theory nut. For as many fans who recognized him, Flynn also had his opponents and detractors who believed he was nothing more than a charlatan.

He heard their laughter die down and spotted one of the men coming his way. Flynn discreetly planted his feet firmly on the floor. If something was to go down, he wanted to be able to react quickly and decisively.

He turned his head to face the man and saw that his three buddies were all holding back laughter. The one coming his way was the "brave" one who'd been chosen to confront the crackpot writer with a witty one-liner.

Flynn rotated his body toward the man and caught him off guard by speaking first. "How's it going, pal?"

The man stopped and stammered, seemingly unsure how to proceed.

"Good," he said, sounding more like a question than a statement. He looked at his crew and then back toward Flynn, desperately trying to get back on script. He paused for a beat before blurting, "The pretty ones never look crazy, do they?"

"Is that some sort of pick-up line?" Flynn said. "I have to say I'm flattered but I don't think that's gonna seal the deal for ya, Cowboy."

The three men at the end of the bar howled with laughter at their friend, who stood stunned, his mouth first agape in surprise before snapping shut and tightening at the jaw. He took another two steps forward and hovered over Flynn. The man was big, a good two inches taller than him. Flynn adjusted himself with a subtle twist of his torso, ready to strike if it came to that.

The big man said, "I'm talking about that girl you was with. Pretty. But not all there in the head."

Flynn relaxed. "How's that?"

"She got a few screws loose," called out one of the other men.

"Tell you about her boyfriend?" the big man asked.

Flynn said nothing.

The second man made his way to Flynn's side of the bar.

"We met that fella," he said. "Good kid. A real soldier. But not the settling-down type if you know what I mean. Told us he came up here to get away, but damn if that pretty girl of his didn't chase his tail clear to Nowhere, Alaska."

Flynn took a swig of his beer.

The big man spoke again. "She ask you to find him for her? Say he disappeared?"

"She's always talking crazy about that research station down the road," said the second man. "All that boy did was some light guard duty over there. But Natalie got herself an imagination and made a glacier out of an ice cube. You ain't the first one she's asked for help."

"No?" said Flynn.

"No sir," said the second man. "She hired a private investigator and everything. Never seen that fella again. Probably took her money and ran. Like we said, she's pretty, and that can be enough to get a man to do things that just don't make sense. Hell, we all been there."

"Well I sure am lucky to have run into you boys," Flynn said. "You saved me a lot of time. Thanks for clearing that up."

The men exchanged proud smiles, happy to do a solid for a fellow man in danger of being led astray by the flighty whims of an attractive woman. One of them patted Flynn on the back and said excitedly, "Let us buy you another beer."

A third man reached to shake Flynn's hand, and that's when Flynn saw it. Just for a split second, clipped to the inside of one of the men's jackets was a badge that looked identical to the ones worn by security personnel at HAARP.

"Then again," Flynn said. "Maybe it's easier to label someone crazy than to admit there might be truth in what they're saying. Especially if it implicates one of our own, right?"

The men's faces melted into uneasy glances.

Flynn continued. "It's fascinating, really. How quick we are to dismiss someone's concerns just because it makes us uncomfortable. Or is it because deep down, we're afraid they might be right and we might be wrong? Or worse yet, on the wrong side of what's right?"

The four men looked at each other for an answer or even a clue on how to react to this unexpected turn.

One of the smaller men spoke up. "You think you're some kind of smart guy? We know Natalie; we know her type. She sulks around here and tries to rile folks up. Every once in a while she cons some stray do-gooder who stumbles along into her path. Is that you? Are you here to cause trouble?"

"Trouble? I'm just having a conversation," Flynn said. "But if facing a few hard truths is too much, I understand. Not everyone can handle that."

The big man pushed his way through his friends and stopped just inches from Flynn. His massive fists were clenched.

Flynn took a half-step back, ready.

"Alright, boys," the bartender barked, speaking for the first time. "We don't need this kind of talk here. Let's just leave it alone. Miss Natalie hasn't done anything to any of you. Sure, she might be a bit odd, but who of us who came to live in these parts can say anything different?"

The remark elicited a faint chuckle from everyone, and the mood felt substantially lighter. The four men mumbled to each other about needing to get home and how it was going to be an early start in the morning and how it was better to not even get involved with strangers these days.

"Thanks for that," Flynn said to the bartender as he slid a generous tip across the bar.

"If you want some free advice, convince that girl to just get outta here," he said. "It's the best move you've got."

Flynn drained what was left of his beer and trudged back to his room. As he reached the top of the stairs he was met by a pair of familiar faces.

25

ST. PETERSBURG BEACH, FLORIDA

Samantha Blackwood had read the police report about Flynn's confrontation with Liam Baxter. She also read the account of Baxter's murder that happened that very same night. The reports were what they were: written documentation of the facts as discovered by law enforcement. Combined with what she saw firsthand on Arthur Tillman's boat, at Flynn's apartment, and what she gleaned online about Dr. Keller, she was beginning to create a clear picture in her head of what was going on.

But clear or not, was it believable? Without Minter, Blackwood needed someone else to bounce ideas off of. The primary investigator on the Baxter case was a detective named Block. She called him and asked if they could get together to compare notes.

Detective Block and Special Agent Blackwood sat opposite each other across a small table in a hole-in-the-wall Italian restaurant just outside the city, two beers and a half-eaten pizza between them.

"I gotta be honest with you," Block said, waving a mammoth hand toward the three case files Blackwood had dropped on the table. "I don't like Flynn for any of these. I talked to him. He's not a murderer. He definitely has a knack for being in the wrong place at the wrong time, but he's not a murderer."

Blackwood removed some photos from the files. She didn't like what Block was saying. She wanted Flynn to be the guy. She wanted to wrap this up. She wanted to close the case. For Wayne Minter.

"You know his history?" she said. "He was CIA."

"Yeah, I checked into him. Some sort of analyst."

"His file has more thick black lines than any I've ever seen. The man's entire intelligence career has been redacted. They don't do that if you just sit around at Langley and monitor communication between alleged terrorist cells. Flynn was deep into something. He's skilled, resourceful. If he wanted someone gone, he could make it happen."

Block nodded his massive head.

"Okay, let's say you're right. Do you think a well-trained government agent would be so sloppy that he'd leave the murder weapon in his room? Would he make a police report to start an investigation into a crime where he was already the primary person of interest?"

Blackwood shrugged.

Block continued. "This looks like an unfortunate coincidence to me."

"How many bad guys have you locked up?"

"Total?"

She nodded.

Block thought about it. "I couldn't give you a number, but it's well into the triple digits," he said.

"Of all those hundreds of criminals, what's one characteristic they all shared?"

Block shrugged. "Their parents didn't love them enough?"

Blackwood smiled. She liked this detective.

"Would you say any of them were what you might call smart?"

"I see where you're going," Block said. "No, I guess not. Like this one guy, a suspect in a drug-related killing. We picked him up with the murder weapon stuck in the waistband of his baggy jeans; a brand new Glock nine mil. We had him in the back of the car on the way to the station, my partner goes, 'Why didn't you dump the gun?' And the guy says, 'I couldn't. It was a present from my mom.'"

Blackwood nearly spit out her beer.

"I kid you not," Block said.

"That's some mom. It's not every woman who's going to give her boy a handgun for Christmas."

"This is Florida. It's more common than you think."

"So you see my point. Sloppy is more the norm than not when someone commits a crime."

"But Flynn's no dummy." Block thumbed through the crime scene photos. "I mean look at this. The section of wall where you found the weapon, the paneling was flipped upside-down. No way he makes that mistake. That speargun was planted in there, and they wanted someone to find it easily."

"Maybe Flynn wanted it to look like it was planted."

Block scowled.

"Alright, maybe not," Blackwood said. "But, why run?"

"Who said he ran? He was on his way to Alaska for an assignment. Maybe it's a coincidence that he left just before you busted into his place."

"Something tells me you wouldn't be so quick to accept 'coincidences' in your own murder investigations."

He sat up straight.

"Baxter *is* my investigation, don't forget," he said. "Flynn was my number one suspect, but I don't think he did it. I don't see any motive. No, I don't normally believe in coincidences, but I also don't jump to conclusions just because I'm climbing the walls to close a case. It needs to make sense, and none of this makes sense—you know it just like I do. I was hoping you'd have more for me, but I think you're stuck at square one with the rest of us."

He was right. About everything.

"Maybe he didn't kill anyone, but James Flynn is wrapped up in this somehow. I can promise you this: I'm going to Alaska and I'm going to find Mr. Flynn, and he's going to give me some answers."

26

Brice Holland and David Bailey, two of the men Flynn had met at the Ultra convention, stood shoulder to shoulder, each other's faces knotted in a grimace as if a foul odor had invaded the top floor of the inn.

Their presence just outside the door to Flynn's room caught him by surprise. He had assumed since they were so hell-bent to have him investigate the lab in Alaska that they had no interest in getting out to see it for themselves. Something urgent must have pried them out of their anonymity and into the light.

"Holland. Bailey. In the neighborhood?" Flynn said.

Holland huffed. Bailey shifted his weight ever so slightly from one leg to the other. Neither man spoke.

"Excuse me, boys," Flynn said as he wedged himself between them to get to his door. "It's been a long day and I have an early start tomorrow if I want to get out of here and back home by dinner time."

"Not right now," the voice came from behind him. Flynn recognized the tone.

"Nellis," he said as he turned to face Ultra's head of security. "I didn't think these two would go out after dark alone. What's this about? Why are you guys here?"

Holland spoke up, braver now with Nellis at his shoulder.

"You're in big trouble, Flynn." Like he heard it in a movie.

Flynn ignored the older man. He spoke to Nellis. "What is this?"

Nellis shrugged. "Let's just go talk."

Bailey poked Flynn in the chest. "Move it."

Flynn gave a look that caused Bailey to flinch.

"Alright, boys," Flynn said. "You got me curious. Let's talk."

They drove a few miles down Tok Cut-off Road, which served as the main highway through the region, Bailey at the wheel, Flynn next to him, Nellis and Holland in the backseat. The car's tires crunched over the snow as they turned onto a side road that was clearly a route less-taken. Their destination was an abandoned concrete shipping depot, a remnant of a bygone era, its gray, weather-beaten walls standing in stark contrast to the white snow and towering pines surrounding it.

Inside, the air was cold, the only light coming from their flashlights as they herded Flynn, hands hastily bound by Bailey, into the heart of the building. They secured him to a chair they had prepared for this moment, the flashlight beams highlighting serious looks on the men's faces.

Holland flipped a switch on the wall, turning on a single light that hung from the ceiling directly over Flynn's head.

"This is quite a little operation you've got going here," Flynn said, scanning his stark surroundings. "Anyone going to tell me what this is all about?"

Bailey and Holland faced him, their eyes filled with a mixture of fear and accusation.

"You killed Baxter," Bailey said with an unexpected wind of conviction.

"Is that what this is about? You think I killed Baxter and you flew all the way to Alaska to tie me up in a chair and say it to my face? What are you going to do exactly? Execute me?"

The two men looked at each other. It seemed feasible that had been the plan, but now that they were all there in the room, they appeared to be less sure how to follow through. Holland and Bailey were not violent men.

"Nellis," Holland barked.

Nellis, lean and serious, stepped forward, gun in hand. Flynn was sure that he, unlike his partners, was no stranger to violence.

"Think about it," Flynn said. "I mean use your head here. Why would I kill Baxter? My goal is to uncover the truth, not to silence it. Baxter came to me. The man was seriously troubled. I wanted to hear what he had to say. I wanted to help him. Instead, he attacked me, and I never saw him again."

"What about Arthur Tillman?" Nellis said.

"What about him?"

"He doesn't even know," Bailey said, nodding toward Flynn. "Dear lord. I thought we were dealing with a skilled investigator, someone professional and discreet. Instead we have put our faith in a buffoon."

Nellis extended his palm toward Bailey as he spoke to Flynn. "The FBI believes you killed Tillman."

Flynn couldn't believe his ears. "You know that's not true. I was at your meeting at the time Tillman was said to have been killed. So why do they think I'm a suspect? I didn't even know the man."

Holland shook his head. "You misunderstand. We don't care about Tillman or who killed him. The fact that you were our guest gives you an effective alibi, which is advantageous for you but problematic for us."

"You're worried the FBI is going to start poking around your little secret club," Flynn said. "Trust me, the feds don't care about your photos of Bigfoot or blurry VHS tapes showing UFOs flying over New Mexico."

Nellis, always with Ultra's security his primary concern, said, "Our meeting was off the record. If they start digging, it could compromise our members, who trust us to protect them. Exposure is not an option."

Flynn looked at each of them in turn. "So, what's the plan?

You know I'm being set up. We need to find out who's behind this and why."

Holland nodded. "We're working on it. But until then, we need to ensure Ultra remains in the shadows. That means keeping you here, out of sight, until we can clear this up."

"You've mucked this up, bigtime, Flynn," shot Bailey.

Flynn ignored the dig. "What do you mean 'clear this up?'"

"Nellis is investigating the Tillman murder," Holland said. "Mr. Bailey and I are going to keep you company here for as long as it takes him to identify the real killer and get the FBI off your trail."

"We trusted you," Holland said. "But with Baxter murdered and you being the last one to see him alive, they will come to you. They'll ask questions. You'll put us all at risk."

Flynn noticed a slight hesitation in Nellis's demeanor; an almost imperceptible twist of the neck that told Flynn that Nellis wasn't completely on board. He seized the opportunity.

"You're the most rational man in this room," Flynn said to Nellis. "You know what I do. Do I strike you as someone who'd jeopardize his mission for a senseless murder? Do you really think I'm going to spill your secrets to the police?"

Nellis paused, his eyes betraying a moment of doubt.

Flynn continued. "Someone else is pulling the strings here, and Baxter was just a pawn. We should be working together to uncover the real threat."

The suggestion sparked an immediate reaction. Bailey turned towards Nellis, his voice rising.

"Are you actually falling for this? He's manipulating us."

Holland joined in, his tone accusatory. "Nellis, you're not seriously doubting our objective, are you?"

As the three argued among themselves, Flynn noticed the rope binding his wrists was loose. In his haste, Bailey had botched the restraints. While the three men argued, Flynn fought against the bindings, expertly working the already slackened knot, coaxing it looser with each careful twist and turn.

"Look at the bigger picture," Flynn urged, his voice steady. "We're all caught in a larger scheme. I'm trying to expose the truth, not just for my sake, but for everyone's."

Nellis's expression shifted from suspicion to contemplation, his internal conflict becoming more apparent. Bailey, sensing the shift, turned back to Flynn, anger flaring in his eyes. But it was too late.

With a quick jerk, Flynn freed his wrists and surged forward, catching the trio off guard. He pushed past Holland, knocked the gun from Nellis's grip, and broke for the door.

27

LOUDOUN COUNTY, VIRGINIA

The Danbury home, a majestic testament to American colonial architecture, stood proudly amidst the lush greenery of its expansive grounds. Its facade, a harmonious blend of red brick and white trim, exuded a sense of time-honored grandeur. Tall, white-columned porticos graced the entrance, inviting visitors into a world where history and elegance intertwined.

Symmetrical windows with traditional shutters, along with the gabled roof, captured the essence of colonial design. The house's large porches, adorned with intricately carved wooden railings, offered a picturesque view of the surrounding landscape.

Senator Danbury's wife, Elena, known for her grace and poise, welcomed Leslie Vanderwaal into the grand hallway of their home. A former school teacher with a Master's degree in Education, Elena had long been an advocate for educational reform and children's literacy. Her passion for these causes was evident in the way she had infused elements of history and learning into her home's decor.

Senator Danbury, always charismatic and impeccably dressed,

even at a casual time like this, joined them, extending a hand to Leslie with a warm smile.

"Welcome to our little piece of history," he said.

As they began the tour, Leslie was immediately struck how the classic decor and furnishings combined to craft a modern tribute to American history. Elena, ever the educator, took the lead, her knowledge and love for American history bringing each room to life.

Tomas, the freelance photographer *The National* contracted to accompany Leslie, trailed behind them, snapping photo after photo of the home's interior as well as candid moments of its owners.

The home's architecture paid homage to its colonial roots throughout, with high ceilings, ornate crown moldings, and hardwood floors.

"The portraits you see," Elena began in the living room, "are not just decorations. They are teaching tools, reminders of where we come from." Her voice held a reverence for the past, a sentiment echoed in the grand fireplace that dominated the room. "This has been a part of Quinton's family for generations. It's more than an heirloom; it's a piece of history."

The furniture echoed the rich history of its architecture. Each room boasted elegant, antique pieces, from ornately carved mahogany dining tables to plush, velvet-upholstered settees, exuding a sense of timeless luxury.

"We often host student groups here," Elena said as they reached the dining room and its long mahogany table. "It's important for them to feel connected to our nation's past."

Outside, Quinton pointed out various plants and flowers, each carefully chosen by Elena for their significance in American history.

"Elena's passion for teaching extends even to our garden," he said.

Throughout the tour, Leslie was captivated not just by the grandeur of the house but by Elena's depth of knowledge and dedication to her cause. The Danburys' wealth and status seemed secondary to their commitment to education and preservation of history.

As they concluded the tour, Leslie was left with a profound sense of respect for Elena Danbury. Her efforts to weave her passion for education into every aspect of their home and life were noteworthy.

A pang of remorse tugged at Leslie's conscience. Surrounded by the tangible evidence of the Senator's apparent love for history and his wife's dedication to education, she found herself questioning the morality of her assignment. The task of digging up dirt on Senator Danbury, a man who, at least on the surface, seemed to embody integrity and commitment to public service, now felt like an intrusion into a world that was far more complex and honorable than she had anticipated.

Leslie's typically sharp journalistic instincts had been somewhat dulled by the grandeur and historical significance of the Danbury home, until a particular detail caught her eye. As they moved along the hall, a closed door with a small security panel and a surveillance camera perched above it stood out amidst the colonial elegance.

Curiosity piqued, she turned to Senator Danbury, "What's behind this door?"

He paused, a hint of discomfort flashing across his face before he replied with a chuckle.

"I'm almost ashamed to admit it, but it's an elaborately modern sauna and workout room for my family and the staff."

He gave a self-deprecating smile, as if to downplay the extravagance of such a facility in a home that otherwise paid homage to American history.

"It sounds fascinating. It would make a great setting for a feature photo in the article," she suggested, watching his reaction.

The Senator's response was swift, almost rehearsed.

"Oh, I don't think so. I'm afraid that a room full of high-end exercise equipment at my 'farm home' might send the wrong message to my voters," he said. "It's a bit too modern and indulgent for the image we're trying to convey here."

Beside him, Mrs. Danbury shifted her posture, her eyes darting momentarily to the door before meeting Leslie's gaze and then falling away toward the floor.

At that moment, Leslie's earlier reservations about her assignment vanished. The Senator's dismissive attitude, coupled with Mrs. Danbury's evident anxiety, reignited the enthusiasm for her original mission. Something was being hidden behind that door — and it was more than a luxurious sauna, that much she was sure of. The guarded nature of the room, so starkly different from the rest of the house, served as a glaring anomaly.

Her mind raced with possibilities. What could the Danburys be hiding? Leslie knew she had to find out. She could be on the verge of uncovering a potentially explosive story.

* * *

Quentin Danbury sat across from Leslie, her smart phone resting on the small table between them recording the conversation. The fall breeze gently rustled the leaves, adding a serene soundtrack to the interview. Danbury, leaning back in his rocking chair, aimed to portray the very image of a seasoned politician at ease in the sanctuary of his stately rural home.

She thanked him for the opportunity to meet and talk with him for the upcoming story. Danbury said the pleasure was his and made sure to add a bit more honey to his already sugary southern drawl that had become his trademark over the years. It was his experience that women, especially Yankee women like this cub reporter, were often taken with his charm as a proper Southern gentleman.

The young woman smiled and asked, "May we get started?"

Danbury liked her politeness right off the bat. "I'm all yours, Miss Vanderwaal."

She charged right in.

"Senator, your constituents admire your commitment to avoiding corporate influence," she said, calm and casual, but with a bite that Danbury immediately found surprising and off-putting. "How do you maintain such integrity in the complex landscape of Washington politics?"

His smile was affable, his response smooth. "It's simple. I stay true to the needs of Virginians. They're my priority, not the deep pockets of corporations."

"Navigating such waters must be challenging. Have there been instances where you've had to make difficult choices to uphold this principle?"

Danbury felt himself flinch inside, but he was certain his reaction went unnoticed by the young reporter. Where was she going with this? His people assured him this was going to be nothing more than a human-interest piece to bolster his image for the stretch run against Calloway. Nothing but softballs, they said. Now this girl, some rookie, no less, was going to start grilling him right off the bat?

The senator chuckled to give himself an extra two seconds to suppress the irritation that was building up.

"In politics, difficult choices are the norm. But I assure you, every decision I make is for the benefit of our state and its people as well as all Americans."

The young woman's gaze held Danbury for a tiny bit longer than he felt comfortable with. Her eyes were serious, almost accusatory. She looked down at her notes for a moment and then brought that stare back to him.

"Speaking of decisions," she said, "there's been talk about federal funding for various research projects. Where do you stand on those?"

She locked eyes with him, her stare as intense as a lion stalking its prey. It was like she already knew the answer and wanted to see if he had the stones to say it out loud.

Danbury squinted, the look trying to tell this young woman to back off. A click and a flash from Tomas's camera startled him.

"Research is vital, but we must be judicious with taxpayer money," he said. "I advocate for projects that promise tangible benefits for our citizens. I'm sure you can respect that I can't speak specifically about any of these projects publicly, as most are of a sensitive nature that involve national security."

Vanderwaal was set to follow up, but Danbury cut her off. He leaned forward and cupped his hand over her cell phone to muffle the recording.

"What's happening here?" he said, dropping his voice and speaking just a few inches from the reporter's nose. "This was supposed to be a profile on my life outside of Washington. My wife and I invited you to our farm home as guests. I was not prepared for a political interrogation or to discuss specifics about one of the many committees on which I sit."

"I'm sorry. You are of course a well-known political figure, so I didn't feel it would be out of line to ask a few job-related questions. I will strike them from the record, and we can start over if you prefer."

The girl tried to sound contrite, but the bratty tone in her voice gave away her true motive. Danbury smiled.

"No," he said. He leaned back in his chair, easing himself back into character. "The questions are fine. I just wasn't expecting *that* kind of interview today. You may proceed. But, I believe that's all the political talk I'd like to engage in today, if you don't mind."

The reporter nodded and said that it was fine and that she was willing to switch gears to discuss less serious topics. Danbury was happy to have here change the subject, but he couldn't help but wonder what this girl already knew.

28

GAKONA, ALASKA

Flynn burst through the door, the cold air slapping him like a snowball to the face, his breath forming vapor clouds as he sprinted into the dense wilderness. The snow crunched under his boots accompanying the sound of his heavy breathing.

Behind him, the trio of Nellis, Holland, and Bailey emerged from the building in disarray. Nellis, Flynn expected, was an experienced tracker, but Bailey and especially the older Holland, would be a liability in any type of pursuit. Flynn's survival skills, honed from years in the CIA, were not to be underestimated, even if he felt to be a little out of practice for such things lately. He darted between trees, calculating his every move to throw them off his trail, his breath laboring as the cold air filled his lungs.

Definitely have to get back in the gym more often.

The moon, barely visible through the heavy clouds, provided scant light, but Flynn used the darkness to his advantage. Once he determined he'd established a healthy lead on his pursuers, he doubled back, circled around a large rock, and paused to catch his breath. It had already been cold during the day, but once the sun went down, the temperature had dropped twenty degrees. Flynn wasn't used to the extreme weather, and he hadn't had to run away from someone in these conditions since Svalbard. He needed to sit and rest, if just for a moment.

The muffled sounds of his stalkers grew closer, their flashlights slicing through the trees searching for him in the snow. The rock provided fair cover from a distance, but it wouldn't do once they came upon him. They were getting closer now, and Flynn could hear their voices bickering at one another, each blaming the other for his escape.

Flynn needed a plan. Running aimlessly into the frigid darkness would no doubt lead to hypothermia. Staying put behind the rock would get himself captured. Then he remembered an old trick.

He quickly gathered a handful of snow and pressed it against his mouth to muffle his breathing. As he laid flat against the snowy ground near the large rock, he covered himself with a layer of loose snow and branches, effectively camouflaging himself.

Nellis and his team passed by mere feet from Flynn, unable to spot his hiding spot in the darkness. Flynn waited, his heart pounding, until their footsteps faded into the distance. He almost had to chuckle. Years of military and CIA training to draw from, and it turns out a simple tactic from his childhood was all he needed.

Once Flynn was sure they were gone, he carefully emerged from his cover and hurried in the opposite direction. The melted snow on his face burned in the cold air. He wiped at his bare skin with his gloves as he ran, trying to dry his face. Using the stars as his guide, he navigated his route until he was a safe distance away.

Flynn, adrenaline still pumping, knew he couldn't outrun his trio of pursuers for long before they doubled back on him. The temperature was dropping. He needed to find shelter soon. A few minutes later, he ducked behind a thicket when he heard their voices and saw their flashlights sweep the snowy landscape. He decided he needed to end the pursuit on foot as quickly as possible or else he would be too exhausted and eventually get caught or freeze to death.

One more push. You got this.

Flynn took a deep breath and broke into a dead sprint back toward the depot and the car they had used to get there. He retraced his steps, using his recent knowledge of the terrain to avoid leaving a clear trail. He'd done the same thing in the rocks and mountains of Afghanistan many years ago. The constant snowfall helped, covering his tracks almost as quickly as he made them. He reached the concrete building and, to his relief, found the vehicle parked haphazardly outside, the engine still warm. Bailey had left the keys in the ignition.

You should've let Nellis drive, boys.

He could hear their voices drawing closer as the beams from their flashlights illuminated the darkness in wild arcs. Flynn collapsed into the driver's seat and fired up the engine. The car roared to life, and he popped the clutch to tear off in a storm of gravel and snow, leaving the three Ultra members stranded behind him.

Once Flynn returned to the Explorer's Inn, he found things quiet. He waved to the bartender, who was giving the evil eye to a solitary customer, who sat slumped on his stool like a man far past his limit for the night.

Flynn's phone vibrated. It was Michael Harrison.

"Mike," Flynn said. He glanced at the clock. It was going on midnight; Washington, D.C. was four hours ahead. "Don't you sleep?"

"I'll sleep when I'm dead," Harrison quipped. "I've been looking into your General Tillman. I think I got something that could help."

"I could handle some good news right about now."

"Interesting tidbit: did you know our esteemed General made rank at age forty-five? That made him the youngest general in the U.S. Army since the end of the Cold War. A guy doesn't just fall into that. It means the younger Tillman was a rising star. It means he did stuff to get attention. It means he was trusted with a lot of sensitive information. It means he had a lot of friends in high places."

"And?"

"Aaaand," Harrison said, knowing he had Flynn's anxious attention. "He was all over the planet, making decisions that greatly affected the safety and security for the good ol' U.S. of A."

"Get to it, Mike."

"He spent the majority of his time in the Middle East fighting Saddam in 1991, and the Taliban in the early 2000s. In addition to those deployments, he bounced to other hotspots such as South Korea, Somalia, Bosnia, Syria, and Ukraine."

Flynn grumbled his impatience.

"And Alaska," Harrison said.

29

LOUDOUN COUNTY, VIRGINIA

Leslie crouched low behind the thick trunk of a large oak tree, maintaining a focused eye on the Danbury home. The sun, now a deep orange, was sinking into the horizon, its fading light casting long shadows over the estate's rolling grounds.

She'd purposely pushed the interview longer than had been agreed upon. Senator Danbury had said he and his wife had to be in Washington that evening for a dinner event, and Leslie wanted them to be in a hurry to leave. She hoped that in their haste, the Danburys and their campaign entourage would be more likely to overlook the tiny breach in their home's security.

She could see them now, scrambling to pile into three black SUVs. She was too far away to hear anything, but the body language told her that everyone appeared to be quite frazzled about getting out on time. The sudden surge of adrenaline made Leslie's hands tremble and she could feel her heartbeat quicken in her chest.

She bounced her attention from the frantic scene going on in the driveway to the small bathroom window on the second floor

—her entry point. She had discreetly left it ajar, a slight push of her fingers during her earlier visit, after excusing herself to the restroom midway through her interview with the senator.

She desperately wanted to see inside the room that Danbury called his "sauna." Danbury had something hidden behind that door that he didn't want her to see, which made her crave that secret information even more. Christopher Mays had sent her to dig up some dirt on the senator, and Leslie knew there was dirt in that room.

At last the group was loaded and en route. As the last of the sleek SUVs rolled down the driveway, a rush of excitement washed over Leslie's body. She gave herself a full minute, deliberately counting each second, allowing the procession of vehicles to disappear down the road. Like a shadow, she slipped from her hiding spot, her movements fluid and deliberate.

The realization of just how much she was willing to do for this story took her by surprise. Breaking into a senator's house was not what she had envisioned when she started her career in journalism, yet here she was, driven by an ambition to reach the top of the mountain.

The estate was silent, a stark contrast to the buzz of activity that had surrounded it just moments before. Her eyes craned up toward the window, and she located the trellis she had mentally marked earlier. The idea of scaling it felt far more daunting now than it had earlier in her imagination.

Climbing the lattice up the side of the house would only be the first real challenge. If no one had noticed the open window, she would get inside the house. But what after that?

For a moment she considered calling the whole thing off and running back across the grass to her rental car parked a ways down the road. She paused, closed her eyes and took a deep breath.

She thought of James Flynn, the seasoned investigator whose audacity she admired.

Flynn would do this. He'd take the risk for the truth. The thought bolstered her resolve to press forward.

Leslie reached out, her fingers closing around the first rung. It felt solid, reliable. With a deep breath, she began her ascent.

Navigating the trellis was like solving a puzzle. Each movement was calculated as Leslie's hands and feet sought secure holds. She'd changed clothes in the car, swapping a skirt and heels for sneakers and yoga pants. The trellis groaned under her weight, sending spikes of fear through her. She stopped halfway up, listening for any signs of activity from inside, but the house remained silent. Up she climbed, her muscles burning, her mind racing as she imagined every possible outcome of her actions.

She reached the window and pushed gently against the glass. It moved silently inward, just as she hoped. For a moment, she was awed by her own audacity, by the sheer boldness of it all. Then, with athleticism she hadn't called upon since her high school days running track, she hoisted herself through the opening, her body contorting to fit through the narrow space.

The weekly yoga classes are really paying off.

She smiled. She was inside.

Is it really going to be this easy?

Inside the bathroom, Leslie paused, her breath ragged, her body tingling with adrenaline. She was inside the house of a high-profile senator, uninvited and unnoticed. The gravity of her situation was not lost on her.

A few deep breaths helped Leslie slow her breathing and regain her composure. She stepped out of the bathroom, her eyes adapting to the dim interior. The house was impossibly quiet, and the silence seemed to amplify her every step and action.

She moved with care, her mind focused on the task at hand. This was her moment, her chance to uncover the truth, and she was determined to seize it.

Leslie crept through the upper corridors of the Danbury mansion with heightened senses. Her eyes reacted to every shadow and every flicker of light.

She descended the grand staircase, and the portraits lining the walls seemed to watch her, their eyes following her every move.

Elena Danbury had described these portraits as teaching tools, reminders of America's past. Now, to Leslie, they felt like silent judges, stern witnesses to her transgression.

She thought of the long, elegant dining table where Mrs. Danbury proudly hosted student groups, connecting them to the nation's history. Now, it stood empty, the chairs like solemn spectators to Leslie's surreptitious mission.

Leslie reached the ground floor. Her destination loomed before her—the door to what Senator Danbury called his sauna and workout room. She hovered her fingers over the keypad. The security measure, an unwelcome obstacle, stood between her and the truth. She was momentarily stymied, her mind racing for a solution.

Leslie reflected on her actions. She thought of the American revolutionaries, those historical figures who graced the walls of the very house in which she now trespassed. They, too, had engaged in acts that were illegal in their time, driven by a belief in a greater good. With that thought, a resolve settled within her. Like them, she was breaking the law, but she was driven by a quest for truth, for a story that could change the narrative of power and corruption.

Leslie stepped back, her eyes scanning the room for any clue, any hint that might help her bypass the security and unveil the secrets that lay beyond the door. She knew she had to act quickly, for every second she spent in the house increased her risk of being caught.

What is the code?

She considered the senator. He was not a complex man. The numeric code to unlock the door would be something relatively simple for him to remember, thus hopefully something easy to crack.

Leslie punched the key pad: 1-2-3-4.

Nothing. It was worth a try, she mused.

She tried 1-1-1-1. Still nothing.

She then cycled through a series of related simple combinations (5687, 4321, 9999, etc.), but the door remained locked. Maybe the code is a five-number sequence or even six, she thought to herself.

She felt hopelessness settle in. Her quest to find the secret seemed destined to end before it even got started.

She tried one last sequence: typing in the current year. She turned the knob. It did not budge.

Then Leslie looked around her at the home's Colonial American decor. She realized the obvious answer was all around her. She slowly pushed the buttons:

1-7-7-6.

Click.

And she was inside.

30

ORLANDO, FLORIDA

Blackwood stood at the periphery in the main exhibition hall of the Orange County Convention Center, her gaze fixed on the throng of attendees. Tonight's event, a charity gala recognizing the nation's top high school students who best represented the future of communication technology through a variety of impressive experiments and research projects, had drawn the elite from various sectors—innovators, celebrities, and philanthropists alike. It was a science fair on steroids, Blackwood thought.

Central figure of the night's proceedings was Blaine Jacobs, the visionary tech and social media mogul, whose many contributions to the world of advanced technology over the years had stirred both awe and controversy in equal measure. Jacobs, a pioneer of social media, who had raced neck-and-neck with the likes of Mark Zuckerberg and Elon Musk, was the keynote speaker. Jacobs was a self-described "passionate devotee of the advancement of artificial intelligence." His topic for the night's final presentation centered on using AI to improve the way people communicate.

Following a raucous introduction of loud music, lasers, and enough fog to rival any arena rock show in history, Jacobs burst onto the main stage behind a literal explosion of smoke and fire. He wore an all-white suit custom tailored to perfectly fit his athletic body. As a juxtaposition to the formal aesthetic of his clothing, Jacobs adorned himself with a plain, black ball cap and black high-top sneakers. The two styles should have clashed, and would have looked ridiculously out of place on anyone else, but Jacobs somehow made it work.

His charisma was immediately palpable to Blackwood, who was able to sense it even from the back of the massive room. For those standing closer to the stage (no one sat down for the entirety of the presentation), Jacobs' performance came off like a religious experience. Part Ted Talk, part rock concert, and part stand-up comedy, Jacobs had those kids in the palm of his hand from the moment he appeared.

For Blackwood, it was a rare opportunity to observe Jacobs in his element, to gauge the reactions of those who moved in his orbit, and perhaps to glean something of the man behind the grandiose visions.

Jacobs was ostensibly featured to share his vision for a world that could be transformed by technology—specifically, his advancements in communication that promised to break down barriers and foster understanding on an unprecedented scale. Yet, Blackwood suspected his motives were not entirely altruistic. His presentation didn't try to disguise his disdain for government oversight, and the ethical quandaries surrounding his projects suggested a complexity to Jacobs that warranted closer scrutiny.

The performance lasted the better part of an hour, followed by thirty minutes of questions from the audience. As the applause died down and the last of the fog dissipated, Jacobs stepped off the stage, his presence commanding the room even without the aid of microphones, flashing lights, or special effects.

Blackwood made her way through the crowd, her eyes locked on her target. She found Jacobs, his face slick with sweat, surrounded by a group of eager young developers wearing VIP passes, each hanging on his every word. She waited patiently until the crowd thinned, presenting her moment to approach.

She stepped forward but was stopped by the stout outstretched arms of Jacobs' burly bodyguard.

"Mr. Jacobs?" she called out, leaning around the security man to make eye contact with him. "I've been looking forward to speaking with you. Your work in communication technology is truly groundbreaking."

Jacobs turned to her, a practiced smile on his face. She wore her normal work-day attire: a crisp white blouse paired with a charcoal blazer, dark slacks, and black leather shoes with just a tiny bit of a heel. His eyes held her with a subtle, disapproving gaze that lingered just a moment too long for her taste.

"Thank you. And you are?"

"Special Agent Blackwood, FBI," she said.

Jacobs' smile drooped for just a moment, but quickly recovered. "FBI. So, you're not just a pretty face. I would ask to see some identification, but I suppose your outfit says it all, doesn't it? I mean no woman would dress like that if she didn't have to."

Jacobs laughed at his own joke and gestured to his bodyguard to let her through. He wiped his face with a towel and invited her to follow him backstage where they could talk in private.

"I'm here to discuss something that might be of mutual interest," she said when they reached his dressing area.

He took off his jacket, revealing a white t-shirt that had gone gray with sweat, clung to his chest, and showed off a lean, muscular build.

"Mind if I change?"

Blackwood gestured that he was free to do as he liked and turned her back to him as he peeled off his sweaty stage outfit. She wasn't sure if it was his normal M.O. to undress in front of women he just met, but she knew that Blaine Jacobs was doing his best to make her feel uncomfortable.

Still facing the wall, she heard the rustle of clothing coming off and asked, "Did you know Arthur Tillman?"

The room went silent for a moment.

Seconds later she heard him step into a pair of pants, and when she turned to face him, Jacobs was pulling on a fresh black t-shirt over a pair of dark jeans.

"What was the name again?" he asked, as if he'd not heard the question.

"Arthur Tillman."

Jacobs' face tightened in recollection like a fifth-grader staring down an algebra equation. "Uhhhh, nope. I don't think that name sounds familiar. Would you like something to drink?"

Blackwood waved away the bottle of water Jacobs held toward her. "Are you sure? Take a look at this picture."

She removed a photo of Tillman from her bag and handed it to him. Jacobs glanced quickly and shook his head.

"Sorry, no," he said. "Should I know this man?"

"Project Hermes," she said. Her eyes searched Jacobs' face for any telltale sign of discomfort.

Jacobs maintained his composure and nodded. "What about it?"

"That's a research program you hired Dr. Ethan Keller to lead, is it not?"

If he was surprised, Jacobs didn't show it. He flashed the hint of a smirk and waved a finger playfully toward her.

"Someone's been doing her research," he said. "Gold star for agent—what was your name again?"

"Blackwood. *Special* Agent Blackwood," she said.

"Yeah Okay, Special Agent. What's your interest in one of my former research initiatives?"

"Former?"

"Sounds like your Reddit discussion didn't give you the full picture. Hermes was shut down almost a year ago; been dead ever since."

"Why did you—"

"I didn't," he said. "It was Big Brother. Once the Feds heard what Keller and I had going on, they swooped in and shut us down. They confiscated an entire lab constructed and appointed solely for Hermes. In one afternoon, they took everything. Said our research was a danger to national security."

"Was it?"

"I've always believed that technology should be used to enhance human connections, not replace them. We're aware of the risks our research poses and we take the appropriate precautions. What is all of this about, anyway?"

"An empty folder labeled 'Project Hermes' was found at the crime scene where Tillman was murdered."

Jacobs laughed. "That's why you're hassling me? A folder with some words scribbled on it? Project Hermes? How do you even know it's my Hermes? Do you realize how many tech firms, research facilities, and government programs name their projects after Greek mythology? I'm not proud to admit it, but I'm not always the most creative man when it comes to words. I venture to guess there are at least a dozen enterprises called Hermes active at any given moment. So, you're here because why? You think I killed this Tillman?"

Blackwood stiffened. Jacobs was doing his level best to make her feel foolish, as if she were overreacting to an otherwise innocuous piece of evidence.

"No one is accusing you of anything, Mr. Jacobs," she said. "We found the empty folder and have solid evidence that causes us to believe it refers to your research. We're merely trying to see if there's a connection that can lead us toward putting this case down."

Jacobs took a long drink from his water bottle and stared Blackwood in the eyes, his jaw clenched and his eyes narrow.

Blackwood switched gears: "When's the last time you spoke to Dr. Keller?"

"Keller was here to lead the Hermes project. When it was over, I had no further use for him. People come and go in this industry; it's the nature of our work."

Jacobs paused. The smirk returned as if he'd finally solved a clever riddle. "You're suggesting I had something to do with Keller's disappearance. Should I have my attorney present?"

"Just trying to piece together the puzzle," Blackwood countered, her gaze never leaving his. "Learning more about Tillman's connection to Hermes could help me solve his murder, and I believe Keller can shed light on that. Since you and Keller worked closely together, I'd hoped you'd have insight on where he might have gone, or who might have taken him."

* * *

LESLIE EASED the door shut behind her. Her adrenaline surged again and her hands fluttered. She stood motionless in the dark room and pulled her phone from her pocket. The room felt unnaturally still, as if holding its breath.

Leslie hesitated to turn on the lights, fearful of drawing attention to her unlawful presence in this hidden area of Senator Danbury's home. There were no windows, and with the door closed it was safe to turn on the light, but she chose instead to use her phone's flashlight.

She allowed her eyes a few moments to adjust, then quietly began her search. The room, she noticed, was less an ostentatious display of wealth and more a functional office, filled with books and cabinets, and a large desk that dominated the space.

Leslie edged her way toward the desk, her fingers trailing over the surface, feeling more than seeing the scattered papers and files. She picked up a file, squinting to read its contents in the meager light. It was mundane, routine political mumbo-jumbo, nothing of interest. She replaced it and moved on to the next, her movements slow and inquisitive, her breath slowing as she once again gained control of her nerves.

She scanned her light over the desk. One file folder immediately stood out. It was the only one stamped with red ink.

Project Titan — Eyes Only

She reached for it and held it up to her phone's bright LED. A shiver ran down her spine. Even before opening it, she knew she had stumbled upon something significant, something she wasn't supposed to see.

Leslie opened the file. Inside, she found photographs that made her blood run cold. They were more than just unsettling; they were grotesque, displaying scenes that her mind struggled to process. Each image was a scene of human suffering, a stark testament to some unknown horror.

Her initial impulse was to document what she found. She clicked the camera app on her phone. She clicked photo after photo, creating a macabre slideshow of evidence of some manner of wrongdoing that she couldn't quite piece together.

As she turned off the camera, a wave of uncertainty washed over her. The evidence she'd held in her hand, the photos she now possessed on her phone, the frightful possibility of what this all could be was just too big to comprehend. It was of course what she wanted—the bigger the story, the better—or so she'd thought. Standing in the middle of it she felt uncertain and ill-equipped to proceed.

She needed help, someone to guide her through the implications of what she had just uncovered.

Flynn.

He was the obvious answer. He would know what to do. He could guide her through to the end. But her pride, her ambition, the very ego that had driven her to this point, now held her back. Calling James Flynn would mean admitting she was out of her depth, that she wasn't ready for the big leagues.

Leslie stood in the dark, her thoughts a jumbled mess. She needed to make a call, to reach out to someone. If not Flynn, who? The decision weighed on her. The enormity of the story she had uncovered loomed over her, a shadow too vast to navigate alone.

She dialed a number on her phone.

31

GAKONA, ALASKA

Flynn stood by the window, staring through the darkening woods outside. Natalie's car pulled into the parking lot and he went outside to meet her.

He put his hands on her shoulders.

"We can't stay here," he said. "A circus is missing three of its clowns who are on my tail with bad intentions. Once they find out I'm not here, it won't take them long to figure out I'm with you with the way the people in this town gossip. Going back to your place is out of the question."

He didn't tell her that the FBI was also seeking him as a murder suspect—no reason to pile on the unpleasant developments. They had enough to worry about.

Natalie nodded. "I know a place."

Without another word, they hurried to Natalie's car.

"There's an empty hunting cabin in the woods," she said. "The owners live in Anchorage and almost never come out here to use it. I gave them a tour of the area a while back, and they said I could stay in the cabin if I needed a place to stay during my sight-seeing excursions. It's isolated, which should keep us off the radar for tonight."

Flynn nodded, his mind working through the implications. "Sounds like our best option for now. How far is it?"

"Not too far, but off the beaten path. It's hidden well; I doubt anyone will find it, even if they're looking."

The car's engine hummed as they drove deeper into the dark forest. Flynn's thoughts were a whirlwind of strategies and contingencies, but part of him was acutely aware of Natalie's presence beside him, a reminder that in his line of work, trust was a rare and valuable commodity.

The headlights carved the darkness and cast an eerie strobe effect as the towering trees whizzed by. Natalie steered off the main road and took a few twists and turns until the car's beams finally revealed a small rustic cabin nestled in a secluded clearing.

She parked the car close and killed the engine, plunging them into silence. They both sat for a moment, collecting their thoughts before stepping out into the cold night air. The cabin, a lone structure out here in the middle of frozen nothing, was a welcome sight.

They hurried inside, the door creaking as Flynn shouldered it open. The inside matched the rustic exterior, with minimal furnishings and a thick layer of dust covering everything. It was cold, the kind of cold that seeped into your bones, and Flynn wasted no time in getting a fire started.

Natalie watched as he arranged the kindling and logs in the fireplace. His movements were methodical and efficient, a testament to his training and experience. Within minutes, the flame took hold, casting a warm, flickering light across the room.

As the fire grew, the cabin lost its chill. They settled near the fireplace, the light dancing across their faces. Natalie had carried in two heavy blankets she kept in the trunk of her car. She handed one to Flynn and wrapped herself in the other as she sat on the dusty floor. For the first time since they had embarked on this dangerous journey, she seemed at peace, almost comfortable, even if Flynn knew it was temporary.

The crackling of the fire was soothing. Flynn and Natalie exchanged a look, an unspoken agreement that, for now, they could afford a brief respite. They were alone, hidden from the dangers that lurked beyond the cabin walls, wrapped in the momentary sanctuary the fire provided.

Outside, the forest stood silent and watchful, the snow-covered ground reflecting the faint glow from the cabin's windows. Inside, Flynn and Natalie allowed themselves a moment of peace, gathering their strength for the challenges that lay ahead in the morning.

Natalie broke the silence, her voice hesitant.

"What's next?"

Flynn's gaze met hers, intense and probing.

"I think I know where Keller is," he said. "Here in Alaska."

Natalie leaned forward, eyes wide with intrigue.

Flynn continued. "You're right that something was going on at HAARP. Something that likely started with good intentions but turned very ugly. Whatever this Hermes is, it's not good."

She shuddered, pulling the thick blanket tighter against her body.

"Whatever it was, it really messed Richard up." Her voice wavered as she spoke. "Before we came to Alaska, Richard was a really nice guy, the kind of man who could fit in anywhere, talk to anyone. Real easy-going. But once he was stationed at HAARP, he changed. He became irritable. Nothing I did was right or good enough. He started picking fights with the locals. He wasn't himself anymore."

"Whatever this Hermes is, it certainly seems to be what changed Richard," Flynn said. "I wonder how many more went through a similar ordeal."

"We have to help them all, Flynn. You said you know where Dr. Keller is."

"Yeah," he said. "Alaska was a huge asset for the United States during the Cold War. It was assumed that any invasion from the Soviets would come through here. Also, any air assault launched from the USSR would come from over the Arctic. So, Alaska was very strategic, and a series of radar and early warning missile detection installations were constructed all over the state."

"I've seen some of those," Natalie said. "Aren't they abandoned?"

"Some are. We still have 15 installations active. Most of the original sites were well-known and easily identified, their conspicuousness acting as a deterrent to any Soviet operation."

"Most of them?"

"There were a handful of bases that were definitely top secret facilities known only to a select few individuals. Men like General Arthur Tillman. One of those bases was built in 1964. It was shut down in 1993."

"The same year the HAARP research facility was built," shot Natalie. "Are you saying—?"

"The original base is allegedly a large underground bunker," Flynn told her, recounting the information he'd received from Harrison earlier in the night. "It was being set up as a potential missile silo for ICBMs we could lob toward Moscow, but it never came to that. It wound up being used as a storage facility and became a bit of an embarrassing expense that was never really needed. The Pentagon swept the whole thing under the rug. It was vacant for decades. When it came time to build HAARP, someone up top had the brilliant idea to cut some costs and use the old bunker as a solid foundation for the new facility."

"So, Keller is holed up in the basement under HAARP?"

"Yes and no. He's likely there, but it's not exactly the basement, not officially anyway. It's doubtful that many, if any, of the staff at HAARP even knows the bunker exists. It was sealed up in ninety-three. I'm not even sure you can access it from inside HAARP."

"Then how do we get inside?"

Flynn showed Natalie his phone. On it was the image of a map.

"A friend of mine gave me these GPS coordinates that he says mark the location of a separate underground bunker, built in the fifties as a bomb shelter. We believe this bunker shares ventilation with Keller's lab and would have been used for expansion if the missile facility grew."

Natalie examined the map. "There are no roads that lead to this location. We'll have to go in on foot, and that's no easy hike. That's rough ground, and the temperature is dropping. It will take the better part of the day or more just to reach the entrance."

Flynn nodded. "Understood," he said. "But, we need to get in and find out what's happening. I'm running out of time here."

Natalie's eyes reflected the fire's glow and something more—a mix of fear and resolve.

"I'll get you in," she said. "We'll find out the truth. For Richard, and for everyone else affected by whatever Hermes is. It's going to be a long day. We need to rest."

They sat in silence, and Flynn pondered the dangerous mission in front of him. Was he right to drag this woman into what he knew was going to be certain danger? He had no choice. She knew the area, and he needed her to guide him to the entrance to the abandoned bunker. He leaned back on his elbows and watched the fire spark and dance.

Natalie yawned, and Flynn watched as she curled up on the floor, pulling the blanket up to her chin. She closed her eyes and was asleep in just a few minutes. The cabin, with its rustic charm and crackling fire, could have been a scene from a different life, he thought, one where danger and conspiracies didn't lurk in the shadows, one where he and Natalie could share a different experience more pleasant than the one staring them in the face. He allowed his imagination to wander briefly, but then brought himself back to reality. He fell asleep and dreamed of her.

32

LOUDOUN COUNTY, VIRGINIA

Tucked under the cover of the dense woods, Sergeant Richard Mahler lay prone, his unblinking eyes staring through a pair of binoculars. The night air was cool, the darkness punctuated by the distant glimmer of light that illuminated the front entryway of Senator Danbury's home.

Mahler's attention was riveted on the young, dark-haired woman, who had, minutes ago, shimmied up the wall and through the second-story window. He squinted, trying to ascertain why she was breaking into the house, but his mind was jumbled with confusion, and he couldn't put reason to her action.

A splitting headache tormented Mahler, a relentless pounding that seemed in sync with the chaotic thoughts that had been swirling in his head for days, if not weeks. There was something he was supposed to do, a purpose he couldn't quite grasp. He watched, almost mechanically, as the woman vanished into the house.

He checked his watch. Time seemed agonizingly slow. Forty-five minutes slipped by. It was dark now. Finally, the woman reappeared, this time slipping out a side door. She moved with the haste of someone who was being pursued. She ran in the opposite direction of where he sat and disappeared over the grassy hill toward the county highway. Mahler tried to puzzle out her motives, but his thoughts were knotted, an incomprehensible mess of orders and urges he couldn't untangle.

With the woman gone, Mahler, dressed in full forest camouflage, knew it was time to move. Despite his mental turmoil, his military training kicked in and he gained a burst of clarity regarding his mission. He bolted from the trees, and his path wound to, from, and around each piece of natural cover that could conceal his movement toward the Senator's house. He dashed through the darkness like a ghost.

As he advanced, Mahler's mind raged across a battlefield of conflicting directives. His thoughts simply refused to align, as if the words in his brain lacked proper definitions; he felt a drive to move forward but couldn't understand where or why he was going. He shook his head, trying to clear the fog, but it clung to him like a relentless adversary.

Mahler crossed a clearing and paused at a small clump of trees to survey the Senator's house, which was now just about a hundred meters away. He crouched low, blending into the shadows to scan the area for any sign of movement. He needed to get inside, to complete his mission. One last objective.

With a deep breath, Mahler moved again, his steps deliberate, his training overriding the chaos in his mind. He approached the house from the side, avoiding the main entrance, seeking a quieter way in.

As he neared the house, the vague sense of purpose that had been nagging at him grew stronger. There was something important he needed to do here, something critical. But the clarity he sought remained elusive, just out of reach, obscured by the maelstrom of thoughts that refused to settle into coherence.

He pressed on, driven by a sense of duty, moving steadily towards the violence that awaited him inside the senator's house.

33

WASHINGTON, D.C.

Leslie hustled through the busy concourse of Washington Dulles Airport while clawing through her purse for her phone. She was in danger of missing her flight if she didn't hurry.

She had stumbled upon something colossal, something potentially catastrophic and needed guidance and reassurance. She needed someone to anchor her in this storm of revelations.

Back at the Danbury home, she'd called Christopher Mays, the publisher of *The National*.

"I—I've found something during my investigation," she told him. "It's big, possibly bigger than anything we've handled before."

There was a brief silence on the other end before Mays replied with a calm, measured tone. "Leslie, that sounds intriguing. Tell me more."

She took a deep breath, trying to steady her voice.

"I don't have all the pieces yet, but from what I've gathered, this Project Titan might be some sort of secret government research program. I'm not sure of the specifics, but it feels enormous, and frankly, a bit overwhelming. People are dead because of it. I have pictures. It's the most horrible thing I've ever seen."

Mays' soothing voice said, "I understand it must be a lot to take in, but Leslie, this is exactly the kind of story I was hoping you'd find. It's actually far better than I could have hoped for. You're doing a fantastic job."

She shifted uncomfortably. "I'm not sure I can handle this alone, Chris. This story—it's not just big; it's dangerous. Maybe we should get Flynn involved. He has experience with this kind of thing."

"No," he said, his tone sharp. "I don't think that's necessary. Flynn is working his own thing. This is your story, and you're more than capable of handling it. We believe in you. *I* believe in you."

She felt a flicker of doubt.

"If Flynn is already investigating something similar, wouldn't it make sense to collaborate? To share information?"

"Flynn works his way, and you work yours," he snapped. "You're proving yourself to be an exceptional journalist. Don't disappoint me now. This is your opportunity to shine, to step out of Flynn's shadow. You don't need to rely on anyone else."

"I guess you're right. It's just that this feels bigger than anything I expected to run into. I'm worried about the repercussions, the risks involved."

"I understand your concerns, but remember, you have the full support of *The National* behind you. You've uncovered a potentially huge story. When you get back, we'll sit down, go over everything, and plan your next steps. And of course, there's going to be a significant raise in it for you. You deserve it. You're going to make people forget about James Flynn. You're my star now."

Leslie slipped out of the Danbury house and drove in silence, Mays' words repeating in her head.

Now, amidst the bustling airport, a sense of achievement

mingled with an uneasy feeling about the path she was heading down. Mays' words echoed in her mind, both uplifting and, in a way she couldn't yet fathom, deeply troubling.

34

NEW YORK CITY

Christopher Mays had been in this game long enough to know a golden opportunity when he saw one, and this one was like striking oil in his own backyard.

He could barely contain his own elation. Truth be told he was beside himself with giddiness. He wanted to rip open his shirt, beat his chest, and shout from the window of his corner office on the thirty-fourth floor that he was indeed "one bad-ass son of a bitch and everyone needed to take notice."

Instead, he sat in his leather office chair, shirt on, and grinned like a sadistic little boy burning ants with a magnifying glass.

Leslie Vanderwaal, his cub reporter, his special project, his own gorgeous protege, had practically fallen into a story that could redefine *The National* from its status as a struggling small-time publication. He would give her the raise she deserved.

He imagined giving her much more, and in this moment of jubilation and triumph, it seemed possible. He knew that beneath that nun-like, buttoned-up veneer, Vanderwaal was a gorgeous woman, and one he wanted to add to his long list of conquests. He knew her type and could read between the lines.

Normally a woman like her wouldn't give him the time of day, but this one would be grateful for the opportunity and willing to repay him for the success he'd thrown her into. Miss Vanderwaal would be the cherry at the top of his victory sundae; he was sure of it.

But he wasn't there yet. He had work to do. *She* had work to do.

Project Titan—the name just reeked of clandestine operations and government secrets. Hollywood couldn't have crafted a better script for him. The deaths linked to this project were tragic, of course, but for him, they were the keys to a kingdom he had always aspired to rule. Every victory had collateral damage.

What were a dozen dead soldiers, give or take?

Victory was assured—almost—and an eager and indebted Leslie Vanderwaal awaited him at the end. But first he needed to set a course of action, of which he determined there were two.

His first option was straightforward—run the story and blow the lid off of this Titan whatever it was. It was the kind of scoop that could send magazine sales and ad revenue through the roof. A story that could put his magazine back on the map, turning it from a fringe publication read by crazies and stuffy academics into a household name. And he'd absorb all the credit. Under his leadership, *The National* would be thought of as one of the top publications in the country, if not the world.

But then there was the juicier option—blackmail. Senator Danbury, with his freshly lined pockets of new-found grassroots campaign funding and political clout, would be an easy target. Danbury might not be the ringleader of this thing, but he'd be the one left holding the bag, and Mays could make those bad optics pay off for years.

He felt a thrill at the thought of the power play, the risk, and sheer scope of the potentially ongoing rewards. Blackmailing a senator wasn't child's play, but the payoff could set him up for life.

Vanderwaal had notified him that she was on her way to him

from D.C. right now. But until she arrived, he had no one with whom to celebrate his victory. What good was winning if no one knew you won? Plus, he could use some advice.

He picked up his phone, dialing Blaine Jacobs, a man shrouded in as much mystery as the stories Mays' nerdy reporters loved to chase. If anyone could help him navigate these treacherous waters and cash in big, it was Jacobs.

Mays didn't waste time with small talk.

"I've got something big, Blaine. Project Titan. Ever heard of it?"

He paused, gauging Jacobs' reaction. There was a brief silence on the line.

"Can't say that I have. But I'm all ears."

Mays outlined the basics, careful not to reveal too much, which was easy since he really didn't know a fiddler's damn about the whole thing.

"We've uncovered a story about this government project. It's big, man. Deadly big. But I'm torn on how to play it."

"Sounds like an opportunity. What are your thoughts?"

"I could run the story, sure," Mays said before dropping his voice to a whisper. "But I also have a chance to leverage this against Senator Danbury. You know, a little—aggressive persuasion if you catch my drift."

"A tempting prospect, Chris. But what if you could have both? The story and the leverage?"

Mays felt a sudden jolt, like someone injected a cocktail of adrenaline and dopamine straight into his bloodstream.

"Both?"

"You have to be smart about it. Don't go after Danbury directly. If you play this right, the story alone could be your leverage. It's all about timing and how you present it."

Mays nodded. "I see your point," he said, realizing Jacobs didn't understand his gesture. "But there's a lot at stake here."

"You got that right," Jacobs said. "You have a gold mine and it's just waiting for you. I can show you how to extract every last nugget. But I would like to meet this young lady reporter of yours. She sounds resourceful."

Mays frowned. "Sure, I can arrange that. But why the interest in Leslie?"

"Just curious about the person who unearthed this story. I like to know who I'm dealing with, Chris. It's how I stay ahead."

Mays agreed, though a nagging suspicion tugged at him. Jacobs always had an agenda, but right now, his advice seemed sound.

"Alright, Blaine. I'll set it up. Thanks for the insight."

"Let's make it tomorrow morning," Jacobs said. "I can be there by nine o'clock."

The suddenness caught Mays off guard, but he was excited to launch this plan into action, so the earlier the better worked great for him.

As he hung up, he felt a mix of excitement and unease. Jacobs was a shark in a sea of little fish, and Mays knew he needed to swim carefully. But the potential rewards were too big to ignore. He just hoped he wasn't biting off more than he could chew.

35

LOUDOUN COUNTY, VIRGINIA

Senator Quinton Danbury stifled a yawn as he and his wife drove down their long driveway, returning home from their lavish Washington dinner party. Maybe it was the two glasses of wine he'd consumed or the fact that it was well past eleven o'clock, but he was struggling to keep his eyes open for the last hundred yards. He rolled down the window, inhaling the sudden introduction of the cool night air tinged with the lingering aroma of autumn leaves. After pressing the button to open the garage, he waited a moment before easing his car inside. He hustled around to open the door for Elena. As they approached the front steps, the senator took Elena's arm and bid goodnight to his security team, escorting his wife inside.

Danbury led his wife out onto the balcony that extended from their second-story bedroom, giving them an expansive view of their property illuminated by the moonlight. Gentle rolling hills and large swaths of trees formed an idyllic setting whether by day or night. The senator sat down and drew in a deep breath as he peered out across his domain. He chuckled to himself, prompting Elena to ask him what he was laughing at. Then Danbury recounted Senator Gil Justice's antics. Elena of course witnessed the entire scene herself, but Danbury couldn't help but break it down once more. He was an infectious storyteller and she could listen to him talk all night whether it was a new tale or one she'd heard a dozen times or more.

"And then he, believe it or not, tried to serenade the waitress with Springsteen's 'Born to Run.' It was—it was just too much."

His laughter echoed across the empty countryside, a joyful sound under the starlit sky.

Elena, her arm still linked with Quinton's, laughed along.

"Only Gil could turn a formal dinner into a karaoke concert," he said, barely able to get the words out through his own laughter.

In truth, Justice had made quite the fool of himself and his poor wife, who had to bear witness to his antics. He had a reputation as a man who chased younger women, but he typically had the sense and decorum to do so discreetly. But for Senator Gil Justice of Florida, an open bar and a young attractive waitresses were the perfect ingredients for an embarrassing evening. Elena assumed it would mean the end of his career, but Quinton waved it off.

"Gil is made of Teflon," he said. "They love him down there in the panhandle. He'll be just fine."

The couple stood up and clasped each other's hands without a word between them, taking up a starting dance post. Even without the music, their steps fell into a synchronized rhythm, shuffling back and forth across the balcony. After a few seconds, they both laughed at the moment. They, too, had let the wine flow freely during the evening and were feeling a bit delirious themselves.

"Why don't you say we finish off the night with some ice cream?" Danbury said.

Elena grinned and spun on her heels, heading straight for the kitchen downstairs. Once they reached the main floor, she stopped, lingering in the grand foyer and admiring all the patriotic decor. Elena looked beautiful in her red dress, and the senator caressed her back as he guided her down the hallway to the kitchen. The house was silent, save for the soft clicks of their shoes against the marble floor.

In the kitchen, Elena leaned against the bar, a contented sigh escaping her lips, while Danbury prepared two bowls of ice cream.

"You know," she began, "despite all this election craziness, these moments with you—they're what I treasure the most."

He leaned in and kissed her. She wrapped her arms around his neck and kissed him back. She felt dizzy from the alcohol and euphoric from the entire evening. Quinton's latest surge in the polls had made him the talk of the evening, and she was proud to be his wife.

"No campaign, no political drama could ever take away what we have," he said.

Elena leaned into him and laid her head against his shoulder. "I love you," she said. "No matter what happens in the election."

Quinton raised her chin with a gentle motion of his finger and kissed her again. After a moment, she pulled back from him and looked into his eyes.

"I know how we can put the perfect ending to this night," she said with a wry smile.

She stepped away from him and strutted up the stairs, looking back at him over her shoulder with a look that guaranteed he'd follow her to the bedroom.

Senator Danbury eagerly began to pursue his wife up the staircase when something caught his eye.

The door to his private office was ajar.

That door was never open.

He froze.

There was something else.

"What is it?" Elena said. "Quinton, your face is white as a sheet."

The senator held his hand up toward his wife. "Go upstairs, Elena. Now."

She took a few steps back toward him, trying to see what had her husband so alarmed. "What—"

"Now" he shouted.

His tone frightened her. He'd never raised his voice to her, not in thirty-five years of marriage. He shot her a look that said, "Go." and she pivoted on the steps and scampered upstairs toward their bedroom.

Danbury turned back to the source of his fear.

A man dressed in green camouflage stepped out of the senator's office. He was holding a .45 caliber pistol at his side. As he locked eyes with Senator Danbury, the man raised the gun and aimed it at Danbury's head. At this range any person who was even slightly proficient with a firearm couldn't miss the kill shot, and Danbury assumed this man was a trained soldier, which meant his very life was literally in this intruder's hands.

The soldier looked weary, sleep-deprived or possibly strung out on drugs. Danbury held up both hands.

"Go easy, Son," he said. "Whatever you're after, we can get through this. No one needs to get hurt."

"People are already hurt," the soldier said. "Because of you."

"Is it money? I've got money. I'll let you take what you can carry and walk away. Put the gun down and we can talk about it."

The soldier squeezed his forehead with his spare hand and winced as if he was suffering from a migraine.

"Money," he said.

The soldier tried to smile, but only managed to twist his face into a malformed grimace.

"Sure thing," Danbury said. He reached into his back pocket and tossed his wallet toward the intruder.

The soldier slapped the wallet out of the air and took a step forward, the barrel of his .45 stabbing closer toward Danbury's face. A surge of cold fear gushed through Danbury's body and for a moment he feared he would lose control.

The soldier's face was distorted with anguish. The migraine or the withdrawal or whatever he was dealing with was appearing to get the upper hand.

"Tell me why I shouldn't do this," he said.

Danbury dug deep inside himself for any scrap of courage he could gather. He was gripped by fear, but knew if this young man was willing to talk, there was a chance for a peaceful solution.

"Do what, Son? Tell me what's going on, and I swear to you, I'll try to help you."

Elena shouted from the bedroom. "I called 9-1-1! The police will be here in two minutes."

Danbury sighed. Her timing couldn't have been any worse.

The soldier wracked the slide on his .45.

"Sounds like we have two minutes."

"Plenty of time," Danbury said. "What's your name, Soldier? I'm Senator Danbury; I assume you know that. But, you can call me Quinton."

The soldier paused and then said, "Sergeant Mahler, Richard J., United States Army."

Danbury breathed deeply. This was progress.

"I'm pleased to meet you, Sergeant Mahler, but I have to admit I'm not enthusiastic about having a gun pointed at my face."

"At least I have the guts to hold the gun."

"I'm not sure I understand what you're saying."

"You kill people every day and you don't even have the courage to look them in the face and pull the trigger."

Mahler took another step closer. His pistol was about a foot from the tip of Danbury's nose.

"Whoa. Hold on. I haven't killed anyone."

Mahler began to recite the name and rank of multiple military personnel representing all four branches. Danbury counted about fifteen names.

"You killed each one of them," Mahler said.

Danbury stood clueless for a moment, and then he understood.

"Project Titan," Danbury said.

Mahler closed his eyes and began to sob.

Danbury attempted to take a step back, but the young soldier opened his eyes and snapped to attention. He stepped forward and held his gun six inches from the senator's face.

"No!" Mahler shouted, tears streaming down his face. "You don't get to walk away."

"I didn't know," said Danbury. "I just saw the photos. I didn't do this."

"You know. Told you, you don't get to walk away from it."

Senator Danbury stood on the stairs of his grand county estate knowing he was about to die. He thought of his wife and how much he loved her and how fortunate he'd been to live the life he'd lived. He closed his eyes and waited for the inevitable end.

There was a flash. The sound was deafening. For a few seconds Danbury was disoriented. Disoriented but not dead. Not injured.

He opened his eyes and saw Sergeant Richard Mahler on the floor bleeding from a self-inflicted gunshot wound to his head. At that moment, police officers burst into the house, and Elena came screaming from the upstairs bedroom.

Elena ran to her husband's arms, and Danbury hugged his wife, shaking with fear but thankful to be alive. One of the police officers knelt to check on the young soldier. He looked at the Danburys and shook his head.

"What's he holding?" said Quinton, noticing what looked like a folded piece of paper in Mahler's hand.

The officer plucked it from Mahler's grip and handed it to Danbury. It was a photograph of a young woman.

36

TAMPA, FLORIDA

Blackwood read through the case file again. She could almost recite every detail by heart. She knew there had to be something there, something that could connect the dots in the Tillman murder case. The more she pored over the evidence, the more it drove her crazy.

She closed the folder and pushed it away from her toward the edge of the desk.

"Dammit," she whispered.

She sat in silence for a moment and reached into the cardboard box that housed all the information surrounding the case. There was one detail that never sat well with her: Tillman's unloaded gun.

Wayne Minter waved it off as though maybe Tillman was just out to scare the man with whom he'd argued, the man who eventually killed him. Waving a nickel-plated revolver would certainly startle someone, Blackwood had to admit, but she just couldn't picture Tillman wielding a weapon just for show.

"Hey, Marcus," Blackwood called out to Special Agent Marcus Reed, who was walking by.

Reed stopped and poked his head in the door with arched eyebrows.

Blackwood knew Reed, a former Marine, was a collector of classic and modern revolvers, and that he preferred their reliability compared to the standard issue Glock .40-caliber automatics FBI agents were mandated to carry. It was a terribly kept secret that Reed kept a .357 revolver in his bedside table. He called it his "home security system."

"Quick question," Blackwood said. "Your .357 at home. Do you keep it loaded?"

"Wouldn't be much good to me if I didn't," Reed said without the tiniest hint of humor.

She nodded. *Just what I thought he'd say.* "Thanks," she said.

"No problem," Reed said. He tapped the side of the door jamb and continued on his way.

Blackwood knew there was no way that Tillman intentionally reached for an unloaded gun the night he went to confront his would-be killer. And the fact that the weapon was found wiped clean of fingerprints was a detail that stuck in her brain like a splinter. It seems unlikely that the killer would have touched the gun at all, so there was no logical reason to worry about fingerprints. The only other person who had access to it was—

Blackwood pulled the case file back toward her and flipped through the pages until she found Debbi Dixon's address.

* * *

DEBBI SAT down in front of her and placed a glass of iced tea on the coffee table between them. The young woman's apartment was just as Blackwood expected: trendy, flashy, and visually pleasing without much personality, very similar to Debbi herself.

Blackwood watched her without speaking. She'd learned when interviewing persons of interest, silence was often a powerful weapon. The room ached with unspoken tension, the only sounds coming from the faint hum of traffic on the busy Tampa streets below.

Debbi fidgeted in her seat and fumbled with a bracelet on her right wrist. Her eyes darted around the room, looking anywhere but at Blackwood. The silence stretched, growing heavier by the second.

Blackwood bent forward and lifted the glass of iced tea to her lips, eyeing Debbi the whole time. She took a long drink and placed the glass back on the table. Blackwood figured it was a good five minutes before the girl broke—a damn good effort. She'd seen hardened killers open up in less than 60 seconds of pure silence. This young woman was tougher than she looked.

"It's just so hard, you know? With everything that's happened," Debbi finally said, her voice tinged with a mix of frustration and desperation.

Blackwood nodded slowly, her demeanor calm and open, inviting Debbi to continue, but not saying a word.

Debbi breathed deep, seeming to gather her thoughts. "It's just—I feel like I'm caught in the middle of something much bigger than I first realized."

Another nod from Blackwood.

"I'm not sure of all the details," Debbi continued, twisting a bracelet around her wrist. "But I know Arthur was involved in things. Secret things. Projects. Investments. Sometimes he'd have meetings at his condo. He'd ask me to leave, sometimes for a few hours."

Blackwood broke her silence. "Why didn't you tell us these things when Special Agent Minter and I talked to you before?"

For the first time Debbi looked Blackwood directly in the eye. "Because I don't want to get killed, too," she said.

"Killed by who, Debbi?" Blackwood leaned forward toward the girl. "Do you know who killed Arthur Tillman?"

Debbi shook her head and covered her face with both hands. "I don't know," she said. "I swear I don't."

"You touched Arthur's .45 revolver that night, didn't you? You took the bullets out."

Debbi pulled her hands away from her face. Her eyes were glossy with tears and surprise.

"I had to," she said, the pace of her speech growing frantic. "I mean—I didn't know what to do. How did you know?"

"I didn't know," Blackwood said. "Not for sure. It was just a guess, really."

Debbi fell back against the plush sofa and exhaled. It sounded to Blackwood like the girl was relieved and scared at the same time, a very suitable reaction for someone who was mixed up in a murder investigation.

"Tell me what happened, Debbi."

As the young woman reluctantly detailed the events of the night Arthur Tillman was murdered, Blackwood couldn't believe what she was hearing.

37

GAKONA, ALASKA

The blast of late-night cold wind coerced Special Agent Blackwood into tightening her coat as she approached the Explorer's Inn. Her breath fogged in the air, a stark reminder that she was far from the tropical weather of Florida's gulf coast.

Earlier that day she'd heard a shocking revelation from young Debbi Dixon that compelled her to hop the next flight to the farthest corner of the United States. Blackwood replayed the conversation in her mind.

"I'd done a couple of videos advertising WhisperShout," Debbi had said.

"The social media network?"

"Yep. Just a couple of short things, you know? Trying to get people to make a profile and stuff, get them interested in the whole thing."

"Sure."

"And one day he told me he wanted me to meet a friend of his, someone who had celebrity influence and could help my career, so I—"

"Wait a minute," Blackwood had interrupted. "Who is 'he'?"

Debbi, seeming almost embarrassed to say it, replied, "Blaine."

"Blaine Jacobs?"

Debbi nodded.

"Blaine Jacobs introduced you to Arthur Tillman?"

"He said Arthur could get me into movies."

Blackwood couldn't believe what she was hearing. "Go on."

Debbi dove headlong into a roller coaster of a narrative describing the early moments of her romantic relationship with Arthur Tillman. Anecdotes about expensive dinners, lavish gifts, and exotic locales spilled in a stream-of-conscious ramble that was nearly impossible to follow. The woman, who had just sat teary-eyed and fearful that she, too, could be murdered had transformed into a giddy teenager recounting a series of dream dates with a rich man more than willing to spoil her at every turn.

Blackwood held up a hand, signaling Debbi to stop.

"Let's get back to the night General Tillman was murdered," she said. "You said you *had to* remove the bullets from the gun. Why?"

Debbi's appearance collapsed into fear once again.

"He made me."

"Who made you?"

"Blaine Jacobs."

Flipping her hood over her head to shield her from the wind and snow, Blackwood scanned the hotel and its surroundings, her expression a mixture of irritation and determination. Not only had Jacobs lied to her about knowing Tillman, he now appeared to be very much a participant in his slaying.

She'd gone straight from Debbi's apartment to Jacobs' office only to find that he'd left the country, sort of. She'd forced his assistant to divulge that Jacobs was on his way to Alaska. So, because of Jacobs, Blackwood was freezing her ass off in the arctic.

There weren't many options for lodgings in the area, so this was the best place to start her search. It all started with James

Flynn. The fact that Flynn and Jacobs both ended up in Alaska was no coincidence. They were both somehow wrapped up in Tillman's death, and Blackwood was going to get to the bottom of it.

She stepped inside, and the warmth from the large fireplace was a welcome upgrade from the single-digit temperature outside. The bartender maintained an unimpressed look as Blackwood displayed her badge. She'd expected to meet some resistance. The people choosing to live mostly off the grid in Alaska weren't eager to share each other's secrets with law enforcement.

"I need information on someone who may have come through here in the past few days," she said. "His name is James Flynn."

The bartender shrugged, a well-rehearsed look of indifference masked his face.

"Lots of folks pass through. Don't remember everyone."

"The man I'm looking for is a person of interest in a federal investigation. It really is in your best interest to cooperate."

"Am I not cooperating? I just said I don't remember every traveler who walks through the door."

"Fair enough." Blackwood pulled out her phone, showing a picture of Flynn. "Have you seen this man recently?"

The bartender flashed a half-hearted glance toward the photo, his expression unreadable. He shrugged.

She pressed him further. "Would it matter to you if I told you this man may have been involved in three homicides? Or that he himself may be in grave danger?"

The bartender didn't blink.

Blackwood sized the man up with a piercing stare. She'd dealt with his type before and knew she wasn't likely to get far with him. She thought for a moment and considered the fact that people in these parts could very well be a hotbed for fans of Flynn, the type of people who had a natural distrust of authority and who would eat up his tales of conspiracy theories and government cover-ups. Getting info from this lot might turn out a lot harder than expected.

"Thanks," she said, her tone dripping with sarcasm, and shifted her attention to an older gentleman at the corner of the bar, whose eyes seemed to reflect a flicker of recognition. She approached him, her voice softer this time but still authoritative. She showed him the picture of Flynn.

"Any help you can provide would be appreciated," she said.

The old man met her gaze, then looked away, his voice barely audible.

"Don't know where he went," he said. "But he was with a woman."

Blackwood nodded, sensing the man had spoken the truth. "Do you have a name for this woman? Have you seen her before?"

"Natalie Mercer," the man said, looking like he'd realized he was better off staying quiet, but that recognition had come too late. "She's a local guide for tourists who want to get out and see nature up close and personal."

Blackwood thanked the man and looked around. No one made eye contact. She'd gotten all she was going to get from this place.

As she stepped outside into the frigid night air once again, her mind evaluating the information she'd gleaned from the old man. She called her office and asked for any information they had on Natalie Mercer.

Energized even with the tiniest of leads, Blackwood got into her car, the engine sputtering to life. She knew the path ahead would be challenging, filled with uncertainties and potential dangers. But her resolve to find Flynn and uncover the truth behind Tillman's murder was stronger than ever. As she drove off into the darkness, the snow-covered Alaskan countryside loomed ahead, a vast expanse of secrets waiting to be unearthed beneath its unforgiving terrain and hardened permafrost.

38

GAKONA, ALASKA

Reaching the front door of Natalie Mercer's residence just outside of Gakona, Blackwood paused, listening for any sign of activity inside. There was none.

She tried the door—it was locked. She removed her gloves and knelt to examine the lock. It was a simple pin tumbler lock; Samantha expected no more than three pins. It would be a breeze to pick.

Of course breaking and entering into the residence of a person of interest was not even remotely in line with FBI protocols, and evidence acquired in such an event would be inadmissible in court. But Blackwood had just flown 4,500 miles and wasn't about to see her investigation get bogged down by a three-pin lock.

She pulled a pair of bobby pins from her purse. She opened one and fashioned a straight piece of metal that she would use as a lock pick. The second pin she bent into an 'L' to act as a simple tension wrench.

Her hands were freezing, but this would take no more than a few seconds. She inserted the tension piece into the bottom of the lock and maintained rotational force on the lock's cylinder. Then she used the straight pick to manipulate the pins into a straight line. It was dark, and she hadn't attempted to pick a lock in years, but within ten seconds she had all three pins in place. The knob twisted, and the door opened.

Blackwood couldn't stifle a smile.

Her flashlight swept across the room, revealing a cramped house, cluttered and lived-in. A table took up the vast majority of the small kitchen area, and it was littered with papers and a large map draped over the table. Blackwood stepped closer and shone the light on the map.

It outlined the local area, with various markings and notes scrawled across it. One particular section was marked prominently: the HAARP facility in Gakona. But what caught her attention was another hand-written note. Blackwood leaned in to read the words: "HERMES? RICHARD—What is going on there?" Underneath, Natalie Mercer had written, "James Flynn."

A quick sweep of the rest of the cabin revealed nothing of immediate interest. She needed to act quickly and follow this lead while the trail was still warm.

39

NEW YORK CITY

Mays paced back and forth in front of the large window that overlooked the Manhattan skyline, anticipating the arrival of Blaine Jacobs. He had dealt with Jacobs before, most notably when the social media billionaire strong-armed Mays to use his magazine's resources to investigate the rumored mind control experiments being conducted in Alaska. James Flynn was up there now, poking his nose into what was going on.

Truth be told, Mays didn't care what kind of articles ran in his magazine as long as they made him money and kept the board of directors off his damn back. He knew Flynn was good at his job and was beloved by a legion of crazy people who devoured his conspiracy theory exposés. If he could hit another home run with this mind-control nonsense, then it could be a very big month for Mays and *The National*.

Despite their intended agenda this morning—how to handle Senator Danbury and capitalize on Leslie Vanderwaal's discovery of the horrifying Project Titan—Mays wondered what twist

Jacobs had in store for him. Jacobs certainly wasn't flying in simply to do him a favor.

Leslie was already there, pouring herself another cup of coffee. She'd arrived at eight as Mays instructed. Jacobs said he wanted to meet her, a detail Mays found concerning.

"Don't say anything stupid," he told her. "I don't know what he wants with you, but you just smile and be polite. Say as little as possible."

Leslie scowled and looked at Mays over the top of her dark-rimmed glasses as she sipped her coffee.

"Good," Mays continued. "Get that attitude out of your system before he gets here. You need to be on your best behavior."

Leslie placed her coffee cup down with a deliberate motion, her eyes narrowly locked on Mays. "I'm not just some intern, you know. I can handle myself."

The situation with the young reporter was not going the way Mays had imagined. He'd expected her to be grateful for the opportunity and frightened about how to proceed. She was supposed to come to him for guidance and protection. He'd expected to be able to control her and use her to get what he wanted. Now he wasn't so sure.

Mays sighed.

"Look, I'm not questioning your abilities. It's just that Jacobs has a way of twisting things," he said. "He doesn't do anything unless there's something in it for him. If we want to control how all of this plays out, we need to be careful. This story, it's big. It could be dangerous."

"That's what I'm afraid of," Leslie said. "We don't even fully understand what Project Titan is, and Danbury's involvement could be deeper than we suspect. Shouldn't we consider confronting the senator or digging deeper before talking to Jacobs?"

Mays paced some more before stopping to face her, his expression serious.

"Confronting Danbury without more evidence could backfire spectacularly. You need to keep gathering information, quietly. Jacobs may have a plan to do that. He has eyes everywhere."

Leslie chewed the inside of her bottom lip.

"What about bringing Flynn in on this? He has the experience and resources that could help us. Maybe he's already onto something that could tie into Titan."

Mays shook his head firmly.

"He's a loose cannon. We can't afford that kind of unpredictability. This is our story, and we're going to handle it our way."

She nodded. "I'm worried we're walking into a lion's den with Jacobs. We should at least be prepared for what he might throw at us."

Mays turned back to the New York skyline and the sun rising over the skyscrapers.

"Don't worry. I've dealt with Jacobs before. He's a shark, but I know how to swim with sharks. Just follow my lead, and we'll get through this."

Even as he heard the words come out of his mouth, Mays wasn't sure he believed them.

* * *

LESLIE WATCHED the door swing open as Blaine Jacobs marched into the room.

She had seen pictures of Jacobs, but this was her first time meeting him in person. Her initial reaction was that his reputation did not match reality.

Jacobs was approaching forty years old but dressed like a kid just out of high school. He was shorter than Leslie expected and wore skin-tight black pants and a faded denim jacket over a white hoodie. White designer sunglasses masked his face that appeared expressionless as he accepted a handshake from Chris Mays.

"Blaine, good to see you again," Mays said.

Jacobs, with a nod and a swift scan of the room, locked his gaze on Leslie.

"Ms. Vanderwaal?"

Striding past Mays as if he was invisible, Jacobs approached Leslie. She noticed a look of irritation flash briefly across Mays' face.

"Yes, Mr. Jacobs. Pleasure to meet you," she said, extending her own handshake, but Jacobs gently held her fingertips aloft and kissed the back of her hand.

"Talented, ambitious, and beautiful," Jacobs said. "Where've you been hiding this one, Mays?"

Jacobs rotated on his heels to face Mays. Leslie lowered her arm and discreetly wiped the back of her hand against her skirt.

Mays opened his mouth to speak, but Jacobs had already lost interest and faced Leslie once more.

"I've heard a great deal about your work on this Danbury thing. Quite impressive," he said.

"Thank you, Mr. Jacobs." Her eyes flicked toward Mays for some sign of silent support.

Jacobs kept his gaze on Leslie as he said to Mays, "You've got a real gem here. It's rare to find such a combination of loyalty, talent, and <u>other</u> intangible traits in one package."

Mays responded with a tight smile.

"Leslie has potential to be one of our best, no doubt."

"Potential?" Jacobs turned away from Leslie, and she exhaled in relief. "Other than the mercurial James Flynn, who else do you have who even comes close?"

Mays didn't answer. He merely shrugged a response.

"I want her," Jacobs said.

Leslie gasped, "What?"

Chris Mays' eyes widened.

"I want her on my team," said Jacobs. "I'm always on the lookout for ambitious and talented people."

Leslie glanced to Mays hoping he'd intervene, but he looked

like he'd been slapped in the back of the head with a frying pan. He wasn't going to be of any help.

"I appreciate the offer, but I just got started here," she said, hoping to take control of the situation. "This is my first big assignment, I don't think I can just leave."

"Sure you can," Jacobs said. "Mays totally understands. He doesn't mind at all."

He winked at Leslie and turned to Mays. "Right, Mays? You don't have any issues with me taking Miss Vanderwaal off your hands, do you?"

Mays was still dumbfounded with that blank look on his face. Leslie was worried he'd slipped into a coma.

"Chris?" she said.

"No," Mays said, finally coming back to reality. "I mean, no, we can't afford to lose her. Like she said, she just started. She's off to a great start, but she still has a lot to learn."

Jacobs frowned. "Don't be silly," he said. "I'll pay you for her, and you," he turned to Leslie, "I'll make it worth your while."

Mays looked as though he'd slipped into a trance, and Leslie knew the idiot was actually contemplating selling her services to this ego-maniacal billionaire. She shot him a look, and he shrugged as if to say he didn't know what to do. He shifted uncomfortably, his eyes darting between Jacobs and Leslie.

"Blaine, I get it, but Leslie is critical to our operation here," he said finally. "She's not just another journalist. We've invested in her."

"Invested? I'm talking about a life-changing leap here, not just another step on your little corporate ladder. Leslie, you understand the magnitude of what's at stake? Don't be short-sighted. I can offer you opportunities beyond your wildest dreams."

Leslie, feeling cornered, spoke up.

"Mr. Jacobs, your offer is flattering, but I'm committed to my role here. It's not just about the job. I believe in what we're doing at *The National*."

"Beliefs? In journalism? We're talking business. And in business, you go where the opportunity is biggest. I'm offering you the chance to be a part of something groundbreaking."

Mays intervened. "Let's not pressure her. Give her some time to think about it."

Jacobs snapped towards Mays with a menacing look that quickly faded to a more agreeable expression. He removed his sunglasses and tucked them inside his jacket.

"You both seem hell-bent on throwing this away, but I won't let you," he said.

Jacobs paced the floor for a moment, steepling his fingers before turning to Mays and continuing. "I'm especially disappointed in you. I truly thought you had more vision than this. I'd really hoped you could see how we could all profit from a simple agreement. All I needed was your cooperation."

Jacobs took his phone from his pants pocket and thumbed a quick message. When he was finished, he slipped the phone back into his pocket and took a seat without saying a single word.

Leslie felt uneasy with Jacobs' change in demeanor. He'd instantly transformed from energetic manipulator to serene bystander, and this new persona seemed to be relaxing in the calm before the storm.

"Should we, uh, talk about this Danbury situation?" Mays asked. "That's why you came all this way, isn't it?"

Jacobs sat silently.

Leslie spoke up, recounting to Jacobs her earlier conversation with Mays about possibly confronting Senator Danbury or even enlisting James Flynn to help investigate. Jacobs continued to ignore them both. The meeting, it seemed, was over.

"I told her that pursuing either option was unwise until we spoke with you first," Mays said. "We were hoping for your guidance."

Jacobs looked at his phone and stood up. "Mr. White," he said.

Leslie turned toward the door to see a meticulously dressed man step into the office. His dark suit was impeccably cut to fit him flawlessly, which must have taken a master tailor due to the man's incredibly slight physique. If not for the evident flesh on his hands and face, Leslie might have mistaken him for a walking skeleton.

Jacobs introduced Leslie and Mays to Mr. White, calling him his "most trusted and valuable employee."

Leslie felt a sudden impulse to just walk out the door and not look back. Something about Mr. White told her things were about to get very bad inside that office. She told herself to go but ignored her own instincts.

"Mr. White knows Senator Danbury quite well," Jacobs told them. "You could say that he's put a lot of time and money into making the senator useful. You see, Senator Danbury is a crucial component to the success of a major initiative I have in the works."

"You're responsible for this Project Titan," Mays blurted.

Jacobs laughed.

"You see, Mr. White? The level of intelligence I have to endure."

He stepped toward Mays until the two men were nearly nose-to-nose.

"You don't even know what Titan is and yet you associate me with its existence," Jacobs said. "The man who walks into darkness without a light is bound to stumble and fall."

Mays stepped backwards to create separation between himself and Jacobs, who had fully regained his aggressive nature.

"I'm sorry," Mays said. "I shouldn't have said that."

Jacobs stepped toward him again until Leslie interrupted.

"You're using Senator Danbury," she said.

The three men turned to face her before she continued.

"Danbury serves on a committee that approves federal funding for secret government research projects. It's in a file I found while researching the fluff piece I was originally assigned to write. You want him to control funding for Titan. But why?"

With a slow, dramatic clap, Jacobs strutted to the middle of the large office, his face beaming like a proud parent.

"Do you see, gentlemen? Do you see? This is what I'm talking about. This is why I must have Miss Vanderwaal at my side."

He strode toward her and cupped her left hand between both of his.

"You are truly as brilliant as you are lovely," he beamed.

Mays stared blankly at Leslie. "Why didn't you say something earlier?"

"Because, Mays," Jacobs interrupted, releasing Leslie's hand and moving toward Mays, "she knows when to keep quiet. Miss Vanderwaal knows the value of information and the importance of proper timing. Unlike you."

"You're the only one I told," Mays said. "I came straight to you with what I knew."

"And that's why you're in this predicament," Jacobs said. "Had you kept your mouth shut and better understood the information you'd been given, you'd be in a much stronger position right now."

"I don't understand."

"Of course you don't. That's why I've called Mr. White. He's here to explain it to you. He has a way of making things very clear."

Jacobs reached his hand toward Leslie.

"Please, young lady, come with me now. Trust me, you won't want to be here much longer."

Leslie, believing she had no other option, took Blaine Jacobs' hand as he escorted her from the office. As she passed through the doorway, she looked back over her shoulder and saw Mr. White step toward Christopher Mays, whose face had gone pale with fear.

Jacobs closed the door behind them.

40

GAKONA, ALASKA

Natalie sat straight up, awakened by a nightmare that she couldn't remember. A feeling of dread washed over her, but the feeling faded as quickly as it came.

Flynn was asleep on the floor next to her near the fireplace.

She leaned forward, keeping her blanket wrapped around her shoulders as she stabbed at the glowing logs with a metal poker to keep the fire going. She checked her watch. The sun would be up soon and she would show Flynn how to get to the bunker he'd located on his map. The bunker that led to Dr. Keller and his secret lab.

Natalie's mind raced to sort out the details of their upcoming mission. She needed to be meticulous; the snowy terrain and weather were unforgiving. She carefully planned the route in her head, considering the terrain and the obstacles that could slow them down. Natalie knew the area well, but she still took the time to formulate a plan to make sure everything ran smoothly.

She watched Flynn sleep. A mix of admiration and concern filled her thoughts. He was smart and capable, but his ego could make him reckless. He wouldn't have a plan. She knew he believed he was at his best when he improvised on the spot; he was quick on his feet. She hoped that together, they could balance each other's strengths and weaknesses and find some answers.

Her thoughts shifted to Richard. She reflected on their relationship, her eyes drifting away, lost in memories of those early days filled with excitement and passion. The uncertainty of their current situation and Richard's well-being weighed heavily on her, creating a mix of fear for his safety and anxiety about their future together.

She remembered feeling a deep connection to Richard but couldn't rekindle the way she felt about him before Dr. Keller's experiments altered the man she loved. And now, so much time had passed since he was the man with whom she'd originally fallen in love.

Natalie rose quietly, careful to not yet wake Flynn. She gathered their supplies, checking each item against the mental list she had prepared. Food, water, first aid supplies, and navigation tools —everything they would need for a safe and successful hike through the woods. She packed with perfect efficiency, fitting each item carefully into two backpacks.

Outside, the first light of dawn was breaking. Natalie stepped out into the frozen morning air, taking a moment to appreciate the stillness. In a few hours, they would be deep in the wilderness, facing unknown dangers. But for now, she allowed herself a moment of peace.

Returning inside, Natalie gently nudged Flynn.

"Time to get moving."

Flynn sat up, rubbing his eyes. He looked around the cabin.

"You've been busy," he said with a tone of what Natalie could only describe as embarrassment. "You shouldn't have let me sleep so long."

She said nothing but handed him a cup of hot coffee and a small plate of breakfast she had prepared for him. They needed their strength for the journey ahead.

They ate in silence. Natalie's mind was already on the path ahead, plotting, planning, and preparing for every possible scenario. The stakes were high, and failure was not an option. With Flynn by her side, she felt a surge of determination. She was ready to uncover the secrets of Keller's lab, no matter what it took.

41

Bundled in heavy jackets to ward off the morning chill, Flynn and Natalie each shouldered a backpack filled with essential supplies. Flynn scanned his surroundings, his mind on the lookout for potential dangers and discoveries that awaited them.

He could tell the journey would be grueling, demanding every ounce of their physical and mental strength. The wooded terrain, vast and rugged, stretched out before them, a forest of black spruce trees dotting a pristine blanket of snow. Icy patches threatened to send them sliding downhill and dense thickets clawed at their clothes. Each step forward was hard-won.

"Stay close," Natalie said. "The terrain can be treacherous."

Flynn nodded. His investigative instincts were keen. The forest was eerily silent, save for the occasional rustle of leaves underfoot and the distant calls of wildlife.

Ever the astute observer, he took mental notes of their route as Natalie led the way. He admired her expertise and the way she moved through the forest with such swiftness, agility, and confidence.

As the sun climbed higher, its rays offered little in the way of warmth, doing nothing to thaw the chill that had set into their bones. They took brief breaks, conserving their energy and supplies, well aware that their search could extend well into the evening. Conversation was sparse, limited to essential communication and the occasional word of encouragement. The isolation of the region enveloped them, a reminder of how far they were from the beaten path.

Wildlife sightings were frequent, and Natalie would quietly point out animals that were within view. They stopped for a brief lunch of protein bars and warm coffee, and a moose crossed their path, its massive form arresting their attention. They watched in awe as the mammoth animal lumbered through the trees with ominous grace.

The journey was not without brief moments of despair. Twice, they thought they'd found the entrance to the bunker, only to discover a rotted tree stump and a large rock. But they pressed on despite the disappointment, driven by a shared sense of purpose and the thrill of the unknown.

As the sun began its descent, casting long shadows across the snow, their persistence finally paid off. Natalie's keen eye spotted an anomaly in the pattern of the snow and underbrush, a hint of something man-made lying beneath. With renewed vigor, they cleared the area, revealing the rusty hatch that marked the entrance to the abandoned bomb shelter.

"This is it," she said, her voice barely a whisper.

Flynn looked around, ensuring they were still alone. The hatch was ingeniously camouflaged, blending perfectly with its surroundings. A steel cable held the hatch shut.

Flynn slid his pack off his shoulders and removed a pair of bolt cutters, which he used to bite through the cable.

They lifted the hatch open to reveal an iron ladder descending through a dark shaft. Flynn felt a surge of adrenaline. This was the moment he had been waiting for. The secrets of Hermes were just within his reach, and with each step he moved closer to the truth that could expose this mystery and clear his name.

At the bottom, the old fallout bunker was cramped and cold.

Their flashlights illuminated their path as Flynn led the way with Natalie just two steps behind.

Natalie tapped Flynn on the shoulder and aimed her light toward the top of the wall in the corner of the room, revealing a grated vent. Flynn nodded and slipped off his backpack and removed a screwdriver. Natalie dragged a worn desk over to him, which he used to boost him closer to the vent in the corner of the room. He worked quickly to remove the screws that held the vent cover in place. Once the screws were gone, Flynn pulled the grate off and climbed inside the ventilation duct.

He offered a hand to Natalie, but she stood pat, arms at her sides.

"I can't," she said.

"Come on we're *this* close," Flynn said.

"I know," she said. "I want to know what happened to Richard and how to save him and whoever else was involved, but I can't go in there."

Flynn nodded, and before he could turn around and begin the journey through the vent, Natalie clutched his hand.

"Be careful," she said.

He winked. "I'll be right back."

They held onto each other for a moment longer than Flynn expected, and he turned toward the ventilation shaft.

But before he crawled inside, his phone vibrated in his pocket. It was a single text message from TruthSeeker47.

Your friend is here to stop you

Flynn grumbled and stuffed the phone back into his pocket. He was done with the enigmatic messages.

42

Flynn's breath came in short bursts, fogging the narrow space of the ventilation duct as he crawled forward. Fighting through his claustrophobia, he worked hard to stay focused and remain sharp. He hoped his pal Harrison was right, that there actually was a secret lab and that he'd find answers he was looking for.

The ductwork twisted like a cramped metal maze, but Flynn belly-crawled and wriggled his way through the tight confines. The low hum of machinery grew louder as he advanced, guiding him closer to his target.

When he reached the end of the shaft, a grate offered a view into the room ahead. Flynn switched off the flashlight. The lab sprawled out like a scene from a dystopian nightmare. Jars of strange tissues ensconced in pink- and blue-tinged formaldehyde covered one shelving unit in the middle of the lab. In a fish tank against the opposite wall, a pale fish with dark spots, a long snout, and sharp teeth haphazardly spread across its crooked mouth patrolled the waters. Against the near wall, pale fluorescent lights shone down on makeshift jail cells containing the lab's true horror.

Locked inside the ominous cages, feeble human figures gazed

through steel mesh. Some lay listless on the cold floors of their cells, their eyes vacant. Others paced or rocked back and forth, mumbling incoherently. An air of despair and madness wafted up even through the small vent.

Flynn noticed a few who bore physical injuries, bandages crudely masking unknown wounds. But the eyes struck him the most—their foggy, unseeing stare that seemed to look right through the walls of their confinement. Were these the victims of Hermes, their minds ravaged by whatever experiments Dr. Keller had conducted?

The grate, like the one he'd used to enter the duct, was attached on the outside via four screws. Flynn contorted his body so his feet swung toward the grate. With a swift motion, he kicked against the aluminum grate with both feet. The first attempt merely bent the metal, but a second effort knocked it loose and onto the floor, landing with a clang.

Flynn felt a surge of anger and pity. He grabbed a chart hanging next to one of the cells and read aloud off the top: "Titan Project: Sgt. Landon Vance."

Flynn sighed and shook his head, realizing that this indeed was Dr. Keller's secret, whoever—or whatever—they were. Victims, part of a larger scheme, discarded shells of human beings whose sanity was the price of military research. He snapped photos of the scene with his cellphone. This was evidence, and he needed every bit of it to expose the truth.

Flynn hustled but did so cautiously. The information he gathered would be vital, not just for his investigation, but for the unfortunate men who had been reduced to the status of lab rats.

He took a deep breath. He had seen the consequences of rogue intelligence operations before, but this was different—this was the first time he'd seen it created by his own nation. It was hard for him to believe what he was seeing. He wondered how many people knew about this project.

How deep does this go?

He took more photos of the cages and their captives. He

wanted to text the images to Theresa, but his phone had no service in the lab.

The caged men shifted their attention toward Flynn. Some of their faces maintained the blank and lifeless expressions, while others appeared agitated. One of the men yelled an obscenity toward Flynn, causing others to do likewise. In mere seconds, the room erupted into rage-filled chaos as the captives beat on their cages and yelled at the intruder.

Besides the open-air duct from where Flynn entered, there was only one door that left the confinement area. Flynn knew someone would come investigate the ruckus. He didn't have to wait long.

The racket of fury and frenzy halted as Dr. Nestor Keller, flanked by an armed guard, stepped into the room. His mere entrance caused a stark shift in the prison's atmosphere. The captives, upon seeing Keller, ceased their outbursts, retreating into a haunting silence that filled the space with an uncomfortable tension. Their eyes, once alight with fury and confusion, now flickered with a mix of fear and recognition.

The guard's hand rested uneasily on his weapon, his eyes darting between the cages and Flynn, assessing the situation. Keller's expression was one of fatigue, as if he were shouldering the weight of the world.

The doctor motioned to the guard, who pointed his gun at Flynn, directing him to walk out of the main containment area and down a corridor to Dr. Keller's office.

"What have you done?" Flynn said, his voice charged with controlled outrage.

Keller's features hardened into a mask of resigned recognition.

"I suppose it was only a matter of time before you found your way here."

Flynn moved closer, his eyes searching Keller's.

"How could you let it go this far?"

Keller motioned to the broken grate and the exposed ventilation shaft.

"I often wondered where that went," he said with almost a chuckle. "So much to worry about, I just couldn't concern myself with every detail. What a silly oversight."

"You're a monster."

Keller's expression shifted, a flicker of surprise and then understanding crossed his face.

"Far more than you realize, Mr. Flynn. You think Titan is the cause of these poor men's suffering." There was a hint of sadness in his tone. "You can't even begin to understand what I've done here. Titan isn't the problem; it's the solution."

Flynn said nothing.

Keller sighed, the burden of his knowledge apparent in his slumped shoulders.

"The original research was called Project Hermes," Keller said. "It started off as a civilian project. I was on that original team. We had financial backing from a corporate investor and big plans to develop a subliminal method of communication. We had a former military general on the team who leaked some information to his buddies at the Pentagon. In less than a week, we were up to our necks in military intelligence. They told us they were shutting us down."

Flynn began to connect the dots.

"The former general," Flynn said. "Was it Arthur Tillman?"

Keller nodded.

"Art brought in his Army buddies and they took the project from us. They said it was too dangerous, but what they really meant was that they wanted the research for themselves. They stole the data and offered to keep me on as the project lead. I had put nearly a year of my life into it so I was happy for the chance to continue my work."

Flynn recalled the note Liam Baxter had handed him at the Ultra convention: *Find the son of Zeus. Find the truth.*

"Hermes, the Greek messenger god, was a son of Zeus," Flynn said. "What did it do?"

"It was based on technology that we created known as Whisper-Shout," Keller said. "Subliminal messages are sent to the brain via a two-channel audio communication. One half of the message is audible. This is the shout, and it can be anything: 'It looks like it could rain this afternoon,' or some other innocuous piece of information. The other half is received subliminally by the brain, but not heard out loud. The second message—the whisper—feels similar to déjà vu. The sensation is a clear visualization of something vaguely familiar that you can comprehend but can't pinpoint where the information comes from.

"If you've ever experienced a memory from your childhood that is represented by a photograph, but you can't quite ascertain whether you truly remember the event or you're just reacting to the photo or possibly a story you've heard over and over from your parents, you have a bit of an idea how Shout-Whisper works."

"So you're saying it works?"

Keller straightened his posture. "Absolutely. For a while." He paused for a moment to adjust his glasses. "Simple messages can easily be received. Test subjects were able to identify images of animals or colors or even a short series of numbers sent as whispers. But repeated Shout-Whispers or ones that tried to convey more complex information, such as a series of instructions caused problems."

"What kind of problems?"

"At first it was just mild confusion, but it evolved to extreme frustration and aggressive anger."

"And violence?" Flynn thought of Sergeant Richard Mahler and Natalie's story about how her boyfriend became more agitated and aggressive after coming to Alaska.

Keller lowered his head.

"Subjects eventually became prone to acts of extreme unpredictability and violence. We learned, too late, that the human brain isn't able to process these bits of information effectively beyond very limited and simple bursts. There are similar, yet far milder, reactions from people who experience repeated episodes of déjà vu. Often those people struggle with substance abuse or other mental health issues or even chronic migraines. The brain begins to labor to determine what's real and what isn't."

"Why didn't you stop once you realized the research was dangerous?"

"A question I ask myself daily," Keller said. "But, you know why. It's the same reason why you never stop seeking answers to your questions. Regardless of personal peril or even potential collateral damage, you drive forward in your life's work, James. I'm no different. I saw that my technology worked but that I needed to iron out the bugs. I needed to find the answer. Find my truth."

Flynn clasped his hands together.

"Work out the bugs? The men in the cells. You were killing them and you kept going—to work out the bugs?"

"I don't expect anyone to understand. I don't expect forgiveness. But Project Titan is my new mission. It's my attempt to rectify the situation, to cure the remaining survivors, to reverse the damage that I've caused. But it's been an uphill battle, with limited success and mounting pressure."

The pieces were falling into place for Flynn, but they painted a far more complex and tragic picture than he'd initially thought.

"How did Liam Baxter fit into all of this?"

Keller looked down, his face unable to mask the sadness.

"Liam was my assistant," he said. "Before we tested Hermes on military personnel, Liam volunteered. He was Patient Zero, if you will. The experiments worked on him. He was a willing subject, and took the initial rounds of messaging well. We were optimistic right off the bat. But then Liam began to complain about confusion. His work became unreliable. We were testing soldiers at that point, and my focus was no longer on his progress or condition. There was so much pressure to get results quickly, Liam was no longer a priority. Then he told me he wanted to leave the project. I was barely present in the real world by that time—I was so consumed by my work that my concern for anything outside of Hermes dropped to nil. I accepted Liam's resignation. The last time I saw him he complained of a headache."

Dr. Keller stood stone-faced and wiped an index finger over his eyelid.

"I told him to take two aspirin. He left, and I never saw him again."

Keller continued, "I've been trying to save them all. Titan is my responsibility to the lives Hermes destroyed."

Flynn felt a surge of conflicting emotions. Anger at the military's reckless experiments, sympathy for Keller's plight, and an overwhelming sense of urgency to bring this story to light.

"I need to tell the world about this," Flynn said. "People need to know the truth about what happened here. Families of these men need to know what happened to their sons, brothers, fathers, and husbands."

Keller nodded, a look of resignation in his eyes.

"I understand why you believe that. I even agree with you on a philosophical level. It's the right thing to do. But—"

Keller stood akimbo and cocked his head to one side while taking a pregnant pause.

"—I can't let you do that. If you tell the world about me, they'll come here. They'll shut me down. I'll go to prison. I'll die before I can set things right. And I can't allow that to happen."

Two more security officers entered Keller's office. He made eye contact with them before nodding at Flynn.

"What are you doing?" Flynn asked as the two guards flanked him and then tightened their hands around his biceps.

Keller ignored the question as he shook his head subtly.

"You can't say you weren't warned, James. I tried my best to tell you. But you wouldn't leave well enough alone."

Then Keller nodded at the guards and they moved toward the door, forcing Flynn forward with them.

43

The clank of the heavy metal door echoed through the dimly lit corridor as a third guard joined the previous two and dragged Flynn back to the lab. With a shove, they tossed Flynn into one of the cramped cells, the door slamming shut with a resounding clang. He barely had time to regain his balance before he heard the sound of approaching footsteps.

Dr. Keller, his white lab coat a stark contrast to the gray, dull atmosphere of the containment wing, approached Flynn's cage. He motioned with his hand, and the guards left the room. Keller's face was a canvas of exhaustion and regret, but his eyes reflected a storm of unspoken emotions.

He spoke in a low voice, one tinged with a weary sincerity. "I apologize for this outcome. But you must understand, what I'm doing here with Project Titan is of great importance."

Flynn, leaning against the cold metal bars, met Keller's gaze with a mix of skepticism and curiosity.

"You can't do this," Flynn said. "You're exhausted, and your efforts aren't working. You said so yourself. Let me push this into the open so other bright minds can get involved. Then these men will have a fighting chance to find a cure they so deserve."

Keller sighed, a gesture that conveyed his shame along with a steely resolve.

"I know how it looks, but the work I'm doing here, it's going to pay off. I'm trying to undo a grave mistake. I have to fix what was broken."

"And the men in these cages? How much time do they have?"

"I'm trying to give them back their lives. I'm fighting against the clock, and sometimes I lose. But I have to try. I owe them that much."

Heavy silence settled between them, broken only by a distant thud from somewhere deeper in the HAARP facility.

Keller, seemingly unaware of the sound, stared at Flynn, a resolute determination in his eyes.

"I know you're a danger to me. I know that I should have one of my guards kill you and dispose of your body somewhere it would never be found. But I've been responsible for too much violence and far too many deaths. I will not have you on my conscience as well."

"So you'll have me rot in here with these other poor bastards you've condemned to die?"

Keller closed his eyes. "I must return to my work."

Flynn watched him walk away. In the stark confines of his cell, surrounded by the echoes of despair and madness, he couldn't help but wonder where the line between Keller the savior and Keller the tormentor blurred.

The thud he'd heard just seconds earlier was back, but this time it was louder and seemed to be rolling this way, increasing in volume as it drew closer. Then the room went dark.

Red emergency lights flickered on. Flynn surveyed the room. The soldiers in the cages seemed to be unfazed by the sudden darkness or the clunking sound that came before. Something deep within the facility had knocked the power out, and the lab was now operating on backup generators.

Flynn heard a click and realized it had come from the lock on his cell door. The cages were secured with electric locks that must've been released down by whatever had caused the blackout. He slowly opened the door and closed it behind him. None of the other captives moved. They either didn't understand that their freedom was a mere push of a door away or they thought their prison was defined more than by the bars that kept them physically confined.

Flynn feared what would happen if they did comprehend the situation. As tragic as their existence was, being captive was the only thing keeping them safe and from potentially hurting others.

The darkness was almost absolute, save for faint illumination from the flashing red emergency bulbs. The power outage had plunged Dr. Keller's lab into chaos. Flynn heard distant shouts and moans along with the scurrying of feet.

Slowly, he crept along the wall, his hands feeling for obstructions, his ears straining for any sound that could spell danger. He edged forward, only able to see a few steps ahead. As he inched down the dark corridor, the realization that he had no clue where he was going made him wish he'd just climbed back up into the ventilation duct and crawled back to Natalie, who he hoped was still safely waiting for him.

A sudden noise ahead made him freeze. Footsteps. Measured, deliberate. Approaching. Flynn's mind raced. He was unarmed, vulnerable. His only advantage was the darkness, and that was a fragile shield at best.

Then the footsteps stopped. He could only make out the shadow of a figure standing maybe ten feet ahead. Flynn prepared himself for confrontation, every muscle tense and ready to act.

A man's voice cut through the silence, low and controlled.

"Flynn."

He recognized the voice and called out to the shadow. "What do you want, Nellis?"

"You're not the least bit surprised to see me," Nellis said. "I like that. You don't rattle easily."

"I knew you'd keep coming until you found me," Flynn said. "I can't say I was necessarily expecting to see you in an abandoned, classified, cold war-era underground missile silo, but I suppose I'm not exactly shocked either."

Nellis stepped forward into the light, half of him bathed in the red glow of the emergency lights, the other hidden in shadow. He set his jaw and narrowed his eyes.

"Keller's a madman."

"I got that impression," said Flynn, who just then saw the gun in Nellis's hand.

"I came here to stop him. And for you—"

Nellis raised his weapon and fired two shots in quick succession. Flynn barely had time to flinch. The sound of the gunshots reverberating off the concrete corridor was deafening, and it took him a second or two to realize that Nellis's target was an armed guard approaching Flynn from the rear. Both of the shots struck the guard, who doubled over onto the floor. If he wasn't dead yet, Flynn figured he soon would be.

He picked up the man's gun and glanced at Nellis.

"Just to be clear, you're saying we're on the same side, right?"

"There are so many sides, who can keep track? Let's say today we're not enemies and leave it at that."

"Why should I trust you?"

"You shouldn't," Nellis said. "But right now, I'm your best chance out of here. I've been investigating Keller and Project Titan. I know what's going on. The world needs to know, and I'm sure not the one to tell it."

Flynn weighed his options. Nellis was dangerous, but if he was telling the truth, this could be his only shot at escape. And if it was a lie, Flynn would rather face the threat head-on than be caught fleeing like a rat in a maze.

"Lead the way," Flynn said. His senses remained on high alert, ready to react at the first sign of betrayal.

Nellis moved with speed and confidence that proved he'd spent some time examining the route in and out of Keller's hidden lab. Flynn's steps were nearly as agile as he followed him through the twists and turns of the bunker's many rooms and hallways.

"How do you know about this place?" Flynn asked.

"You're not the only retired spook in the world, Flynn."

"Let me guess: NSA?"

Nellis ignored the question. "Up this way, quickly. It won't take long for them to get the main power back on."

Nellis stopped at an iron ladder painted bright yellow. He looked at Flynn and said, "Let's go. Keep your head down when we get up there. They're going to be swarming like wet hornets."

Flynn followed Nellis up the ladder and could only smile as he found himself in the supply room he'd searched earlier during his initial visit to the HAARP facility. A small hidden panel in the wall was the access point to Keller's lab, and Flynn had overlooked it entirely. His intelligence buddies would never let him live it down if they ever found out.

He'd have to find another time to be embarrassed about his diminishing spycraft skills because as he and Nellis exited the storage room, they were met by a dozen armed security guards in the large computer lab.

The guards fired first, their shots wild and well off the mark. Flynn and Nellis took cover behind a bank of computer workstations and tried to wait them out.

Nellis was a pure marksman with a handgun, and Flynn was glad they were no longer adversaries. He thought about Truth-Seeker47's message: "your enemy is not your enemy." He then wondered which of his friends was not his friend?

Nellis used six shots to put down four guards, while Flynn took out four more using the nine-millimeter pistol he retrieved from the fallen guard.

Watching half of their numbers drop in just a few seconds took some of the resolve out of the remaining guards. A few of them dropped to the floor behind cover, while others simply threw their guns down and ran.

All except for one.

Dr. Simon Grant trained his rifle on Flynn, creating a standoff.

"I told you not to go snooping around," Grant said. "And look where it got you. Neither one of you will make it out of here alive—and the sad thing is I think you'd soon see we were on the same side if you took a moment to listen."

Flynn narrowed his eyes. "Dr. Keller just tried to throw me into a cage. That doesn't exactly scream that we're on the same side, now does it?"

"Do you have a death wish, Mr. Flynn?" Grant asked.

"No, but I do," Nellis said.

The sudden injection into the conversation was enough to throw Grant off. His eyes darted toward Nellis's. And Flynn seized the moment, pumping several rounds of lead into Grant's chest, before sending the final fatal shot into the man's forehead.

"Well done," Nellis said.

Flynn thanked Nellis but felt an uneasiness about doing so.

Why thank me for killing a man?

Flynn decided to revisit what he thought about his decision later.

Nellis, seeing the opportunity for them to escape, gestured to Flynn to make a run for it. Flynn didn't hesitate, sprinting from the computer room toward the main lobby and the front door. Nellis fired two more shots to cover their getaway.

44

Flynn burst through the double doors into the lobby of the HAARP research station. He had to shield his eyes from the sunlight blasting in through the front windows and entrance. It took a few seconds for his eyes to adjust to the brightness of the day after straining to make his way through the darkness of the interior of the facility and Dr. Keller's underground hidden lab.

Once he got his bearings, Flynn sought cover, as no fewer than twenty men outfitted in body armor and armed with assault rifles strode toward the front of the building. Flynn scrutinized their attire, layered for Arctic survival with equipment not in compliance with standard military gear. The lack of consistent uniform insignia, the eclectic mix of civilian and military-grade weapons and clothing, and their undisciplined alignment confirmed Flynn's suspicion: These were not U.S. military personnel but mercenaries.

He ducked behind a receptionist's desk and braced for the onslaught. He had his doubts on the effectiveness his defensive position would have against live rounds in the event that the men outside decided to open fire. But he had to do *something*. His only hope was that they hadn't seen him, or that he was not their target.

Seconds later, Nellis came through the door, and Flynn grabbed him and pulled him behind the desk.

"These guys with you?" Flynn asked.

Nellis rubbed his eyes and held up a hand to shield against the bright sun as he peeked around the edge of the desk.

"I wish they were," he said. "Those boys look to be geared for war."

Flynn took another glance. The mercs stopped maybe twenty yards from the front door as if they were waiting for further orders before they stormed the building.

"I'll be damned," Flynn said.

"What do you see?"

"It's Jacobs."

"What are you doing?" Nellis asked.

Flynn gave him a thin smile, placed his hand on Nellis's shoulder, and stood straight up.

"Don't move," Flynn said. "No matter what happens. You'll know when it's time."

Nellis tried to protest, but Flynn held an open palm toward him and signaled for him to stay quiet. Then Flynn headed to the entrance, pushed the front door open with both hands and stepped outside.

The armed mercs, who obviously weren't expecting someone to come out of the building, brought all their weapons to bear on Flynn as he walked through the doors and offered a friendly wave. He squinted and used one hand to shield himself from the sun's glare. Then he slowly raised both arms above his head.

45

The armed men standing outside the facility slowly aligned in a loose semi-circle and then advanced toward Flynn. One shouted instructions to him to keep his hands raised and to not move. Another shouted to "anyone inside the HAARP facility" that they should put down their weapons and exit through the front door. They stopped just a few yards away from Flynn, their guns still raised and aimed toward him.

"You can stand down," a man shouted from a short distance behind the mercs' line.

"He isn't our enemy. He isn't going to do anything foolish. James Flynn is a calm man, of that you can be sure."

A gap formed between two men in the center of the formation, and Blaine Jacobs strutted through, wearing forest camo, a red beret and mirror sunglasses. He approached Flynn with an outstretched hand.

"It's good to see you again, Flynn," Jacobs said. "It's not exactly how I expected things to play out, but, well, here we are."

Flynn looked at Jacobs' hand but refused to offer his own in return.

Jacobs smiled. "I assume you're figuring all of this out, so I'm surprised you're not happy to see me. You saw what Keller is up to in there. You can write a huge piece about what was going on here; blow the lid off of this whole thing and become even more famous than you already are."

"I talked to Dr. Keller," Flynn said. "I *do* know what's going on in there—he told me about Projects Hermes and Titan. And now that you're here, I have an even clearer view of the big picture."

Jacobs' smile melted.

Flynn said, "You must have been supplying the corporate dollars that bank rolled Keller's original subliminal message research before the military came in and shut you down."

"Before they stole it from me." Jacobs' demeanor instantly changed, as he wagged a finger inches from Flynn's nose. "That was my project. It was my idea. Keller did the work, but he was following my orders and spending my money. Tillman and Barrow came in and just took it. I could have revolutionized human communication and increased the security of sensitive information for billions of people. I could have made identity theft a thing of the past. Possibilities were endless. We had a long way to go, sure, but despite Keller's strange behavior, the man truly is a genius. He was discovering things about the human body with massive implications for humanity. We were making progress. But once the military caught wind of what we were doing, their small mindedness took over. They failed to see the big picture, choosing only to focus on their own short-term limited objectives. They stole my research."

"It doesn't work, Blaine," Flynn said. "You do understand that."

"It didn't work for them because they are too impatient, too hasty. It was going to work."

"Keller doesn't share your optimism. He said it was a massive failure. You saw the dead bodies so you know as well as anyone what happened."

"Small setbacks in the wake of overwhelming progress," Jacobs said. "Do you know how many people died trying to perfect the airplane, or break the sound barrier, or travel into outer space, or land on the moon? All of society's greatest advancements have suffered collateral damage."

"You're talking about dangerous and controversial scientific research that affects the human brain, not the invention of the internal combustion engine, here," Flynn argued. "The gains you were hoping to achieve are not worth the cost of human lives, especially since none of your live tests were successful."

A hint of Jacobs' smile returned.

"I see Keller didn't tell you *everything*."

Jacobs motioned to two of his men and then toward Flynn. The mercs approached Flynn, confiscated the pistol from the back of his waistband and gestured for him to walk back into the research facility.

The rest of Jacobs' men flooded into the building past Flynn and his two guards. When Flynn re-entered he saw the mercs disappear deeper into the research center. Seconds later he heard gunfire as HAARP's security force engaged the intruders. He scanned the lobby and glanced toward the reception area where he'd left Nellis.

An abrupt, violent nudge from behind coaxed Flynn to keep moving. Sounds from the fighting had mostly died down, and as he moved past the set of double doors in the lobby, he saw clear signs that HAARP's limited security presence had been defeated. The ones fortunate enough to still be alive rested on their knees with their hands zip-tied behind their backs. Flynn felt an odd sense of guilt looking at the guards, the same men he himself had shot at just a few minutes earlier as he and Nellis fought to escape Keller's secret bunker lab. They were men simply doing their job, almost certainly unaware of the secrets that had been operating underground. They were there to protect the facility and stop intruders. And now some of them were dead. More collateral damage from Project Titan.

* * *

NELLIS CAME out from behind the desk after the last of Jacobs' men filed into the inner workings of HAARP. He tucked his pistol into its holster, which was concealed by his large coat. His Sig Sauer nine millimeter wasn't going to be much use against those mercs and their high-powered assault rifles.

He wondered why Flynn gave himself up. He couldn't hear what he'd said to Jacobs, but whatever it was, it resulted in Flynn getting hauled away.

He felt like he was out of options. He could slip out the front door and head back home with Holland and Bailey. No one would ever know that he was even there. Just another sideways op, a mission that was FUBAR. He'd been there before. And while the taste of failure and the pain of defeat were never things he enjoyed, he knew that walking away alive was always the most important thing.

But what about Flynn? What about Keller? What about those servicemen locked behind those cages? Would they go home? Would they walk away alive?

He cursed himself under his breath for what he knew he had to do. It was almost certainly a suicide mission, but he truly believed he had no choice. He had to try and get those men out of there.

Just as he was about to venture back inside the depths of HAARP and Dr. Keller's lab, Nellis heard the front door open. He flinched and began to dive back behind the desk, but he stopped.

Coming through the door was a woman, her dark, shoulder-length hair flaked with snow. She advanced toward him with purpose. Her gaze pierced him with what he could only perceive as malicious intent.

"Special Agent Blackwood," she said. "I'm looking for James Flynn."

46

The door clanged shut, and for the second time in the same day, James Flynn was locked in a cage deep inside Dr. Keller's secret lab. Jacobs' men had restored power to the station, securing all the cells and turning the main lights back on.

With Flynn trapped behind the steel mesh, Jacobs dismissed his guards from the room and took a seat. He removed his glasses and beret and looked toward Flynn with compassion.

"This could work," Jacobs said, nodding toward the haggard soldiers cowering in their cages. "It is working."

"You're delusional," Flynn said. "This whole thing is a massive failure."

Jacobs waved dismissively at the remark.

"There are obstacles in my way, and I need to remove them. Then I'll be back on schedule," Jacobs said. "It's going to be quite a show. I want you to have a front row seat."

* * *

BLACKWOOD LOOKED at Nellis sideways as he told her the entire story from the beginning.

"I had my suspicions about Jacobs all along," he said. "In my line of work, trust doesn't come easy, and it's even less forthcoming when dealing with a billionaire tech mogul. I did a lot of homework on Flynn once this TruthSeeker47 individual requested him to investigate HAARP for us. Once I realized that Jacobs was also interested in what was going on, I dug up some info on him and discovered he'd been involved in some weird projects that operated along the far edges of what we might consider responsible scientific research. I assumed TS47 and Jacobs were one and the same, although it didn't make sense why Jacobs would openly request Flynn to get involved but then do the same thing with some shadowy alias. He didn't need to get Ultra involved at all."

"Maybe Jacobs believed Flynn would be more intrigued by the mystery," Blackwood said, "and decided to add in that extra element to compel Flynn to dive in."

Nellis shrugged. "We were worried that Jacobs was trying to expose Ultra and that this stuff in Gakona was a tactic to get us out in the open. Once Baxter ended up dead, we knew we needed to keep tabs on Flynn. And then when Flynn took one of Jacobs' planes up here to Alaska, we assumed they were on the same side."

"And now you're sure they're not?"

Nellis nodded. "This stuff with Dr. Keller and this mind-control research? Flynn had no clue what was going on until he stepped right into it. He was up here doing a legit job; he was expecting to write a magazine article. And that interaction with Jacobs just a bit ago? Those guys aren't friends."

"Well, I've still got Jacobs as my top suspect in the killings of Arthur Tillman and Special Agent Minter, so I'm going in there after him. If they are friends, and Flynn stands in my way, I'll take him down too."

Nellis narrowed his gaze. "Flynn's not your guy. And, Jacobs isn't going to just let you inside. He's got a platoon of heavily armed thugs in there. If you march inside thinking your badge is going to shield you, you're going to have a fight on your hands, and unless you have your own team of special ops soldiers, you're grossly outgunned."

Blackwood glanced back toward the door as a squad of U.S. Army soldiers paced through.

"This ain't my first rodeo," she said.

47

Flynn couldn't believe his ears. At a loss for words, he managed only to huff a mocking chuckle, expressing the incredulity he felt for Jacobs.

"I sent you here to expose Project Titan," Jacobs said. "I wanted Dr. Keller shut down. I wanted him back working for me on the original program."

"I don't think he's interested," Flynn said. "He's focused on correcting his mistakes."

"That's why I brought you into the picture, Flynn. You could expose the entire project in the pages of your magazine, and Keller would lose everything. Unless of course you reported that you found nothing, just as you initially expected when you took on this assignment—just a government facility studying the ionosphere."

"Why would I choose to hide the truth after I saw what really happened here? What would keep me from blowing the lid off this whole thing and exposing everyone involved?"

Jacobs took a digital tablet from his pack and held the screen so Flynn could see it.

"This is a live video feed from inside my private plane parked at the same landing strip where you arrived a few days ago."

Flynn recognized the interior of the plane on which he'd flown from Florida to Gakona. He also recognized the lone passenger in the cabin. It was Leslie Vanderwaal.

Flynn stared wide-eyed but said nothing.

"Miss Vanderwaal has had a very eventful morning," Jacobs said. "Her boss, Mr. Mays met a tragic and untimely demise, and she's decided to work directly for me in my marketing department, although I do feel as though I grossly overstated her role going forward; mainly that *she* won't be going forward."

Flynn grabbed at the wire mesh that comprised the walls of his cage and violently yanked on them. It didn't budge.

"It doesn't have to be this way, Flynn," Jacobs said. "Your inability to get in and out of this facility without being captured by Dr. Keller is why I had to come here and clean up this mess. And now that I'm here doing damage control, I'm going to tie up all the loose ends, which includes you, of course. Honestly, I didn't expect Keller to be so vigilant. Perhaps, you've lost a step. Maybe this is all for the best. I can just take the original Hermes research and go. It's actually much cleaner this way. I'm sorry I didn't think of it sooner. I actually have buyers on standby ready to take delivery whenever I make the decision to hand it over."

"Buyers? What are you talking about?"

"Tillman and his fat-ass Pentagon pals wanted to see if Hermes could be used on the battlefield. It's time I let them bear witness. Imagine an army of Hermes soldiers wreaking unpredictable acts of extreme violence anywhere in the country at any given moment."

"You're talking about selling Hermes to terrorists," Flynn barked. "You're more delusional than I thought."

Jacobs huffed. "Your world view is so tiny, James. So narrow. So blind. United States imperialism has many enemies. That doesn't make us terrorists."

"Us?"

"I've been at war with our nation's government for most of my life," Jacobs said. "When they stole my research, that was the last indignity that I would allow myself to suffer. I wanted to be part of the solution, but when Tillman sent his thugs in here to tear the fruits of my hard work from my own hands, he made me the problem. I'm only sorry that I couldn't leave him alive long enough to be a part of the end game."

"Which is what exactly, you crazy bastard?"

Jacobs once again donned the flashy red beret and mirror sunglasses. He smiled.

"You know, Flynn," he said. "The complete destruction of American society."

* * *

One of Jacobs' mercs entered the room and conversed quietly for a moment with Jacobs.

Jacobs turned to Flynn. "This just keeps getting better and better. The FBI and that security man from Ultra are here, apparently because of you. Looks like I really am going to eliminate all loose ends today."

"The FBI will have this place surrounded," Flynn said. "There's no way you'll make it back to your plane. It's almost a guarantee they'll have it locked down as well."

"I'm counting on it," said Jacobs with a wide grin. He propped his tablet on the desk so that Flynn had a clear view.

"I want you to have a nice view of Miss Vanderwaal when my private jet explodes. It's a shame, really. She seems to be quite capable. I truthfully could have found a useful spot for her in my organization. I only brought her along to convince you to make a deal, but like General Tillman, you want to push me into the darkness and see me stripped of what is rightfully mine. So, you can watch the repercussions of your decision."

Jacobs held a remote detonator and clicked the switch. A digital clock appeared on screen, counting down from thirty minutes.

"Sorry to be so dramatic," he said. "But I need my explosions to be timed just right to cause as much chaos and confusion as possible out there. When this clock hits zero, I'm afraid it's gonzo time for our lovely Leslie."

Jacobs pantomimed a dramatic explosion and left the room.

Flynn flailed against the side of his cage, frustrated over his helplessness. Then he heard gunfire echoing through the building.

* * *

THE FIRST TWO soldiers who shuffled haphazardly through the door went down almost instantly from a pair of headshots. The brutal and unexpected gore sent a panic through many of the soldiers, most of whom had never experienced any live combat. The rest of the squad scrambled to stack on either side of the double doors as their commander shouted instructions and tried to restore order.

Three soldiers threw flashbang grenades through the doorway. As soon as the grenades exploded, half of the squad sprinted in to take cover as the rest of the soldiers laid down cover.

The battle for HAARP was under way.

48

Flynn stared at the digital tablet and its clock that now read twenty-eight minutes as it counted down. On the screen, Leslie was in full view. Not restrained and not alarmed. Flynn didn't know what Jacobs had told her, but she clearly trusted him enough to just sit tight on that plane until he came back. If he could somehow get a message to her, she could simply walk off the plane to safety. But, there was no way to do that.

The zombie-like figures trapped in the cells next to him also seemed drawn to the screen.

"Who is she?" one of the men asked.

The question, clearly enunciated from someone two cages away, surprised Flynn. As most of the captives seemed to be mostly catatonic, Flynn had almost felt like he was alone in the lab.

"She's a co-worker," Flynn said. "A friend in danger."

"We're all going to die here, aren't we?" the man asked, his voice weak and shaky.

"We're not dead yet," Flynn said, "which means we still have a chance. What's your name?"

"Sergeant Ethan Ramirez, USMC," the man said. "How about you? What's going on out there?"

Flynn introduced himself to Sergeant Ramirez and gave him a brief rundown on the events leading up to Jacobs' assault on HAARP and the apparent counter strike from the FBI. It was hard to tell looking through the cage that was between them, but Ramirez looked to be in much better shape than the other test subjects. The mere fact that he could speak put him alone at the head of the class. His eyes were clear and focused, and he nodded as Flynn spoke.

"I was one of the first to volunteer for this program," Ramirez said, "if you can believe someone being so naive. But Dr. Keller has been giving us new medicine. It wasn't helping at first, but I think it might be now. I feel better than I have in months."

"You didn't know what you were signing up for, Ramirez," Flynn said. "None of you did. You were doing what you thought was right. It's why you joined the Marines, right? To go first?" He smiled at the young man.

"I'd like to help you save your friend," Ramirez said.

Flynn nodded. "We've got to find a way out of this death trap first."

"Maybe I can help," came a voice from across the room.

Natalie had shimmied her way through the ventilation duct and was standing in front of them.

The men in the cages diverted their attention toward her, watching as she approached the cells.

Flynn beamed. He wanted to wrap her in a massive hug and not let go. He thought only of her and how badly he wanted to kiss her right then. He had so much he wanted to say, but the only thing he managed to shout was, "Unlock the damn door."

"Nice to see you, too," Natalie said.

"There's a console against that wall that unlocks the boxes," Ramirez said.

Natalie hit the button to open Flynn's cage. Flynn stepped out and looked over at Ramirez and then to Natalie.

"His, too," he said. "Open all of them. We're all getting out of here."

Natalie paused to make sure Flynn wasn't losing his mind. He nodded.

"Do it."

She slapped her hand against each of the buttons, unlocking the cages, one after another. Some of the men stepped out into the room, but others, too confused or too frightened to leave their cells, stayed inside.

Ramirez approached Flynn and shook his hand.

"I can't help you save your friend," Ramirez said. "I have a bigger mission in front of me."

Flynn looked around at the soldiers, sailors, Marines and airmen who had walked out of their cells. He wasn't sure if they were well enough to be free. He wasn't sure if Dr. Keller's Project Titan efforts were working, or if Ramirez was merely an outlier or simply a tremendous actor. But he knew for sure that these men did not deserve to die in those cages.

"They're your men, Sergeant," he said.

Ramirez nodded.

Flynn turned to Natalie. "We need to get out of here."

49

Blaine Jacobs checked his watch as one of his men hustled out of the room after fastening the detonator to the final piece of C4 explosive. He'd picked five guards to wire the place to blow in succession. They chose key areas that would exponentially increase the damage—as well as the horror—in stages.

By the time the last charges finally went off in the boiler room and the volatile chemical storage area, Keller's underground lab and the HAARP research facility would be little more than a charred hole in the side of the mountain. And the fallout from the chemical exposure would guarantee that anyone who wasn't killed in the blast would die anyway. And it would contaminate the area, making it impossible for rescuers to search the rubble for clues.

But before that would happen, Jacobs would be long gone. He had a helicopter en route to lift him from the soon-to-be burning research station back to a second private jet sitting at yet another small landing strip about an hour away. There would be no survivors or witnesses to put him at the scene. He had the Hermes research in hand. His buyer was waiting for him. The money he stood to make was astronomical, but he'd almost be willing to give

Hermes away to the right party who could bring about the fall of the United States as he knew it. *Almost.* He still had plans to live a long life far from the Western Hemisphere, a place where he could be comfortable and watch the world burn. Someplace like Australia.

The first of the explosions rocked the building. Jacobs checked his watch again. The timing had to be precise.

* * *

BLACKWOOD CLENCHED her jaw as she surveyed her predicament.

Jacobs' mercenaries had a well-planned defensive strategy and had pinned down the soldiers. The battle had devolved into a stalemate, though she felt like she was losing since the private security force had prevented her from moving deeper into the facility with the other troops.

Another blast rocked the room, sending chunks of the ceiling crashing down onto the equipment and igniting a small blaze. Meanwhile, the relentless echo of gunfire added to the overwhelming chaos. Blackwood huddled behind some debris and watched as Nellis crawled through the haze toward her.

"If those mercs don't take out all of your men, this fire will," he said. "You can't hold out much longer. And if you could, I'm not sure what the point would be. They've got that corridor blocked."

Blackwood grimaced. She squinted through the smoke and mayhem and spotted a doorway that appeared to lead to a route that bent behind the enemy position. She pointed in that direction.

"The squad can't get through, but maybe they won't notice me," she said. "Give me some cover, I'm going to make a break for it and see if I can get behind them."

Nellis shook his head at the idea and opened his mouth as if he was going to protest, but Blackwood wasn't interested in hearing it. She dashed toward the door. And it was a terrible mistake.

The mercs had triangulated the entire room and noticed her immediately. But the smoke and flames made her a difficult target, enabling her to slip behind a load-bearing pillar near the middle of the room without being gunned down. She took a deep breath, regrouping in her momentary safety. But she couldn't stay there much longer. She needed to move.

"Well, that didn't work," she shouted back at Nellis, who was still shaking his head in disbelief at her bravado.

"You're a crazy woman," he said. "You alright?"

"I'm fine. Just hurt my pride."

"Now what?"

Blackwood analyzed the scene. It seemed hopeless. Nellis had been right: they were outgunned and outnumbered. She considered the idea that discretion truly was the better part of valor and that maybe it was best to pull back and concede this round.

Another explosion burst in the room, but this one was not as devastating as the first two bigger blasts that sounded as though they came deep from within the facility.

Blackwood leaned out from behind her cover and saw that a grenade had exploded just behind Jacobs' men, who were now disorganized and turning to face whatever—or whoever—was attacking their flank.

Six of the mercs went down and a new group of armed men appeared in their place at the front of the corridor. They were dressed in matching, yet well-worn and tattered outfits that looked to Blackwood like hospital scrubs.

The Project Hermes test subjects?

One of the patients stepped forward and gestured down the hall. "This way is clear," he said.

Blackwood thanked him and introduced herself. He nodded and said his name was Sergeant Ramirez.

"These men need immediate medical attention," he said.

Blackwood handed her radio to Nellis. "Escort these men out

of the facility. Use this to contact the FBI field office in Anchorage and get these men the help they need."

"What are you going to do?"

"I came here for Jacobs, and I'm not leaving without him."

"You have to get out of here," Ramirez said. "He's going to blow the whole place up."

"Then I have to stop him," she said.

"We need to leave now," Ramirez pleaded. "All of us."

Nellis looked at Blackwood and then said to Ramirez, "You're wasting your breath, kid. If she says she's going in there, she's going in there..."

50

Flynn followed Natalie up the ladder back out through the secret entrance in the woods. It was cold, but Flynn was happy to take long, deep breaths of the fresh air.

He looked at his watch: twenty minutes remaining. It had taken them much longer than that just to hike here from the road, not to mention the car ride they had taken from the inn.

Natalie shook her head. "James, it's hopeless. There's not enough time."

"We have to try."

Then they heard it—the distinct sound of a snowmobile ripping through the countryside. It was coming toward them. They both took cover in the trees and waited.

The sound of the engine got louder and soon they saw the Polaris Assault 800 approach their location. Flynn and Natalie took cover behind a boulder before he peeked around the side of it to see if he could tell who was on the vehicle. The rider skidded to a stop and dismounted. After removing his helmet and cradling it in his arm, he scanned the area and started following Flynn and Natalie's tracks.

He was dressed in dark blue with bright yellow letters on the back: FBI, one of Blackwood's men. They had apparently been on to the hidden entrance to Keller's lab.

Quite the sporty ride for a Fed, Flynn thought.

The agent immediately noticed the footprints Flynn and Natalie had left behind and took his service pistol from its holster.

Natalie bounced up from her hiding spot and yelled to the FBI agent, "He's after me. Please help!"

The agent held his outstretched palm toward her and told her to calm down. He was about to ask her some questions when Flynn stepped from behind the tree and approached the agent from behind. He jabbed the end of a branch into the small of the agent's back.

"Don't make a bad decision," Flynn said. "Don't overthink it. Just drop the pistol."

"Assaulting a federal agent is a felony," the agent said. "You'll do serious time for this. You might want to be the one who does the thinking here."

Flynn pressed the branch even harder into the man's back. "It's only a felony if they catch me. Don't push me to do something I don't want to do. Just drop the gun. I need your ride, but I'll bring it back."

The agent, realizing he had no leverage, dropped the pistol in the snow. Flynn tossed the branch and grabbed the gun, which he used to indicate the secret hatch.

"Climb down there," he said. "Wait until we're gone and then get the hell out of this area. This whole place is going to blow."

Flynn and Natalie hopped on the snowmobile and sped away.

51

A third blast exploded and the HAARP facility was ablaze, its walls echoing with the sounds of shouting, panic, and gunfire. Samantha Blackwood prowled through the chaos. She had come for Flynn, the journalist whose trail had led her here, but the situation had escalated far beyond a simple apprehension of a person of interest.

As she navigated the labyrinth of burning corridors, her mind raced. Flynn was the key to this entire puzzle, she believed. Catching him would unravel the threads that had entangled the Tillman case and the murder of her partner, Wayne Minter. But, Flynn could wait. Her priority target had shifted to Jacobs, the man responsible for the day's carnage.

A sudden blast shook the foundation, and a section of the ceiling crumbled. Blackwood dodged the debris, her heart pounding. She clenched her jaw and forged ahead, climbing over a bit of rubble and then crawling through the remains of what was once a perfectly functional wall.

She was dirty and sweaty from the grime and the fire that was beginning to rage around her. Then, through the smoke and flickering flames, she saw him. Blaine Jacobs.

* * *

NATALIE HELD on tightly to Flynn's waist as he navigated the snowmobile at top speed, zig-zagging through the forest toward the main road. She ducked her head against his back when it appeared he might careen into a tree or slam headlong into a large rock.

She closed her eyes and prayed that they reached the road without incident, a request that seemed to be quite unreasonable considering the treacherous obstacles all around them and the speed at which Flynn was trying to avoid them. After a few minutes, the consistent jolting and jarring from the uneven terrain gave way to a much smoother ride. Natalie looked up; they had reached the road and were on their way toward the airfield.

She eyed Flynn's watch. They had just under eight minutes left.

* * *

JACOBS STOOD THERE, eerily calm amidst the mayhem.

"Finally," he said, his voice smooth, acknowledging none of the turmoil around them. "Here for Flynn, I presume?"

Blackwood's hand instinctively reached for her sidearm.

"Not just yet," she said. "I have an annoying nuisance to take care of first."

He chuckled, striding closer. "Always one step behind, aren't you?"

She tensed, but kept her voice steady.

"What's all this about?" she said. "We've got you. There's no way out of this. No way you don't go away for a long time—or worse."

"Destruction, Agent Blackwood, is sometimes an inevitable path to creation. A new world order, beyond the grasp of ordinary minds."

"And the lives lost? Just collateral damage?"

"Necessary, I'm afraid. I have to keep the plan on course. Tillman had become a hazard. He threatened to expose the plan. Initially he was all-in, enthusiastic for what we were about to accomplish. But he quickly lost the stomach for the process. Liam Baxter was nothing more than a fool who stuck his nose where it didn't belong. The only one I almost feel sorry for is your dear friend Special Agent Minter. That was a man who was only doing his job. Unfortunately for him, his job put him in the way of my objective, so he had to go."

Blackwood clenched her fists and narrowed her eyes. Tillman and Wayne's deaths were no longer a mystery. Flynn had nothing to do with them. She raised her nine millimeter pistol toward Jacobs, trained at his head. From such a short distance she wouldn't miss.

* * *

THE POLARIS'S engine roared as the snowmobile glided over the snow along the side of the road. Flynn twisted his wrist and glanced at his watch. Five minutes. The road ahead was twisty and followed the path of the Copper River, which took them off a direct path toward the airfield. They weren't going to make it.

He turned his head sideways so Natalie could hear him speak.

"In case this doesn't work out, I'm sorry," he said.

Before she could ask what he meant, Flynn jerked the snowmobile to the right away from the smooth surface near the road back to the precarious and unpredictable footing of the rocky and wooded countryside, and Natalie got her answer.

She buried her head into his back once again.

* * *

BLACKWOOD'S MIND whirred as she processed everything she'd just heard from Jacobs. The tech billionaire had just confessed, yet

Flynn, the unpredictable variable in her case, remained at large. She knew Jacobs would consider him a threat.

"And Flynn?" she said. "How does he fit into your plans?"

Jacobs frowned. "Oh, him. He's like a pesky fly, always buzzing around when you least want him. But flies get swatted eventually."

"Where is he now?"

"Mr. Flynn is exactly where he needs to be. He was so eager to uncover the truth about Projects Hermes and Titan. Let's just say he's now in a prime position to see everything unfold."

Blackwood figured Flynn was somewhere in the facility, likely trapped if not dead already. The fire and destruction around her made her believe the latter outcome seemed most probable. If things were this bad up here, she could only imagine what the devastation was below the surface where Dr. Keller performed his secret experiments. Flynn would have to wait. She needed to take down Jacobs first.

Her grip on her weapon tightened. She had to act.

"It ends here," she said. "Blaine Jacobs, you're under arrest for the murders of General Arthur Tillman and FBI Special Agent Wayne Minter."

Another thunderous explosion rocked the building, and Blackwood and Jacobs were sent tumbling.

* * *

FLYNN SNAKED through trees with the deftness of a downhill skier weaving through tightly spaced gates. The clock was ticking, but he could finally see the airfield in the distance. Between them was the ice-covered river that Flynn hoped was frozen solid enough to bear the weight of the snowmobile.

He slid to a stop atop the ridge overlooking the lake.

"This is where you get off," he said to Natalie. "You'll be safe here. I don't want you to be any closer to that plane when it explodes."

She started to object, but Flynn cut her off.

"There's no time to argue. Stay here. I'll come back for you."

Begrudgingly, she dismounted the snowmobile, and Flynn launched himself down the hill for a full-throttle sprint toward imminent danger.

He had just over two minutes to go when he hit the surface of the Copper River. The snowmobile glided smoothly over the ice, and Flynn could see Jacobs' jet up the hill on the other side just ahead.

* * *

As the ceiling had collapsed, Blackwood tumbled to the floor. Dazed by the explosion, she got up on one knee and started to stand when, out of the corner of her eye, she noticed Jacobs flying toward her. She glanced at his hand and noticed a knife and blocked his strike with her forearm, knocking him aside. She scrambled to her feet and turned to face Jacobs, ready to strike. But before she could, Jacobs had rolled to his feet and was charging toward her.

Blackwood slid aside, dodging his punches before countering. She rammed her knee into his midsection. Jacobs staggered back, trying to regain his bearings as she struck again.

But she didn't let up. Blackwood followed her knee strike with a quick right hook, but Jacobs ducked. But as he did, he stumbled backward. Blackwood seized the opening, kicking him again, this time in the center of his chest with much more force than before. Jacobs fell backward, hitting the floor with a thud. Blackwood dove to the ground and scrambled to pick up the weapon.

As she wrapped her fingers around the handle, the building groaned under the strain of the fire, the heat intensifying. The room crumbled amidst the fire and explosions. A piece of the wall on her left fell into her and knocked her to the ground. Blackwood's legs were pinned, the debris too heavy for her to lift. She grimaced as she tried to free herself from the material. But she couldn't, relegating herself to that position.

* * *

Flynn gunned the snowmobile, his eyes fixed on the small airstrip up ahead where the sleek private jet sat, its engines lifeless.

Flynn couldn't see the bomb, but figured it was almost certainly attached to one of the wings near the fuel tanks.

Already humming at full speed, well over a hundred miles per hour, when he came off the lake, he began the climb toward the airstrip. He only needed a few seconds to reach the top.

The airfield was less than a hundred yards away but surrounded by a mound of snow that had been plowed up along the perimeter of the strip. He steered toward it.

His clock counted down from just under thirty seconds when his front skis hit the snow mound, the makeshift ramp launching him airborne. At breakneck speed, the snowmobile soared in a high arc toward the parked jet.

* * *

Jacobs stood over Blackwood, her lower body trapped under a steel beam. She winced as she reached for her leg, the pain searing and making her wonder if she'd broken it. The smell of smoke rolled down the hall, causing her to cough. She could taste blood in her mouth. With defeat imminent, she expected Jacobs to gloat as he staggered to his feet. Given his ego, she braced for his boastful parting shot, to mock her and laugh at her failure. But he didn't.

Instead, he knelt next to her, his face almost an expression of remorse.

Behind him, the roof was gone, and the bright blue sky was a contrast to the death and destruction that had gone on inside the facility for years. She heard the unmistakable sound of a helicopter rotor and then saw the chopper overhead.

"You died for a greater cause today," Jacobs said to her. He lightly touched her forehead and waved his other arm toward the helicopter. "What you will know as a personal failure for these final moments of your life will live on forever as a sacrifice for a new world of human communication and understanding. I never got to tell the others. I'm happy I can tell you."

A harness lowered from the helicopter, and Jacobs secured himself in it.

As Jacobs began to rise toward the helicopter, Blackwood spied her pistol just out of reach among the rubble.

She strained to touch it, but it lay just inches from her outstretched fingertips. She surged with all of her strength but couldn't reach the weapon. She watched as Jacobs was hoisted higher into the sky toward his escape chopper.

"Goodbye, Agent Blackwood," he said. "And thank you."

Blackwood felt another violent shake from an eruption further inside the building. The tremor jostled her and the shattered pieces of the wall that pinned her down. It didn't fully release her from the debris, but the blast shifted the room around her just enough to bring the pistol within reach.

She grabbed the gun, and took aim and fired.

"You're welcome," she said.

She fired three shots in quick succession, each of them finding their mark. Blaine Jacobs' limp body was hauled toward the helicopter, and Blackwood saw him smile and pull open his coat to reveal a bullet-proof vest.

* * *

As the airborne snowmobile sailed over the tip of the wing and toward the fuselage, Flynn jumped off, collapsing onto the surface of the wing and dragging his feet to avoid falling off it. His momentum carried him into the body of the plane, and his finger fought to grasp the cold metal. The snowmobile hit the top of the plane and then caromed off the other wing before crashing nose down into a snow bank flanking the edge of the runway.

Flynn looked inside one of the windows and saw Leslie Vanderwaal's face in utter shock.

"Flynn?" she shouted. "What are you doing?"

"I don't know," he said. "Just get out of there. Get out and run."

"But, I don't have a coat. It looks very cold out there."

"Leslie—"

"And these shoes. Run? Are you serious?"

"The plane is going to explode!"

She looked at him in disbelief. "What do you mean, explode?"

Fifteen seconds passed. Flynn knew if the conversation persisted, it was going to be the death of them both.

Flynn slid off the wing, hoping to see the bomb attached underneath. It was not.

He ducked under the cabin to the other wing. There it was.

Housed in a rugged metal casing, the bomb was roughly the size of a large textbook. With the outer shell a matted black, scuffed and worn in places, Blackwood could tell it had been constructed and handled with haste. Through a transparent, reinforced panel Flynn saw a maze of wires and components. Among the tangle of red, blue, and yellow wires, a small digital timer displayed the countdown in bright red digits.

Flynn had worked with explosives before but never against a ticking clock. Defusing the thing was not an option.

He yanked the bomb with both hands. It had been affixed with putty and came free easier than he expected. The timer's display screen showed twelve seconds remaining.

Flynn raced over to the snowmobile, setting it upright and hoping it was still somewhat operational. He secured the bomb to the snowmobile's rear rack, mounted the vehicle and took off.

His fingers worked deftly to wrap his watch band around the

throttle to keep it wide-open. Just before the snowmobile reached the snow ramp, Flynn rolled off.

The snowmobile caught big air and sped nearly to the center of the river when the bomb detonated in a fiery spectacle. The explosion and ensuing heat caused a crack that evolved into a large hole that swallowed the charred remains.

Guess I won't be returning that snowmobile after all.

Flynn bent at the waist with his hands on his knees and watched safely from the tarmac. A minute later Leslie joined him wearing no coat and quite possibly the most uncomfortable pair of shoes Flynn had ever seen.

"Cutting it a little close, don't you think?" she said, her voice calm.

"You're welcome, Leslie."

52

Samantha Blackwood lay pinned beneath debris amongst the bedlam and destruction of the crumbling HAARP research facility. Intense flames burned all around her, casting a fierce and menacing glow. The acrid smoke stung her lungs and forced her to cough. Her thoughts raced, and a sense of finality crept in. Amidst the chaos, her mind drifted to Wayne Minter, her partner, her mentor.

"I tried, Wayne," she whispered.

She tried one last time to pull herself free, pushing against the steel beam encased in a chunk of the wall that had fallen across her legs while trying to wriggle out from under its weight. It was no use.

I'm going to die here.

The building creaked and groaned as the steel infrastructure struggled to maintain the weight of the facility. The question wasn't if it would collapse, but when. The smoke thickened, and the heat from the flames intensified. The wide-open hole that had been torn out of the ceiling helped with the ventilation, as the black smoke had a place to escape; without it, she already would have suffocated.

Just when Blackwood had resigned herself to the idea that she was mere minutes away from drawing her last breath, two figures emerged through the smoke. One was dressed in a white coat smeared with soot—Blackwood recognized him as Dr. Keller from her background work on the HAARP facility. His eyes reflected both fear and determination as he scuttled toward her through the debris.

The other man was Nellis, who bulldozed himself through the wreckage like a fullback. He reached her first with Keller arriving a couple of seconds later.

"Don't you have somewhere better to be?" she said.

"No time," Keller gasped. "We need to get out of here, now."

Nellis bent over and slid both his hands under the largest chunk of debris that held Blackwood down. Keller also bent for a firm grip where he could manage some leverage against the concrete.

"All three of us," Nellis said. "On three."

He counted, and Blackwood pushed upward with every bit of strength she had left, while Nellis and Keller groaned against the weight of the obstacle.

They managed to raise the wall just enough for Blackwood to squirm free. Pain shot through her leg as the two men helped her to her feet. She screamed in agony, certain she had a fracture in her lower leg. She leaned into Nellis just to stay upright. He gave her a concerned look.

"I'm alright," she said. "Just give me some support, we can get outta here."

She wrapped one arm around his neck, and he held her upright to shift her weight off of her injured leg.

Keller led the way. With the assistance from Nellis, Blackwood hobbled down the hallway. Together, they stumbled through the collapsing corridors, dodging falling debris and flames.

53

WASHINGTON, D.C.

The Russell Senate Office Building was a blend of historic elegance and modern functionality, its placid exterior a sharp contrast to the frenetic activity occurring inside as the fate of Project Titan hung in the balance. James Flynn and Leslie Vanderwaal walked down a wide corridor lined with mahogany-paneled walls, their footsteps echoing softly on the marble floor. The air was filled with a sense of dignity and history. Marble fireplaces, wood crown moldings, and nickel lighting fixtures with frosted glass chimney shades added to the building's stately ambiance.

As they neared Senator Danbury's office, Leslie turned to Flynn, her expression serious.

"We need to be straightforward with him. He needs to understand the real impact of his decision."

Flynn adjusted his tie. "How's this look?" he asked, his eyes narrowed and his forehead creased with lines.

"It'll do." Her face said she was none too impressed.

"Don't push too hard right off the bat," Flynn said. "We need to make him feel like he's making the right call on his own. We go in there and make demands, he'll reject us on principle. We have to present the facts about Projects Titan and Hermes in a way that doesn't put him on the defensive."

She nodded that she understood.

"You might be right. But we can't sugarcoat it. This is about more than just politics; it's about all the lives at stake."

"It's about placating the Senator's ego," he said, "to get him to make the right decision."

"Well if anyone is an expert on big egos, it's you."

"You know, I rescued you out of a plane with a ticking bomb, right?"

She waved him off. "Don't be so dramatic."

They paused in front of a door with brass fixtures, Senator Danbury's name etched on a plaque. The office beyond was visible through the glass, showcasing a tastefully decorated space with light blue walls.

Flynn's face went serious.

"Lay out the truth, make it simple. Let him connect the dots himself."

He reached for the door handle, but Leslie brushed him aside and barged past him into the senator's office.

The room greeted them with an air of understated power, the dark wood furniture and historical decor speaking volumes about the decisions made within these walls.

Danbury, sitting behind his grand desk, looked up with a thin, serious smile.

"Miss Vanderwaal, I appreciate you coming to see me once again," he said. "I assume this is the esteemed Mr. Flynn, whom I've heard so much about."

Flynn stepped forward to shake Danbury's hand.

"Thank you, Sen—"

"Senator, we've uncovered something critical," Leslie blurted. "Project Titan isn't causing harm. It's actually designed to reverse the effects of another program—Project Hermes. Hermes is the real problem."

Danbury's brows bent in confusion.

"Hermes? I've never heard of it."

"That's because it's been kept under wraps," Leslie continued. "Project Hermes has been causing severe psychological damage to its subjects. Titan was developed to mitigate those effects. You have to vote to keep Project Titan fully funded. Lives are at stake."

The senator scowled. "Let's not get ahead of ourselves," he said. "I appreciate you making an appointment and flying all the way here to bring me new information, but I've been analyzing these research budgets for six months. I can't be swayed by an unconfirmed report at the last second. My decision will be based on the entirety of the available data and what is best for the American people."

Flynn stepped forward. "Senator, people like Sergeant Mahler are victims of Hermes, not Titan. The outcome of the Titan research could be their only hope."

The mention of Mahler's name forced Danbury's face to flash with pain. Flynn wanted to make this personal, connect it to the incident at his home when Mahler broke in and attempted to kill him. The incident had been mostly stifled from the mainstream media, but Flynn's connections clued him in. He didn't trust the senator to make the right decision for everyone, but he did count on him to make the one that would clear his own conscience.

Danbury nodded slowly, indicating both concern and skepticism.

"I see. This is—quite a revelation," he said. "It is certainly something to think about. I thank you both for bringing this to my attention. I assure you, I'll make the best decision for America, considering all that you've told me."

Leslie took a breath, and Flynn, expecting her to press the issue with Danbury, gripped her by the arm and twisted her toward the door.

"Ow! You're—"

"Thank you for your time, Senator Danbury," Flynn said. "We know you have a busy schedule. We'll see ourselves out."

Flynn kept a tight clasp on Leslie's arm as he ushered her out of the senator's office. Once in the hallway, she jerked herself free and jabbed a well-manicured index finger at Flynn's nose.

She kept her voice low, but her stare pierced Flynn.

"Don't you ever touch me again. What the hell was that?"

Flynn held up both hands, palms out.

"I'm sorry," he said. "But we did what we set out to do. The ball is in his court. Nothing you were going to say was going to help our cause."

Seething, Leslie stomped toward the exit.

"Remember when I said we should work on a story together sometime? Forget it!"

54

WASHINGTON, D.C.

Senator Quinton Danbury sat at his desk with his head buried in his hands, massaging his closed eyes with his fingertips. A course of action that had minutes ago seemed so clear was now as uncertain as a snow-covered road winding down the Blue Ridge Mountains. The confidence he had felt was replaced by a maze of doubt and what-ifs, each possibility branching off into more complex and uncertain outcomes.

The morally right and decent move pointed toward keeping money flowing to Project Titan so that victims like Richard Mahler could possibly be saved. The image of the young sergeant dying in his own home overran his thoughts; he simply couldn't get it out of his mind. If he could make a decision that would erase that incident, he surely would.

But no such outcome was available. What was done was done. He couldn't save Sergeant Mahler. There was no point in spending any more time worrying about it.

Then he thought of the ominous Mr. White, to whom he was in debt. White had delivered a windfall of campaign money that had helped Danbury surge in all of the latest polls. He had not only caught up to Blake Calloway but was actually leading him in most counties in the state.

Mr. White, as scary and mysterious as he might be, was proving to be a useful ally. If he was that valuable as a friend, how dangerous could he become as an enemy?

Danbury was not eager to find out.

But then there was that damn Leslie Vanderwaal. She could expose him. Even though the vote on the research projects was not public knowledge, journalists like her always found a way to get their grubby mitts on that information. Danbury believed he could trust James Flynn, an ex-military, ex-Company man, to keep a lid on things. He'd understand. But the girl would be a problem; he knew for sure. She'd find out how he voted and then put it out there that he knew about the danger of cutting the funding for Project Titan. It would kill his re-election campaign. His political career would be dead.

He couldn't help but feel like he'd been thrust into a no-win situation.

55

NEW YORK CITY

No one had heard a word from Christopher Mays in weeks. Industry pundits speculated that he'd just run off and was living under the radar with some bubbly young intern he'd managed to hoodwink into shacking up with him somewhere off the grid. His quirky behavior and history of burning through girlfriends gave the theory plausibility.

Theresa Halston knew better. She couldn't say for sure what happened, but she knew Mays had met an early demise, possibly at the hands of the father, brother, or lover of the aforementioned bubbly young intern.

He wasn't coming back, that much was agreed upon by the board when it invoked an emergency meeting to deal with the leadership vacuum. When the board emerged, the chairman announced that Theresa had been appointed the new publisher of *The National*, citing, "no other option" as a less-than-shining vote of confidence in her abilities.

She'd always despised the position, despite the pay increase and the better office. But regardless of how she felt about taking over the business side of things, it seemed better to jump into the seat rather than gamble with whatever jackass the board might anoint as her new boss. Even if the job drained the creative juices from her, at least she could somewhat control her own destiny. In her wildest dreams she hoped she could actually make a difference, though she remained skeptical.

After settling into her new corner office, her first task was to squash dreams and be an obstacle to legit journalism, just like a real publisher.

Her first victim? Leslie Vanderwaal.

"Are you serious?" Leslie said as she sat slack-jawed across the desk from Theresa.

Theresa was. She nodded. "I'm afraid so."

"You're killing the entire piece on HAARP?"

"It was Flynn's assignment anyway," Theresa said. "You still have your interview with Danbury—your *original* interview with Danbury, that is. Be happy. We're putting it on the cover."

Leslie sulked. "It's a puff piece. Filler. Some feel-good advertisement for another dinosaur of a politician."

"Those articles pay the bills. The senator will appreciate what we've done for him. It will pay off some day." She felt dirty toeing that tired company line.

"What about Flynn? He's not going to write anything? The biggest story he's ever covered, and he's just going to walk away from it?"

"Flynn is a professional," Theresa said. "He knows the score. He might not be happy about it, but he also knows there will be other stories out there."

Until Theresa could find a replacement for her role as managing editor, she filled the role and basked in the power it afforded her. She gave Leslie the particulars on what she needed from her on the Danbury feature. She provided a word count, topics to cover (and stay away from), potential secondary sources for extra color on the senator and his wife, and of course the deadline.

Leslie's face showed no sign of interest or even comprehension in anything Theresa was saying. The young woman was instead gazing out the window of the plush and modern office previously occupied by Christopher Mays. Theresa craned her neck toward the glass to see what had Leslie's attention. She saw nothing.

"Are you getting all of this?" Theresa asked.

Leslie did not respond. She appeared to be deep in thought, her mind completely preoccupied with something other than what Theresa was trying to convey.

"Leslie?"

Leslie looked her in the eye.

"Did you hear me?"

"No."

Theresa huffed and began to repeat the instructions.

"No," Leslie said again.

Theresa stopped, giving her young writer a look that was equal parts confusion and annoyance.

Leslie said, "I'm not going to do that."

"You're not going to do what?"

"Any of it," she said, smiling for the first time during the entire conversation. She stood and slung a black leather backpack that held her laptop and also doubled as her purse over her shoulder. "I quit."

56

WASHINGTON, D.C.

Mr. White was the last person Danbury wanted to see, but there he was standing in the senator's office like an Armani-clad skeleton. Just as dapper. Just as damn frightening.

Somehow the man managed to appear seemingly out of thin air as if summoned like a genie from a tarnished lamp. His presence seemed to ignore the rules of time and space. He was always just <u>there</u>, no matter where <u>there</u> was. And no matter how many times they met and spoke, his oddly angular physique was never not unnerving to Danbury.

He somehow expected to see him today.

"Of course you did," Mr. White said as if he'd read Danbury's mind.

Or did I speak my thoughts out loud? Danbury felt an odd sensation as if the impending conversation had already taken place yet no words had been spoken—or had they? He couldn't tell.

"It's okay, Senator," Mr. White said.

And Danbury understood.

"So it's all been taken care of?"

"All of it. There's no need to cast a vote today. Project Titan has been removed. Project Hermes never existed. You'll be re-elected."

Danbury felt in a daze. He heard the words, understood them anyway, but Mr. White's mouth never moved.

* * *

WHITE DIALED THE PHONE. A man answered. He knew him only as TruthSeeker47. They had never met in person.

"I trust it went well," TruthSeeker47 said.

"It did. The senator is a friend now. He understands his role."

"Good."

"We have loose ends," White said. "Flynn. The girl. The FBI."

"This is where Mr. Jacobs did us a favor. He was sloppy. Impatient. He put himself in the spotlight, made himself their boogeyman. As for the eager Miss Vanderwaal and our intrepid James Flynn, they have nothing left to chase, no proof that Hermes or Titan ever existed. The magazine is under control. No article about what happened in Alaska is forthcoming."

"What about *him*?"

"I'm afraid he's more of a liability than an asset at this point," TruthSeeker47 said. "I'll leave him up to you."

57

ANNAPOLIS, MARYLAND

Admiral Paul Barrow sat in the dim light of his office, the day's events replaying in his mind like a well-orchestrated symphony. He leaned back in his chair, the leather creaking under his weight, and gazed out the window.

Thoughts of Wayne Minter's death hit him like an unexpected wave, crashing over the stoic facade he had maintained for so long. Wayne had been a friend whose loyalty and camaraderie had been a rare constant throughout Barrow's career as a Naval officer. Memories flooded in—shared laughter, candid conversations, and moments of mutual respect. The weight of Wayne's demise filled the room, reminding Barrow of the personal cost of his ambitions. For a brief moment, the admiral allowed himself to mourn, to feel the sting of loss, before the mask of composure returned, burying his sorrow beneath layers of duty and resolve.

He'd tried to sway Wayne away from the case, but he knew that was going to be a lost cause. Wayne was as tenacious an investigator that Barrow had ever seen, and worse, he actually believed in the noble purpose of his position at the FBI. A zealot was a dangerous foe. A skilled zealot had to be dealt with.

A sudden vibration from his phone interrupted his thoughts. It was a text message confirming that the mission was successful. He didn't reply. He was done for the day.

Barrow stood and tidied his desk, a ritual marking the end of another long day. His office was a testament to his illustrious career: Medals, awards, and commendations adorned the walls. However, one picture, in particular, held his gaze longer than the others—a photograph of him in his Naval Academy days, a star football player with dreams as vast as the ocean in which he would eventually command ships.

He moved to the bar in the corner of his office, pouring himself a glass of bourbon. He took a sip. The smooth, oaky flavor delivered a feeling of warm satisfaction. This week had been challenging, but ultimately, everything was falling into place.

Barrow walked back to his desk, his mind now drifting from fine detail back to the broader strokes. He had maneuvered each piece with precision, guiding events from the shadows, undetected and unsuspected. His adversaries were oblivious to the puppeteer amongst them, each believing they had been victorious.

Sitting down again, he opened a drawer and pulled out a small, intricate model of a Naval cruiser, a reminder of where it all began. He turned it over in his hands, lost in thought. His career had always been about winning, the pursuit of power and influence. He'd learned to always stay a step ahead, always maintain control, even in the face of adversity.

Barrow switched off his desk lamp and made his way to the door. He paused, taking one last look around the room that served as his command center, his sanctuary. His eyes lingered on the framed football photo again. The young man in the picture, confident and victorious. He was still that man inside, only a bit older and much wiser than when he'd donned his favorite number on his jersey—No. 47.

With a final, satisfied nod, Admiral Paul Barrow, Naval hero, and unsuspected architect of chaos, turned off the lights and left the room.

58

SOMEWHERE IN ARIZONA

Dr. Nestor Keller peeked out the curtain of his motel room. The FBI had him under protective custody and were preparing to move him into witness protection. Blaine Jacobs was gone, but Keller was still a target for many seeking revenge against him for his role in the development of the Hermes project.

Special Agent Blackwood had left important details about Keller out of her report. The way she told her story, Keller was an innocent victim and Jacobs was the hidden mastermind behind what went on in that secret lab. It went against her oath to uphold the law—in reality, Dr. Keller should stand trial for his offenses and be locked away forever (or worse.) But Blackwood knew Keller was more useful to society alive and free than he would be incarcerated or dead. So, she skimped on the report.

They would move Keller somewhere remote and allow him to continue work on his Titan research. He'd had moderate success in some of the subjects, including Sergeant Ethan Ramirez. But progress was slow or non-existent in others. The results remained somewhat a mystery for Keller, but he was going to continue to put all of his efforts into finding answers.

In his mind, he was already in prison and he'd never be free until each one of those men was cured of their affliction caused by Project Hermes.

He peered through the curtain. The two agents guarding his door were gone. Keller felt a jolt of pure terror surge through his body. He closed the curtain and stepped away from the window.

They'd found him. *He* had found him.

Keller, frantic, spun around and scanned the room for a place to hide. It was too late to run. The beds were solid frames; no hiding underneath. His only option was the bathroom. It was almost pointless to try. But try he did. He sat in the bathtub, pulled his knees up to his chest and cradled his legs with both arms. He leaned his head forward and tried to silence his breathing between his knees. But his heart was beating so fast, and his breathing was so rapid, he had no chance to remain perfectly quiet.

He heard a sound from the bedroom. The lock clicked, and the front door opened. He closed his eyes and prayed for it not to be who he knew it would be. He wept, knowing death was imminent.

The bathroom door swung open, and Dr. Keller opened his eyes and looked up.

The shower curtain slid open.

Dr. Keller was greeted by a familiar face—the bony visage of Mr. White.

59

MELBOURNE, AUSTRALIA

The taxi driver picked up the man at the airport. The man was average height and average build. He had a thick brown mustache, a pair of dark-rimmed glasses, and spoke with a North American accent.

"Here on business?"

"Always," the man said.

"American or Canadian?"

"American. Does that bother you?"

"Me? No, sir. I love you Yanks. I love everybody, really. Anyone who pays me anyway." He laughed a hearty laugh.

The man smiled. He gave the driver directions and sat back into the seat and closed his eyes.

"Yeah, may as well get some rest," the driver said. "That's a bit of a haul out there."

The drive took nearly two hours. The man seemed to sleep for the full duration, but when they arrived, he sat up straight like he'd been alert the entire time.

The man stepped out of the car and said, "Wait here."

"Meter's running," the driver said.

"Of course."

It was a nice house out here in the middle of nowhere. It was strange to see a place like this so far out. The driver wondered what kind of person would choose to live here. They clearly had means to live in the city or at least closer in where there were things to do and see. It sure was a nice house. Rich man's house.

He watched the man step to the front door and walk right in. He closed the door behind him. Maybe this was his house. The driver kept watching. Only a couple of minutes passed, and the driver thought he heard a sound like the crack of bullwhip. Not once, but twice. Crack. Crack.

Seconds later, the door opened, and the man stepped back out into the sunlight and strode back to the cab.

He got in the backseat.

"Thanks for waiting," he said. He told the driver to head back to the airport.

The driver looked at the man in the rearview mirror and said, "Is that your house? You forget something?"

"No. Only people trying to hide from something live out here. And, I never forget anything."

* * *

THE CAB PULLED up at the airport. He paid the fare and added a generous tip.

"How about you forget about this little trip?"

The driver counted the money and smiled. "I think I was off today. Definitely didn't pick anyone up from the airport," he said.

As James Flynn walked into the Melbourne Airport, he peeled the fake mustache from his lip, removed the dark-rimmed costume glasses, and threw them both in the trash.

Old habits die hard.

60

MANAVA BEACH, TAHITI

The waves lapped the sand in a hypnotic rhythm. The water was a crystal blue that previously only existed in his dreams. The sun was bright and warm, not harsh or uncomfortably hot. The sand was white and felt like finely granulated sugar between his toes.

James Flynn came out of the water and slicked his wet hair back over his head as he approached her. She smiled and it made him smile back. She looked amazing in a bathing suit, leaning back in her beach chair. He went to her and bent down to give her a kiss before taking a seat beside her.

"Beats Alaska," he said.

"Just barely," Natalie joked.

He sat there with her, looking over the beautiful beach and ocean beyond, neither of them saying a word.

Shortly after returning home from the horror show that was the ordeal in Alaska, they discussed Richard Mahler. Natalie was sad to find out that he'd taken his own life. She hated that she wasn't able to save him from the pain that led to his terrible fate. But she told Flynn that she'd already lost Richard months ago when he became one of the first victims of Project Hermes. She had loved him, but knew he would never be the man she knew before. She had wanted to find him and help him, but she no longer wanted to be with him.

Flynn admitted that he was falling for her, but that they should take it slow. Natalie was ten years younger, and he wanted to make sure the age difference wasn't going to pose any issues. They both recognized that enduring a traumatic event like the one they faced in Alaska could intensify emotions between them, leading to feelings that might be fleeting or not entirely genuine.

She reassured him that she was going into it with her eyes open.

"If it's just a fling, then that's what it is," she had said. "I enjoy being with you. If it's only for a short time, at least we had that. Just don't get too old on me too fast."

"Hey, I still do my own stunts," he said with a laugh.

"We're going to need a strict no-snowmobile policy if this is going to work."

It was then that he suggested a getaway. Wanting to adhere to the "take it slow" plan, he secured separate ocean-view cottages, one for each of them.

"No pressure. No expectations," he said. "I just think a chance to get away for a while could help us both decide what's next for us, whether that's you and me or 'we'."

They had taken a plane, a boat, another plane, and another boat to reach the remote location on the other side of the world. It felt like a different planet where there was nothing to do but simply exist and contemplate life.

They weren't sure what was in store for their next chapter, but neither of them ever stepped inside that second cottage.

THE END

NEWSLETTER SIGNUP

If you would like to stay up to date on R.J. Patterson's latest writing projects with his periodic newsletter, visit RJPbooks.com to sign up.

ACKNOWLEDGMENTS

I am grateful to so many people who have helped with the creation of this project and the entire James Flynn series.

I would also like to thank my advance reader team for all their input in improving this book along with all the other readers who have enthusiastically embraced the story of James Flynn. Stay tuned ... there's more James Flynn adventures coming soon.

ABOUT THE AUTHORS

R.J. PATTERSON is an award-winning writer living in southeastern Idaho. He first began his illustrious writing career as a sports journalist, recording his exploits on the soccer fields in England as a young boy. Then when his father told him that people would pay him to watch sports if he would write about what he saw, he went all in. He landed his first writing job at age 15 as a sports writer for a daily newspaper in Orangeburg, S.C. He later attended earned a degree in newspaper journalism from the University of Georgia, where he took a job covering high school sports for the award-winning *Athens Banner-Herald* and *Daily News*.

He later became the sports editor of *The Valdosta Daily Times* before working in the magazine world as an editor and freelance journalist. He has won numerous writing awards, including a national award for his investigative reporting on a sordid tale surrounding an NCAA investigation over the University of Georgia football program.

R.J. enjoys the great outdoors of the Northwest while living there with his wife and four children. He still follows sports closely.

He also loves connecting with readers and would love to hear from you. To stay updated about future projects, connect with him on Facebook or on the interwebs at RJPbooks.com and sign up for his newsletter to get deals and updates.

J.D. KANE, in another life, was an award-winning sports writer and columnist who covered high school, college, and professional sports for daily newspapers in Ohio, Indiana, Georgia, and Florida. He has since left newspapers behind (And who hasn't?) to pursue other opportunities in digital marketing and SEO content strategy while honing his craft as a writer of crime and thriller fiction. A Gen-X musician, Kane loves all things rock guitar and is an unapologetic fan of classic rock and "Hair Metal." He lives with his lovely wife and children in Northeast Ohio, where he can be found cheering for his beloved Cleveland sports teams; "Next year is always our year!"

Connect with J.D. at his website, www.JDKanebooks.com.

Made in the USA
Coppell, TX
28 June 2024